W9-AZD-910

help me please

helpmepleasehelpmepleasehelpmepleasehelpmeplease

barbara d'amato

FORGE®

A TOM DOHERTY ASSOCIATES BOOK
NEW YORK

This is a work of fiction. All the characters and events portrayed in this book are either products of the author's imagination or are used fictitiously.

HELP ME PLEASE

Copyright © 1999 by Barbara D'Amato

A Forge Book
Published by Tom Doherty Associates, LLC
175 Fifth Avenue
New York, NY 10010

www.tor.com

Forge® is a registered trademark of Tom Doherty Associates, LLC.

ISBN: 0-812-59015-5
Library of Congress Catalog Card Number: 99-22195

First edition: October 1999
First mass market edition: January 2001

Printed in the United States of America

0 9 8 7 6 5 4 3 2 1

An infant comes into a world of incomprehensible noises, confusing lights, unfamiliar tastes, frightening hunger, and peculiar feelings of hot, cold, rough, smooth, sharp, and soft. Little children are coping with a blooming, buzzing confusion and fighting for what they need. They are tenacious, persistent, and courageous. This book is dedicated to the courage of small children and especially to my favorite feisty folk, Emily and Adam.

acknowledgments

My thanks for help to David Mechner, Donna Batdorff, Paul Steketee D'Amato, Brian Richard D'Amato, Sheryl Rak D'Amato, and Anthony A. D'Amato, who provided ideas and technical help, and the one who taught by example, Emily Catherine D'Amato. Also to my reading group and severest critics (as they should be) Mark Zubro and Hugh Holton.

day zero

helpmepleasehelpmepleasehelpmepleasehelpmeplease

saturday

one

Golden air filled Holy Name Cathedral. Golden sunlight, weighty with dust motes, sank heavily through the
windows and settled over the amber oak pews and wood-
work. Maggie McKittredge felt bathed in gold and blessed.

Danielle's hair was gold, too, shining in the light, red
gold, fine, curly baby hair.

Danni was three, a pale porcelain cherub, wearing her
favorite long blue-and-white-checked gingham dress, the
one she thought made her look like a queen. But Daddy
called her Princess, which was okay, too.

The worshippers at the Saturday morning mass sighed and
rustled. Maggie, who was used to counting the house in
theaters, estimated about fifty people, which seemed a thin
scattering in the huge cathedral. As she and Neal and Danni
entered, several of them had recognized her. A youngish,
pretty woman, wearing a pale lilac dress and pale lilac
shoes, said, "I'm such a fan. For years, you've been my
favorite singer."

This made Maggie feel a little old.

Several others smiled at her or pointed her out to a companion. An elderly man, walking with difficulty, passed them without any recognition and sat in the pew in front of them.

A woman of about sixty, wearing a worn brown coat, studied them as they sat down. She stopped for a moment, hesitated, wondering whether to speak, and then whispered to Maggie, "Your singing got me through a very bad time in my life."

That was wonderful. Maggie smiled and touched her sleeve and thanked her. The woman turned away shyly and sat across the aisle.

My singing got me through a very bad time in my life, too, she thought. She remembered how it had been, those years of believing she would never have a baby. Years when it seemed to her she saw babies everywhere. Endless tests, some of them what the doctors liked to call "uncomfortable." Tests on Neal, too, that she knew embarrassed him. He'd been very patient, but he'd come home red-faced and silent from the doctor's office.

She ruffled Danni's hair. Danni sat at the end of the pew. Maggie was next and then Neal. Maggie expected Danni to fidget, and it would be easier having the child on the end if she needed to take her out for a walk.

Maggie had come here many times, beginning the day she'd arrived in Chicago for the first tests at Northwestern's fertility clinic, and then while she was pregnant, and then when she was released from the hospital four days after Danni's birth. She had come to Holy Name once every year after that, always four days after Danni's birthday, just like that first time of greatest thanks. It was a pilgrimage.

Little Danni had no real memory of the cathedral, of course. Danni had been here when she was four days, and a year and four days old, and two years and four days, and now three years and four days.

Danni craned her head back, rapt, loving the soaring pillars and golden light, stained-glass windows, and far away, the remote ceiling, its colors made soft by the dusty air.

The priest chanted. His clear voice rose, and the cavernous church pulled it into the upper air, both thinning the voice and elevating it, purifying it. Maggie wondered what it would be like to sing here. Would you sound like an angel?

"Mommy, I hot," Danni whispered.

"You can't be, honey. It's cool here."

"Yeth I *am*."

"Well, take off your sweater."

"Otay."

Maggie relaxed. There was something sleepy and sensuous in the amber light, heavily saturated with incense. She was content. She was deeply aware of how blessed she was, as if there was nothing left in the world to wish for, and she floated on the thought.

Neal put his hand over hers and whispered, "Let's take Danni for an ice cream cone after," he said.

"Neal! She's wearing her best dress."

"They have cleaners in Chicago, just like they have at home."

A minute later, Danni said, "I hot." She squirmed. When Maggie and Neal went to their knees to pray, Danni slipped off the pew, knelt down for a few seconds like they did, then got up and slowly turned around and around in place. Her long skirt flared out a little and brushed the pew seat as she twirled.

When Neal and Maggie slid back into their seats, Danni continued to spin, stepping out into the aisle to get more room.

What should I do now? Maggie wondered. Would it be less disruptive to leave Danni in the aisle or call her back to her seat? But she's having so much fun. So much delight.

As the priest chanted, Danni began to sing. With no idea of what the priest was saying, she sang softly, "It a smaw world affa all, it a smaw world affa all—"

Maggie turned to Neal. "What should I do?"

"Nothing," he said. "Let her—"

The older woman leaned across the aisle toward them and

said softly, "She's perfect. She's what it's all about. Let her dance." Maggie smiled.

And Danni had indeed started to dance. Singing, she rocked from foot to foot, then spun, almost a perfect pirouette. But the old man in the pew ahead of them turned around and hissed, "Shhhh!"

A black-cassocked priest came down the aisle. They had greeted him at the front doors when he'd welcomed them to the church. He leaned over Maggie. He had warm hazel eyes and sandy hair and a wooden cross hung at his neck. "Would she like to walk a couple of minutes? In the back of the nave?"

"Oh, I don't think so, Father. Thank you." She never let Danni out of her sight except with her nanny, Brenda.

Suddenly, there was a gurgling sound from the pew ahead. The old man coughed, made a bubbling sound, and then slid slowly sideways, disappearing from sight. The woman across the aisle stood up and said, "Look, look! What's wrong?"

Neal jumped up and bent over the back of the pew, his hand on the old man's shoulder, trying to keep him from falling from the seat to the floor, but the angle was wrong and Neal couldn't keep his grip. The man sank to the floor.

Several people stood and watched. Half a dozen came to help. A second priest from the front of the church ran quickly up the aisle. He said, "I'm Father Raymond. What's happened?"

Three or four of the parishioners hurried up. One woman said, "I'm a nurse."

The first priest lifted Danni out of the way, saying to Father Raymond, "This man just collapsed."

"Did he say what was wrong?"

"No."

The old man made a gurgling sound.

Neal said, "Somebody call nine-one-one. Quick."

By now a dozen men and women were gathered around asking to help. Maggie stepped out of the pew so that Neal could get past and reached her hand out for Danni.

Danni was not in the aisle where she had been just seconds before. "Danni?"

The aisle was clogged by a large knot of people. "Is my little girl behind you? Danni? Danni!" Maggie pushed through the crowd, but there was no little figure in a blue-and-white dress. She turned back toward Neal, looking for the sandy-haired priest. But only Father Raymond knelt next to the old man.

"Where is that other priest?" Maggie asked the person closest to her. "Where did he go?" Her voice rose.

"I think he went for help," a woman said.

"Did he have a little girl with him?"

"Yes, I think he did."

Maggie said to Father Raymond, who was slowly lifting the elderly man, "Where did that priest take my little girl?"

The old man said, "I feel terrible!" Holding both hands to his head, he climbed laboriously back onto the seat of the pew.

Father Raymond turned to Maggie. He said, "What do you mean?"

"That priest. Who took my little girl. The one you assigned to greet people coming in."

"We don't have anybody assigned to greet people."

two

Chester Gardena, age thirteen, of Newton, Iowa, saw it first. He was roaming around on the net, checking out web sites, looking at things that had interesting names and might be good stuff. Chester had a Gateway 2000, which his parents had bought him for his birthday. Microsoft Internet Explorer had come with it, which he browsed with, plus a free couple of months of activation and unlimited use. He could hack around on the net and tell his parents he was doing school work. They were clueless about computers.

It was 1:00 P.M., and Chester's parents didn't know he was home; they thought he was in school. But they both worked and got home early in the evening, just in time to order dinner from a Chinese delivery. Or sometimes one of them came home with KFC. Chester liked that better, even though he'd really prefer they picked up cheeseburgers and fries.

So Chester had the house to himself, some cold pizza, and a Classic Coke. Life was truly excellent.

A page name struck his fancy and he looked into it. On

his screen appeared part of a bare room with a doll in the corner. This did not seem nearly as interesting as he'd hoped. Truly a waste of perfectly good net space.

"Some *people*," he said, and was ready to look elsewhere when the doll moved.

Chester watched. When the doll put her hands over her eyes, he realized it was a child. Then she whimpered, just once.

There were some bottles near the child. The walls of the room were light gray and the floor was dark gray wood, which was probably brown in the actual signal, but because of the equipment he was using, he didn't get color. Also it was a little pixelated, like grainy film. There was a small patch of white in the foreground. He said, "Go ahead, do something."

Chester watched another three or four minutes, but nothing else happened. He got bored, said, "You're toast," to the screen, killed the site, and went on to try other pages.

John Ado, who lived in Cairo, Egypt, stumbled on the new page less than a minute after Chester, when he brought up his favorite browser. It was then just past 9:00 P.M. local time or, as his screen had it, 21:01:08.

John owned a small computer repair business that catered especially to American and English expatriates. It was open every day from noon until midnight. It was just lucrative enough to keep him in food and shelter—and electricity and phones, of course. He was an avid net surfer. When he was on, he flew from his room out into the whole world. He especially loved the new pages where the action was live— Las Vegas casinos with man-made erupting volcanoes, or the U.S. National Park Service sites of Old Faithful doing the real thing.

As soon as he got free from a customer and his clerk was back from dinner—far too long a dinner, he thought, how could anybody spend forty-three minutes eating *kammooni-yya?*—John went to his desk and dialed up his local net provider. His screen came up and finally the "what's new on the net" crawler. Because he got hardware in the course of his business, his setup was a Frankenstein—a mixture of the latest Intel mother board, tons of memory, a whole series of SCSI devices with hard drives and CD ROMs, and other good stuff all chained together. He browsed until he saw something that looked interesting. Then he checked it out.

There was a child in a corner of a room. The picture was in color, because he had better equipment than Chester, pixelated, but way clear enough so he could see detail. He could even see that she had blue eyes. Her hair was blonde and she wore a blue-and-white-checked dress. And as he looked closer, he realized she was crying.

In front of the child on the floor was a square-shaped streak of paint. It was in the foreground and disappeared into the "front" of the screen, so he could not see where it led or what it was part of, but he thought it was an intentional thing painted on the floor.

There were some bottles near the child and some sort of pad, no visible windows, and a cold, diffuse light in the room. There was nothing particularly remarkable going on in the room, which was strange all by itself. Web page designers usually gave you some serious action or some advertising or some high-impact, high-octane art. John wondered what it could all mean.

The title of the page was weird, too.

It was <**helpmeplease.**>

Several other people across North America saw the page in the next three minutes, but nobody much wondered what it was.

At five minutes past one central time, the page was noticed by Steven J. Saylor's browser. Mr. Saylor was based in Galveston, Texas, and his job was to morph words and pictures in visually interesting ways for CNN. He spent his work day at his keyboard, and his idea of relaxation after work was surfing the net.

Saylor had excellent equipment—two computers, an Ameritech high-speed T1 line that came into a company T1 LAN box. For his job, he could roll off images to play around with or run through his 3-D text image processor or put them on a CD ROM or DVD for CNN.

Mr. Saylor got *very good* resolution.

Mr. Saylor took one look at the action site and immediately recognized both the probable situation and its news potential. He had no information of any specific kidnapping anywhere in the country, but the thing smelled like a breaking story to him. You got a feeling for these things, he would say to his boss later, after a lifetime of working news. He notified CNN headquarters in Atlanta first, by E-mail, and then left a voice mail for a supervisor to make certain somebody who knew what they were doing would scan breaking news bulletins for a likely connection.

Last, with the important stuff taken care of, he called the FBI.

three

My beeper had buzzed at twelve-thirty. I was washing my hands, prior to making my mother a tuna fish sandwich. Quickly drying my hands, I checked the number. The office, of course. Any other day it would have been my mother calling, but she was in the house with me.

The one Saturday I take off, the department can't let me alone.

Sam, my aide, answered on the first ring. "What's today's crisis?" I asked, cheerfully.

"Drop everything. I'm sending a unit to pick you up." There was no joking tone in his voice.

"I'm in the middle of something."

"Not any more, Polly. Don't even think about it. The car will be there in ten minutes. Maybe less. I hope." He'd been my aide for over three years and knew he didn't have to be deferential—at least when nobody else was listening. "Get moving."

"Why? What's happening?"

"First, you need to know Burkholder is yelling for you. And he's panicked."

"Okay, so it's serious. What is it?"

"A kidnapping. I'm sending some info I've downloaded on the principals. And I'm also sending you the first uniform who responded to the scene. Name's Fetterman."

"He's coming in the car?"

"Yup. And the car's already left."

"I have to go out for a while, Mom."

"But we just got started unpacking. You said you had all day—"

"Yes, I did. I'm really sorry."

"I know your job is important to you."

My job keeps you in macaroni and prune juice. "Now, Mom, you're important, too."

"You said you'd help me settle in."

"I *will.* Soon. Tonight. Anyway, we got almost all of your stuff settled on Wednesday night."

"I know you have to live your own life, Polly," she said, her mouth pursed in a lovely, gentle smile.

Today had started out pleasant. Until about half a minute after I woke up. Then I realized this was the day I was moving my mother into my extremely small house. I didn't want to; I'm not a total idiot. But what could we do? We couldn't afford to keep up both my place and hers on my police officer's salary. Even top cops aren't paid like CEOs at Microsoft and General Motors. My dad had been a cop, back in the days when cops were paid a pittance. Mayor Daley—Daley the First, that was, not our present one—said that you didn't need to pay cops much because they could always steal. Things have changed. Cops are paid a decent living wage now, though it isn't princely. And in my opinion, there's a lot less stealing.

A living wage was not enough to keep my mother out of my guest room. It was that or a nursing home, and I couldn't afford a nursing home.

My mother suffers from depression—actually, double depression is what the psychs are calling it these days. This means that she has occasional major depressive incidents when I have to hospitalize her, and the rest of the time she is just plain gloomy. The good news about the major depressions is that her medical insurance will pay for the hospitalization and doctors and medication. Unfortunately, no insurance covers her home care the rest of the time, and she's so morose her shrink and I both think she's in some danger of suicide and needs to be watched. My mother is sixty-three, acts like ninety, and is as healthy as a two-year-old horse—physically. I feel sorry for her, but I have learned that I can't fix her.

Prozac didn't work. Neither did Serzone, Zoloft, BuSpar, amitriptyline, imipramine, doxepin, clomipramine, fluoxetine, lithium, or anything else. We had been paying a neighbor to sit with her in her house, but the cost ate up her savings. She has nothing coming in because she never in her life was able to work. My dad's police department pension had run out. Taxes and repairs and insurance on her small house were impossibly high. A water heater failure was a crisis; a fallen gutter and downspout was a catastrophe. With her living in my house, we will pay just one set of those costs, which should, God grant, mean I can afford to have somebody sit with her while I'm at work.

Thank heavens I'm at work a lot.

I quickly telephoned Mrs. Drobney next door. She would come over right away. Bless Mrs. Drobney, who wanted to make extra money because her daughter had just given birth to twin boys. The daughter's husband had taken one look at the two small obligations and left her, and the family needed financial supplementing.

"Mom, Mrs. Drobney will help you with any other unpacking."

"How do I know she's honest, Polly? She might take something." *Something like sixteen pairs of outdated, outgrown Supp-Hose stockings with holes in them,* I thought. *Faded family photos? The huge box of twenty-five-watt light bulbs, most of them burned out, that you insisted on bringing?*

"You know Mrs. Drobney perfectly well. I introduced you."

"I've met her. That doesn't mean I know anything about her."

"Well then, get to know her better! Make friends!" I was strapping on my holster, realizing that handguns were going to be another problem in a house with a depressive woman. I'd have to get a safe or trigger locks, just like officers with small children. Everything at home had been so easy up to now.

My mother looked reproachfully at me. I didn't know whether she wanted to make me feel guilty for speaking sharply to her or for wearing a gun. It could be either one, and I didn't have time now to worry about which.

Mom is small, sweet-looking, soft-spoken, her white hair fluffy and curled prettily around her face, her face a youthful pink, carefully rouged. Her mannerisms are girlish, a toss of the head to the side, a lowering of the eyes, whispering when discussing certain delicate subjects.

I said, "I'm sorry, Mom. Go out for a walk with her," I said. "She's really very nice. Get to know the neighborhood."

"Oh, I couldn't, dear. It's been raining. My shoes would get wet."

"I have some old shoes you could use."

"Yours are low-heeled. I can't wear low heels. I've worn high heels all my life and flats make the backs of my legs ache."

"Then wear my rain boots over your own shoes."

"I always feel like I'm going to trip in those things. You know, it would be terrible if I fell and broke something. I'd be laid up forever. And I don't want to be a burden on you."

Suddenly, going out to a police emergency seemed like a really excellent idea.

———

The squad car, a three-year-old Chevy, slid to a halt in front of my house and I strode fast down my walk just as Mrs. Drobney came bustling up, chubby legs pumping. "Gotta run," I said, and she nodded.

A skinny, young, uniformed cop jumped out of the driver's side front door and another young one out of the passenger side. They raced each other to open the right rear door for me.

"Let's move!" I said, sliding in. The driver ran around to the far side, jumped back in, and slammed his door. The other cop, a young man with large ears set at a ninety-degree angle to his head, dithered from foot to foot a couple of seconds about where to sit, front seat or back. I motioned him into the back with me; he climbed in and opened his notebook. The driver stepped on the gas.

"What's your name?" I asked the lad.

"Fetterman, ma'am. Officer Fetterman, ma'am."

"Bring me up to speed," I said to Fetterman, cocking my head at the driver, who was up past speed, or at least past the legal limit. I made the small joke trying to lighten Fetterman up, but he just clutched his notebook firmly.

I said, "Driver, use your lights and siren if you're going this fast on a city street."

"Uh, yes, ma'am."

"Always," I said.

"Yes, ma'am."

"Now, Fetterman."

"Sure. Okay, ma'am, uh, boss." He began to read from his notes. "The kidnapping victim is Danielle Gaston. Female white. She's three years plus four days old. Blue eyes, blonde hair, three feet tall, thirty-six pounds, described as being small for her age, wearing a blue-and-white-checked dress."

I closed my eyes for a second, suddenly deeply sad.

"Go on."

"She vanished during the eleven o'clock mass at Holy Name. As near as we know now, she went missing at eleven forty-five, close to the end of the mass. An elderly man collapsed, and during the confusion the child vanished. She was last seen being carried up the aisle by a priest."

"That's nasty."

"Yes, boss."

"You were the first uniform on the scene. What did the situation look like?"

"There were fifty-two parishioners in the church by my count. And three priests. The mother was on the church steps when we arrived, calling, 'Danni!' The father was with a church official, running around looking in alcoves and stuff like that. I don't know what to call 'em because I'm not Catholic. I put the call out downtown right away because I figured the sooner they told the airports and the highway toll booths and so on the better off we'd be."

"You were absolutely right." This downey-cheeked lad was breathless and pink with the importance of it all, but coping. He was intimidated by me. Not me personally, I'm sure. I am five feet five on a sunny day after ten hours of sleep, and he had to be over six feet. But he probably had never been in a car with a top cop. I realized he didn't even know what to call me, so he had settled for the generic "boss." Which all bosses in the department, even the super-intendent, will happily answer to.

It's a cop thing.

I am Deputy Chief of Detectives, North. Chicago also has a Deputy Chief of Detectives, South, and a big Chief of Detectives, who is boss to both of us. That was Burkholder, who was said to be panicked.

Burkholder's panic plus Fetterman's instant call down-town, knowing word should go out immediately, led me to my next question. "And who is this child, Fetterman?"

"Danielle Gaston. Her father is Sen. Neal Gaston."

"Uh-oh."

"Senator from Missouri," he said. "And her mother is the country-western singer—"

"Maggie McKittredge! Oh, my god."

No wonder Burkholder was panicked.

———

"Who's here?" I said to the Area Three commander, Ainslie, who stood on the steps of Holy Name.

The place was swarming with cops, but he said, "Nobody yet," knowing what I meant. "The superintendent is on the way. Burkholder is hiding back in the tall grass—uh—he's at Eleventh and State."

Eleventh and State is the CPD central office building. Ainslie was telling me that Burkholder was keeping his head down until he knew whether we'd done a good job or a bad job. Then he could either take credit or keep on hiding. Burkholder was famous for this.

I could see now that Sam, my aide, had gotten me over here fast so I would be on the scene when the big boys like the superintendent showed up. Must remember to give Sam an "attaboy."

"Sent out her description?"

"The parents had a recent photo with them," Ainslie said. "We faxed it."

"How many have you got canvassing?"

"Twelve."

It was always an even number. They work in teams.

I gazed up at the facade of Holy Name then out at the street and sighed. "We need a whole lot more." This was a crowded area, directly west of Chicago's Gold Coast. The lake front was five blocks away. Some of the priciest shopping in the world was within a few blocks—Armani, Godiva, Neiman Marcus, Georg Jensen, Cartier, Ultimo, Jil Sander, the list could go on and on. Some of the most hideous, unlivable public housing was also within six blocks.

Holy Name rose grandly above a sea of small stores that clung to its north and south shoulders. Its front steps, facade, and glorious rose window faced west across State Street and from there over a wide parking area almost a full block in size. Beyond that were high-rise apartment buildings. Standing on the church steps, I could look to the corner at my right and see a Burger King, a McDonald's, a liquor store, and a patchwork of store-front shops. Behind them to the north was a beige-pink building, probably thirty stories tall.

A little closer and a little taller was the YMCA tower. Beyond the parking lot, over half a block away, was another high-rise apartment building. None of these was close enough to have a really good view of the front doors of Holy Name. A row of trees with billowing new leaves grew along the west side of State Street, softening the look of the parking lot, obstructing the view of Holy Name for people in the lot and for most of the lower floors of all the apartment buildings. Looking to my left, south, across the intersection of State and Superior Streets, I saw a low-rise apartment building, possibly fifteen floors with stepped-back Mayan-templelike walls, all glass. Behind this, facing the south side of Holy Name, was a gigantic high-rise, forty or fifty floors to my quick estimate, with bay windows in all its apartments. I made a rapid calculation that maybe three to four thousand apartments in the general area, with potential witnesses in them, had some view of the street in front of Holy Name. And we expected twelve detectives to canvas the area! Twelve people would take a full day just to do the fifty-floor high-rise.

Ainslie's eyes were sympathetic as he observed me. He knew what I was up against. If I put too many people on the job, I would be criticized for wasting department money and personnel and devoting time to Danielle Gaston because her parents were famous. If I didn't get enough people on the job and she was found dead—well, that would be utter disaster.

Ainslie really wanted to help. He wasn't a Burkholder. We have good guys and bad guys in the CPD—just like in real life.

I said, "Add another dozen for starters. Pull people off everything else."

"Right."

What I hoped for, of course, was major luck—to find somebody, anybody, who had seen the kidnapping. I wished for an elderly person or a shut-in who spent all day looking out the window.

"How many techs here?" I asked Ainslie.

"Three."

"Hey, spiffy." Sometimes you couldn't get one for hours, even with a murder. "Don't forget to print the church doors. I know a hundred people must have handled them, but still."

A police photographer was taking pictures of the front of the cathedral and the street. This was good. It meant that when we were back in the office questioning a witness or trying to figure out where somebody was standing when he saw—or said he saw—an important incident, we wouldn't have to go out to the cathedral to check whether the facts fit the geography. Simple stuff, but it saves many hours.

"You started your canvass with pedestrians?"

"Absolutely."

"They see anything?"

"Not anything that seems important so far. Of course, anybody walking by at the time of the kidnapping wouldn't likely still be walking by fifteen minutes later when we got here."

"You never know. People do errands and then start back home. You're interviewing customers at all the restaurants?"

"Even as we speak." He said this with a "what-do-you-expect" tone that was fully justified. He'd been in the business as long as I had.

It wasn't my job to check on everything Ainslie did anyway or to criticize him—unless he screwed up, of course. But if he did screw up, my reputation and job were on the line, not just his.

I said, "A busy street. Full daylight. People at the Holy Name mass. People passing by on the sidewalk. Cars everywhere."

"I know. Not easy to sneak off with a kid."

"Do we know how?"

"Other than the fact that she was lifted up into the arms of a priest in the church, no, we don't know a goddamn thing. The bad priest is gone with the kid, and the good priest, Father Raymond, is here. And Father Raymond is hopping mad!"

I pointed at State Street in front of the church. It was a no-parking zone. "Could a car stand here?"

"Sure. Especially if it looked important. Limo or something. But if it was *me* making a snatch, I'd set a precise time and have the car pull up at that instant. Or have it watching from a short distance down the block and pull up the second it sees me. Why take a chance hanging around?"

"Do people pick other people up in front of the church?"

"Of course. All the time."

"Damn. Media know about this yet?

"No." He glanced meaningfully at the street, which would have been filled with TV vans if they had.

"Don't let them hear it from you. And don't release any details."

"You got it."

"I'm gonna scope out the church. I'll go directly to Eleventh and State from here. I want the first written reports from the detectives, whatever they have so far, no matter how skimpy, on my desk when I get there."

"Right, boss."

"Good." I started up the steps. "Now, where have you got the parents?"

"They're not here. They're back at their hotel. The Knickerbocker."

I stood up straighter and looked him in the eye. *"Why?"* This was not procedure. They ought to be here. The first interviews should be done on-site.

"Orders from downtown. Burkholder's order."

"Oh, great! He should make up his damn mind. Either come in and help out or keep his stupid hands off!"

Ainslie nodded.

"I don't like it," I said. "It looks like we have one rule for the rich and another for everybody else."

He hesitated, which was tantamount to saying, "Don't we?" What he actually said was, "Of course we have a kid-gloves rule for people who have the media at the end of a leash."

"Which is why Burkholder wants to push *me* out front."

"Naturally."

"Have the parents been interviewed at least?" I demanded.

"Only—uh—very lightly."

"Holy shit. And we're supposed to leap into full response mode on half information?"

"In a word, yes."

"Well," I said, still steaming, "you got stuff to do. I'll walk the site inside for a minute. Then the neighborhood outside. Then I'll go to the Knickerbocker. But I still want those reports on my desk when I get back."

I headed toward the church doors. The rookie Fetterman's quick action and attention to detail had impressed me. I turned around and said to him, "Come with me."

"But my sergeant said I was to report right back—"

"*Trust* me on this, Fetterman."

Fetterman was a patrol officer, which of course put him one rung below his patrol sergeant. The sergeant ranked below the lieutenant. The lieutenant ranked below the district patrol commander, and the district commander's boss was a gentleman on the same command level as me. Fetterman knew which way the wind blew. He said, "Yes, sir. Ma'am. Uh, boss." His large ears turned magenta, but he followed me smartly.

four

The elevator at the Knickerbocker was as big as my whole bedroom at home. Everything in the elevator that wasn't mirrored was gold or marble, and all the mirrors were gold-veined, the kind of mirrors that make you look like you're covered in seaweed when you see yourself in them. There was a bench, gilded in gold, in case you got tired while riding up or down.

It stopped at the twenty-third floor. The top.

I recognized Maggie McKittredge the minute I saw her, huddled on the sofa in her suite. Recognized her and didn't recognize her, in a way. Like almost everybody in the United States, I'd seen her on television, her red hair shining, eyes gleaming with joy as she sang, wearing glittering dresses—different styles and colors, but always made of fabrics covered with something that danced in the spotlights and fragmented light. Even when she sang sad songs, the old Appalachian ballads she loved, she sparkled.

The woman I met now was drab. She sat in the corner of a slip-covered green-and-white sofa. Her face was expressionless; one hand was a fist covered tightly by the other hand. Every color on her, even the red hair, was dull. She did not see us. I stepped back involuntarily and stepped on Fetterman's foot. He gasped very quietly.

Maggie's husband, Sen. Neal Gaston, was pacing behind her and saw us come in. He pulled himself up stiffly and went to stand near Maggie.

I said, "I'm Deputy Chief Polly Kelly. And this is Officer Fetterman."

Gaston was red-faced and walked high up on his toes. He had black hair and black eyebrows. Just a little gray at the sideburns. He was a big man. I could almost believe I saw his shoulder muscles tense and bunch, right through the expensive soft wool of his jacket. He nodded at me impatiently. "Is there any news?" he asked. I had to give him credit. He spoke to me, even though I wasn't in uniform and Fetterman was. Of course, Fetterman was just past being a child.

"No, I'm sorry. There's no news yet. I'm afraid I need to ask you more questions."

"It's been almost two hours! You should have found her by now!"

"We're working flat-out on it."

"She could be anyplace by this time."

"Sir, I've notified the FBI—"

"*I've* notified the FBI!" he said.

"Fine, sir. Two of us is better than one. Of course, they'd take either one of us seriously, I'm sure." Gaston locked eyes with me. I was ashamed of myself. This man's child was missing. It was no time for a power struggle. I said, "There are dozens of officers canvassing. Hundreds on alert. Her photo has been faxed everywhere. It's very fortunate you had it with you. The all-call went out immediately. O'Hare, Meigs Field, Midway, and every commercial and private airfield within a hundred miles is watching for her. Even the military fields, like Glenview. We've got people at the toll booths on the tollways with pictures of your daughter, which we faxed them. The fax is one of the real benefits of the computer age. There are plainclothes officers carrying her picture in the bus station, the Chicago & Northwestern Station, Union Station, on the el, every subway line—"

He waved his hand. All this wasn't the point. "My *daughter* is still missing!"

"Yes, sir—"

Maggie McKittredge spoke quietly. "Let's answer Chief Kelly's questions, Neal." She rose and moved to one of two white overstuffed chairs that faced each other near the sofa. "Come sit here," she said to me.

Fetterman rocked back and forth from one foot to another. McKittredge said, "And you could take the sofa Officer— uh—"

"Fetterman, ma'am." He stared at her, terribly impressed to be in the presence of a celebrity. But he took out his notepad and pen briskly, sat where she said, and placed his notepad on his knee.

Good boy, Fetterman, I thought.

Maggie McKittredge apparently knew that her husband was too tense to sit down. She didn't even suggest it.

I drew a breath. I would approach the questioning carefully. I didn't want to be aggressive, but I needed to extract every possible detail. And not let my sympathy get in the way.

"Ms. McKittredge"—I paused, wondering whether to call her by her professional name or her husband's name, but she seemed to find this acceptable. She raised her head. She said, "Yes?" very quietly, as if she had very little breath left.

"The detectives who spoke to you first have probably asked many of these same questions, but I need to do it again. I'm organizing the search, and besides that, it's best for you to have several different people ask their own slightly different sets of questions. We have a basic procedure, of course, but no two police officers are alike, and no two cases are alike. The fact that investigators differ gives us more scope. We need to bring out as much information as possible."

"Yes, I understand." She was courteous, immediately attentive, and, I thought, tightly controlled. She did not tell me that she had already answered all the questions she could bear to, even though probably she had. She did not tell me that she was too upset to talk. She raised her head, steeled herself, folded her hands, white-knuckled, in her lap, and said, "Let me help however you want me to."

I was proud of her.

Her husband was another story. "Maggie should be lying down. She shouldn't be badgered." There was anger and frustration in every word.

To her I said, "I'm sorry. I know you're suffering. But this really is best done now."

"Don't apologize. Go ahead."

Senator Gaston had been making fists of his hands and shifting from foot to foot. Finally, he said, "I can't stand this!" and walked out of the room into a sitting room beyond. I realized that what I had thought were voices coming from the farther room was instead a television set. It went through my head that Senator Gaston was a politician. Could he possibly want to see whether there was news coverage of the kidnapping? Then I kicked myself mentally for being so cynical. I had dealt with entirely too many politicians in my job. The man was visibly worried.

Maggie caught my gaze. I hoped she hadn't guessed what I was thinking. "I'm sorry," she said. "Neal is very high-strung. He really isn't able to stand still."

"No problem. I can talk to him after you." In fact, I actually preferred interviewing them separately.

"He doesn't take frustration well."

I nodded. "Let's start at the beginning. How did you get to Holy Name this morning?"

"Neal's chauffeur picked us up at the hotel here."

"His name is—?"

"Cal Stamos."

"And he's been with you how long?"

"With Neal seventeen years. We've been married twelve years."

"Did you go directly from the hotel here to Holy Name?"

"Yes. We passed FAO Schwartz on Michigan Avenue on the way and Danni wanted to stop, but we told her we would later." She spoke the last part of the sentence in a rush, as if getting it out would make it less painful. But she didn't weep.

"And when you got to Holy Name, who did you see?"

"To really notice or speak to, a fiftyish woman. Brown coat, hair turning gray. A younger woman wearing a lilac dress and lilac shoes. Dark brown hair. Slender. Both of them wanted to tell me they liked my singing. Other than that, nobody to talk with. There was an elderly man in front of us, who was somewhat crabby. He collapsed later, so I suppose he was unpleasant because he wasn't feeling well. There were a lot of other people but all spread throughout the church, and we didn't have any contact with them. Maybe fifty or sixty people, all told, scattered around."

"Had you ever seen any of them before?"

"Never."

"Anywhere? Anywhere at all? In a crowd at a concert?"

"No. Not that I recall."

"Did you get a look at all of them?"

"No. Four or five to really look at. Quite a few I only saw from behind. I saw the priest, of course."

"I'll get to him. Let's back up a little first. On your way from the hotel to Holy Name, did you notice anybody following you?"

"Traffic was slow, but that's Chicago. Especially Michigan Avenue. I certainly didn't notice any car that stayed behind us."

"Okay. Outside the church, when you arrived, did you see anybody you knew?"

"No."

"Anybody you noticed especially? Anybody watching you?"

"There was a teenage girl and boy. They stared at the car. Not at us, though, the limo."

"What did they look like? Black, white, Asian, Hispanic?"

"White. Dressed in Levi's. I think the boy had a yellow sweatshirt. The girl had long, dark hair, I think. A ruby-colored stud in her nose. I swear they only looked at the car. I'm used to having people recognize me—" she said this as if it was embarrassing—"and they really didn't seem to."

"Any other car? A car waiting?"

"Not that I noticed."

"Okay. Now let me ask you about the priest. Who probably wasn't a priest."

"Who probably wasn't a priest." She shivered. "To take advantage of that trust—" She stopped for a moment and whispered, "God damn him!"

I watched her body curl forward over her fists, which she held, tight but trembling, against her chest. "In your place," I said, "I'd want him cut in ribbons."

She groaned. "I do." She took two or three slow breaths. "But I'm not—it's stupid, but the way I was raised—I'm not at *ease* with feeling hate."

"I would feel hate. I'd be happy to."

She almost smiled at that. She composed herself again. "Let me try to answer your question. He was medium tall, about five-eleven, I would say. He had light brown hair, very bushy. A *lot* of hair. A little overweight. Those cassocks they wear are fitted, and his was quite tight around the waist."

"Eye color?" I was thinking to myself that these days eye color can be changed with contacts, but we had to start somewhere.

"I'm not sure. That probably means they were hazel. I find I notice bright blue eyes. And very dark brown eyes with light brown hair would probably be noticeable, too, don't you think?"

"I guess so." She was right, but it was important for

her to come up with the description and for me not to influence it.

She said, "He had one of those faces that just isn't distinctive. You look as if this doesn't help you much."

"I'm sorry. I didn't mean to."

"And I know it doesn't. People can change eye color. You can wear lifts in your shoes. A thick wig. I believe this actually *was* a wig. You can wear a couple of vests under the outer clothes to add pounds."

I stared at her.

"I'm in show business," she said softly. "I know about illusion."

"I see. Well, let's talk about the parts of a person that can't be changed. Medium tall was one. You can add a couple of inches, and if you walk very carefully stooped, you may take off an inch or two; but we know he's a little above average height."

"Yes, I agree."

"You saw his nose?"

"Yes. You're right again. That couldn't be changed much. I'm sorry to say it was a nondescript nose. You can expand a nose with plugs or rubber, but this was small, if anything."

"Ears?"

"His hair covered the tops. But nothing special about his ears."

"Not extra large or protruding ears or extra long lobes then?"

"No."

"What about the set of his eyes? Deep sockets? Or did the eyes protrude?"

"Neither. Ordinary. I'm sorry I keep saying ordinary."

"Listen, ordinary isn't as common as you would think. One more hard-to-alter feature: his chin."

"Not pointed. Not big, not sharp, not receding either." She shook her head because this, too, meant ordinary. "Oh, my God. We really have almost nothing to go on. Almost nothing at *all*. Isn't that right?"

"We don't have much. So far. But that's because we're

just starting. You'll be surprised how fast information comes in now. And as we get information on possible kidnappers, this description is going to eliminate a lot of people."

"Don't look so sad, Chief Kelly."

"You could call me Polly, ma'am, if you'd like."

She half smiled. "Polly. Please call me Maggie. Everybody does. Even the stuffiest friends Neal has." Her face lightened. For just a split second she had forgotten to think about the horror that had happened to her. I wondered how long she would have to endure this realization process. Would she wake up tomorrow morning, believing for just a couple of seconds it was a normal morning, then realize that her daughter was gone? Or was there a chance we could find the child quickly, before tomorrow?

She was thinking the same thing.

"Polly, will you find her?"

"Yes, I think we will."

She wouldn't let me get away with that. "Will you find her in time?"

I made a decision. It's probably the same thing doctors do in serious illnesses. I had a doctor tell me once there were two kinds of patients, and you could almost guess from their body language which was which. There were the ones who threw themselves on the doctor's expertise and explicitly or silently said, "You take over and make all the choices. And don't frighten me." Then there were the others who said, "Give me all the facts honestly, and I will run my own life."

Maggie McKittredge was the second type.

"What you're asking is whether I think we'll find her alive."

"Yes." She looked directly into my eyes. "That's exactly what I'm asking. This is a time for frankness."

"Then," I replied, "I have to say I don't know. I can't know. Every case is different. We were on it very, very quickly. Officer Fetterman here reacted very promptly. We have a lot to thank him for. There are cases where children are kidnapped playing in a playground alone during the day or from a bedroom at night and sometimes it's hours before anybody knows they're gone. By then they really could be anyplace. Not this time. Whoever has your child—"

"Danni."

"Whoever has Danni has not had much time to run before the police agencies started looking. The kidnappers have gone to earth somewhere. They must have, as soon as they possibly could. I can say honestly that they can't have gone far."

"Yes." She glanced at the window, as if, without the walls in the way, Danni might be within view. And for all I knew, it was possible. For all I knew, the child could be right across the street.

I said, "Besides, this is not a case of some child molester or disorganized serial killer grabbing a little girl who just happened to be available. Those are the worst. Believe me, the very worst. This wasn't impulsive."

"No. Because if he wasn't a priest, he had to get a priest's clothes first."

"Exactly." I was very pleased; she was terrified, and grieving—and *thinking*. "It was premeditated. Even if he's actually a priest, he's not from Holy Name. That means Danni was taken for a reason."

"Which means they want something."

"Yes. Which means, I believe, Maggie, that they will treat her as a thing of value."

"Oh, my Lord. I just hope so. Because she is."

"A thing of great value," I said.

"She's worth all my life."

I said, "You're very strong."

"First, we're going to find Danni. And when she's home and safe, *then* I'm going to break down."

"All right. Now I'm going to have to ask you some really painful questions."

"Go ahead."

"You're famous. Stalkers follow stars like you. Senator Gaston is famous also, and a politician. Politicians have enemies—"

"Yes—"

"And there was no bodyguard with you?"

"No. I wish Cal had come inside with us. But we didn't think—in a church—"

"Why did you take your eyes off your child?"

She clasped her hands together. It was the only sign of the guilt she must have felt.

"I would give my life if I hadn't," she said in a low voice. "First, it was the old man who collapsed. I thought I could help. I have some CPR training. And Neal was going to call nine-one-one if nobody else did. Two priests were standing right there. I was brought up in the church. I was brought up to revere the body of the church, the representatives of the church, the representatives of Christ on earth."

"But—"

"Even then, if some person dressed as a priest came up to me on the street and asked to take Danni for a walk, say for an ice cream cone, of *course* I wouldn't let her go. But I would let the priests at our church at home pick her up and hold her, like this man did. I know them. And I knew, or I thought I knew, that this man was a real and official member of the staff at this cathedral."

"Why?"

"Because when we came in, he was standing at the door, greeting people as they arrived for mass. And the people seemed to know him."

I had only begun to think that through when Senator Gaston yelled, "Maggie! For God's sake, come and look at this!"

We both jumped, up. Maggie staggered, but I caught her elbow and we both ran to the sitting room. Fetterman clutched his notepad and followed.

The television was set to CNN. Sen. Neal Gaston faced it with his hands pressed together as if he were praying. Maybe he was.

On the screen was a small child, a little girl in a blue-and-white dress, huddled in the corner of a large, bare room. We could hear the child singing, "A-B-C-D-E-F-G—"

Neal put his arm around Maggie's shoulders and held her. He didn't say anything, just provided his warmth, and suddenly I liked him quite a lot. He had been angry before because he had been terrified.

"Oh, oh, yes," Maggie said. "Oh, thank God, it's Danni."

five

The room was not large, but it seemed huge to Danni.
She was used to larger rooms and would not have been able
to explain why this seemed so big to her. The reason was
its emptiness. There was no furniture. There were no rugs.
There were boards over the windows, no curtains. There
were no pictures. Her bedroom at home was almost as large
as this, but it was full of toys, especially her favorite rhi-
nosaurus and Hoppo—Hoppo the hippopotamus.

This room made her voice sound funny.

She sang, "A-B-C-D-E-F-G," and it sounded funny, more
like the bathroom at home than a real room.

Danni was three years old. All the world looked big to
her, but she was used to traveling with her parents and used
to different rooms in different places. What she was not used
to was nasty people who didn't talk with her. Everybody
always talked with her.

The priest who picked her up had been nice at first. He
had told her the old man was sick, and he would carry her

outside where she wouldn't catch the sickness. They got in a car.

That was when the priest stopped being nice. He didn't talk to her at all, just shoved her into the car. And there was no car seat for her—no princess seat. Her daddy called it that.

When they slowed down, she tried to get out of the car. Then the other man gave her a shot. And she didn't think he was a doctor; he wasn't dressed like a doctor. She was really angry at him then. She cried. Then she felt sleepy for a little while. And after a long drive, they came here. The man dropped her in this room and left. He didn't say anything at all. Danni knew Mommy would say he was rude.

And then nothing happened. A lot of time went by and still nothing happened. Nothing at all. Danni tried to be very good, and she didn't cry for a very long time. Then she cried a little bit. But she thought that if Mommy was here, Mommy would say she was a big girl, just like the first day of play school.

This thought made Danni feel better. It made her think of another thing she had noticed. There were lights up on the ceiling here that weren't like lights you had at home. She believed they were called flulessen lights, the ones that were long, thin tubes that play schools had and houses didn't. The flulessen lights were all along the ceiling.

Danni decided this was a sort of play school. If it was like play school, she didn't need to be scared. They had a song they sang at play school called "My Mommy Comes Back." They had it on a video. Quite often the teacher allowed Danni to put the video in the TV and turn it on so they could listen to songs.

Danni sang "My Mommy Comes Back" for quite a long time.

She felt thirsty, but there were bottles of water, and she drank some. Then she decided that at play school about now they would take their nap. This room had a nap pad, which proved that it was very much like play school.

Danni napped for what she thought was another very, very long time.

Now it was time to finger paint. Finger painting was her very favorite part of play school. But there weren't any paints here. For a very long time, Danni moved her hands in big circles and waves on the floor, pretending there were colors, as if she were painting, but it wasn't really much fun. It wasn't anything like the fun of painting at play school.

Danni had to go to the bathroom. She was a very big girl now and never wore a diaper any more. Not for a long time. There was no bathroom here. Danni was worried about this, but she didn't really have to go potty too badly yet, and maybe by the time she did, her mommy would come back.

She was hungry, too. She walked around the room again, just checking, because she already knew there was no place to put food.

"No fish eraser," she said. "No fish eraser."

She tried the doorknob, but it didn't turn, and the door wouldn't open.

six

Back in my office at three o'clock, increasingly worried
because there had been no ransom demand, I sank into the
wood swivel chair, thinking, *Hurry! Hurry up and find her!*
My assistant, Sam, had followed me. A guy—not a cop—
from the Division of Electronic Maintenance came in after
him, carrying a small, dusty television for my office. He
plunked it down but left without plugging it in. Sam
frowned at the man's back, shook his head, and plugged in
the TV. Fetterman came in a few seconds later, still holding
his notepad. I said, "Fetterman?"

"Yes, boss?"

"Run out and find a bookstore and get me a book on child
development."

"A what, boss?"

"A book on child development." When he still looked
puzzled, I said, "What a parent can expect at each age. You
know, Fetterman. Think. What is a three-year-old child able
to do?"

"*Oho!*" he said enthusiastically. Then briefly turning pink, he added, "Sorry. I mean, Oho, boss."

"Thank you, Fetterman."

Fetterman nearly ran into Commander Ainslie in the doorway. Ainslie answered the question neither I nor Sam had asked. "No news."

I said, "Gather 'round." Sam and Ainslie pulled up office chairs, Sam to my left and Ainslie to my right. Ainslie always looks freshly pressed, freshly shaved, and generally crisp. I tend to be suspicious of men who are too fond of clothing, but in Ainslie's case there's a good guy under the polish. He's all cop and all professional.

"The earliest the kidnappers could have gotten out of the church to their car with the child—with Danni—is eleven forty-three," I said. "They would likely have left the cathedral within the first moments after they seized her. The parents noticed she was missing at about eleven forty-four. Nobody looked at their watches right at that instant. Father Raymond looked at his watch at eleven forty-six. I'm allowing a minute *at most* for Maggie to discover Danni was missing, a minute for everybody to bustle around ineffectively, and a minute for several of the bystanders and Maggie to rush to the street doors and look around outside."

Ainslie said, "The kidnappers could have hidden her in the cathedral."

"Not for long. It would be very, very risky, and I assume your people have searched it all by now."

"Absolutely. Inch by inch."

"Searched by when?"

"By twelve noon the real priest, Father Raymond, and Senator Gaston and some church officials had looked in all the obvious places. By twelve-forty I had had my people go over the whole building thoroughly."

"Okay. So sometime after eleven forty-three and certainly before twelve-forty the kidnappers had left the church and were on the street with Danni, getting her away from there."

"Right."

"Confirm for me. When did PAP go into effect?"

"Twelve-ten," Ainslie said.

I was referring to the Chicago emergency plan to seal escape routes. It has a truly long bureaucratic name, but some of us call it "the presidential assassination plan," hence PAP. It orders the staffing of transportation hubs—air, rail, and bus—informing toll booths, notifying the Illinois State Police and all suburban police forces, getting helicopter pilots on stand-by, all the things you want to do fast if you need to button up the city. But you cannot throw out an impenetrable net in a city this size.

I said, "I want tapes of all airport radio traffic after eleven forty-five. No, wait, let's back way up. Make it from last evening, in case somebody came in that we need to know about. Especially private planes and helicopters. Include Glenview Naval Air Base, too."

"They'll object that the military is classified—"

"We'll sic the senator on them if they do. Also, private lines that run helicopter rides. And get the itineraries of the TV channels' traffic helicopters."

"They'll object, too."

"Promise them some sort of *quid pro quo*."

"News footage? When we have it?"

"Whatever. Promise them anything that works. Also, find out about any crop dusters in the area."

"They'll be way outside Chicago."

"No kidding! I didn't think we had a blueberry plantation at State and Madison."

He blinked at my tone of voice. "Right."

"I'm sorry, Ainslie. This is making me angry. I'm afraid we may have lost her. Danni could have been driven to, say, Wheaton, for example, in a car and loaded onto a plane there."

"That's possible."

"I want details about the ownership and routes of everything that goes up in the air, including crop dusters. If that Fujifilm blimp that lumbers around over the Bears games at Soldier Field was up, I want to know when it went up and where it came down. Those planes that fly along the lake-front with advertising banners—"

"I get the picture."

"Good. Know what galls me?"

"What?"

"We can do it with the air, button it up tight if we really try. But not with the ground, and the ground is more likely. We can notify the toll booth personnel, sure. Cops along every major highway. We did that. But all anybody has to do is drive sedately on local, residential streets until they get to Indiana or Wisconsin and then move the child—Danni—move Danni into a farmhouse. And televise from there. There is no way on earth to intercept and inspect every car on every street."

"And we didn't. And couldn't have, even with more warning than we had. Plus, you need probable cause to search a car."

"She could be far outside Chicago by now, and we'd never know."

He nodded gloomily.

"All right. Next, let's get a human being to personally phone seminaries and churches to ask if a priest's outfit has gone missing."

"I'll start with my area right away."

"Assign your detective to sit here and call the whole city. I know your guy will be from Area Three, but I'll fix it later. We've got a lot to do."

"I was going to mention that. Chief, frankly, the problem is too much to do and not enough cops."

"I know."

"I could use another hundred, easy—"

My private phone rang. Very few people have this number. I picked up.

"Polly?" It was my mother's voice, and not a good time to hear it.

"What's the trouble, Mom?"

"Oh, no trouble at all. I'm terribly sorry to bother you. I

just was talking with Mrs. Drobney. I told her she shouldn't stay. I was sure you'd be home for dinner."

"She's supposed to stay until I get there, Mom, whenever that is. And I really don't think I can get there in time for dinner."

"Oh. I'm ever so sorry to hear that. It's been so long since we had a nice dinner together. And I wanted to tell you about some awful digestive problems I've been having since I left home."

"Mom, I hope you're going to think of my house as yours."

"Oh, of course, dear. It's a lovely home. I'm sure my little problem is just nerves."

"I may be back late but—"

"Why?"

"Why?" Ordinarily, confiding in my mother about my work only provoked a thousand questions. Or the same two questions repeated five hundred times apiece. Usually, "What will happen now?" and, "Do you have to get involved?" But in this case, she would probably see Danni on television any minute, and she might actually be interested. "We've had a kidnapping."

"Oh, how awful. Terrible. The poor parents!"

"Yes. I'm in charge of this. That's why I really have to stay awhile."

"Well, Polly, don't you think—"

"Think what?"

"Well, I mean, if you're in charge, don't you think, shouldn't they give a big problem like that to somebody who knows what they're doing?"

I took a deep breath and said I'd be home when I could and hung up. I was used to my mother, which meant in a way that I was burned out on her remarks. Averting the mind was best.

To Commander Ainslie, I said, "I'll get you the personnel somehow. Next point: People are creatures of habit. They go back to the same lunch places day after day. I'm not telling you anything you don't know. But I want you to detail the personnel *now* for tomorrow so nobody screws it up for you. Whatever else gets done, this is vital. I want you to have enough cops to go from one restaurant to another in the Holy Name area tomorrow between eleven-thirty and twelve-thirty, and ask patrons if they saw a priest with a little girl. There's a McDonald's, a Burger King, a deli, and a specialty coffee shop on Chicago Avenue at State. That's at the north side of Holy Name. On the south side there's a sandwich place and another designer coffee place. People sit in coffee houses and restaurants and stare out at the street. They're our very best hope. The other businesses aren't as promising, but try all of them. There are a lot of small businesses along State. A bank. Cell phone store. A Greek take-out. And don't forget all of the high-rises will have a management office and maybe a rental office. A lot of the time they're not busy, and the staff just basically stares out the window. Also, if they have special staffers, like janitors, who take over on the staff lunch hour, we need to interview them, too. Do those today. Some will be closed Sunday."

"Right, Chief," Ainslie said.

"Are there any ATMs in the area with video cameras?"

"Two on State Street. And one each on the McDonald's and the Burger King. We already have the tapes."

"Hey, I knew you would. And you looked at them?"

"Indeed."

"Aw, don't make me work for it, Ainslie. Anything?"

"Nobody in a priest suit. I got a guy listing all the makes of cars going through the drive-throughs, as best he can tell. He's an auto-model expert. But of course, you don't see the whole car. And it's black-and-white tape, too."

"You're saying nothing leaps out at you."

"I'm saying nothing leaps out at me *so far*."

The in-house phone rang. Sam jumped, but I answered it first.

"Agent Khalid from the FBI is here in the parking lot, Chief Kelly," the door guard said.

"Okay. Fine. Get him parked and send him up."

Turning to Ainslie, I said, "Has there been any word from the kidnappers?"

"Not at my end."

"Nor the parents' end? You have a tap on their line at the hotel?"

"It was in by one o'clock."

As Area Three commander, Ainslie covered the First Police District, where the Knickerbocker Hotel was located, and the Eighteenth District, where Holy Name was located, as well as districts Nineteen, Twenty, Twenty-three, and Twenty-four. But there are twenty-five districts in Chicago. I would have to involve the other area commanders for specific searches in other parts of the city.

I said to my aide, "Sam, call the police in Jefferson City, Missouri. Get a trace and tape set up there, too. Senator Gaston's home and office. The FBI would probably like to get in on that, but I don't give a rip who does it as long as it gets done. And Ainslie?"

"Yes, boss?"

"We need to learn all we can about the Gastons. Maggie's whole life and the senator's life even more so."

"Right."

"They wouldn't be the first parents in the world to do something hideous to their child."

"Well, I can't do Missouri, but I can certainly start questioning whatever staff they have here in town."

To Sam, I said, "When you talk to Missouri, ask the police for background on the family. And on the Gastons' staff. We'll get more detail later."

"Yes, boss."

Somebody gave a peremptory knock on the door. Chief Burkholder blew in, hair ruffled, breathing hard. Burkholder has cheeks like saddlebags and protruding, muddy brown eyes.

"Good afternoon, Chief," I said.

"This is a crisis."

"Yes, sir."

"What are you doing about it? You have to inform the airports, the rail stations, the bus—"

"Yes, sir, we've done that. And more." *It's standard, you pompous ass.* "We're canvassing the area. There are at least four thousand apartments with sight lines—" This would stop him. Burkholder hated details and didn't like to be told about them.

He said, "Then take care of it. I want her found now! Can't you handle that?"

It was considered bad form in the department to yell at a subordinate in front of anybody. It was medium-bad in front of the cop's superiors, but really bad in front of their inferiors. Bad form, bad for discipline, bad for morale. Either Burkholder didn't know any better or he didn't care. For an instant, I was furious. Then I remembered the missing child.

"I want her found too, sir." *Suck it up and deal with it,* I thought. Burkholder was just an obstruction—a part of the job. Either I wanted my job, or I didn't want my job. And I wanted my job.

"My reputation is on the line here," he said.

"Yes, sir." I'd long since given up calling him "boss." Boss seemed to imply some expertise or virtue.

"We've tolerated you this far, Kelly, but you'd better perform."

Tolerated? Hey, Burkholder, don't forget, I'm carrying a sidearm. I can shoot you.

I got control of my head. I said, "Yes, sir," the way you're supposed to, and didn't know whether to admire my self-restraint or be ashamed of myself for kowtowing to a fool.

Then I thought again of Danni. And I thought of what could go wrong if this stupid oaf took charge of the search for her. And I said very nicely, "We will all give a hundred percent, sir."

"You'd better!" he said, and he went out, slamming the door. Burkholder had always been unpleasant to women; but instead of learning, however grudgingly, he was getting worse. Which was peculiar.

Commander Ainslie and Sam had kept their heads down

during the exchange. This wasn't cowardice but genuine awareness that they could make things worse. Now Ainslie said, "The man's totally hoo-ha."

"Hoo-ha?"

"New expression, boss. Spelled H-U-H-A."

"And?"

"Means 'Head Up His Ass.' "

I laughed. Then I said, "Forget him. We've got to move fast. We need serious Internet experts. Our computer crime unit is working on locating some. And I called the Computer Crime AIC at the FBI. I want to tell you both now, before Khalid gets here, that we're going to cooperate with him fully. This is no time for interagency rivalry."

"As long as we don't get it *from* him. You know how it goes. They love us while we give them our data, and after that we can hold their coats."

"You know the drill. The feebies get to come in on the case, whether we want them or not, if there's a ransom demand. They can come in after twenty-four hours anyway, on the assumption that the child may have been taken across state lines. Kidnapping is a federal crime."

"Sure. But they only choose to come in if they think they can make points on it."

What Ainslie was talking about was a belief shared by a lot of local police departments. He meant that the FBI enters cases where the local cops have collected enough evidence so that the feds are pretty sure they can solve it. And local cops believe that the feds keep their hands off, or hold a "watching brief," when the case looks like it's unsolvable and going to spread around a lot of discredit.

There was an exception. I said, "Yeah, Ainslie, or when it's a high-profile case."

"You're right. They'll have to take this one on. You couldn't get much more media uproar than this is gonna make."

"Well, I'll tell you one thing. If there's any probability that Danni has left Chicago, I *want* the feds to take over.

But if she's still here, I want control. The feds don't know Chicago like we do."

"Hell, even their local agents aren't from here."

"They move them from city to city intentionally."

"Sure. Keeps them honest. Less chance of them getting too cozy with local bad guys."

"If Danni is in Chicago, I'll fight to keep control of the case. I promise you. Now—we don't have time to waste worrying. Ainslie, get cracking. Sam, the FBI guy is on the way up. Get us an appointment right away with DiMaggio or the superintendent."

"Aye-aye, boss."

In the few seconds after Ainslie left and while Sam got on his phone, I pictured Maggie McKittredge as I had last seen her. From the moment Danni had appeared on the television screen, Maggie's gaze had been fixed on her daughter. I had tried to speak to her a couple of times and quit when she wouldn't look at me, only at Danni. Then, belatedly, I realized it didn't matter whether she looked at me; she was willing to talk, unless Danni was saying something at that moment. She was just simply not willing to *look* anywhere else.

"Tell me about Danni," I had said. "A three-year-old child must—"

Just then Danni on the screen had said, "No fish eraser. No fish eraser." Maggie was transfixed a few seconds. Then she told me, "What you need to understand is that Danni isn't just 'a three-year-old child.' She's a person. She has several friends her age she plays with, and they're all different *people*. People, not three-year-olds."

"I understand that. I really do; I have nephews."

"Danni is artistic. She paints and crayons all the time. I expected to have a child who liked to sing, but she only sings a little. Danni is deaf in one ear. I don't think that's why she doesn't sing so much. It doesn't really affect her hearing, although she can't tell where a sound is coming from quite as easily as a person with hearing in both ears.

Her artwork is in a different category. She's *fascinated* by paints and colors and shapes."

"I see."

"Do you have children?"

"No. Just the nephews."

"I wish—" She stopped herself.

"You wish I did have. You think I'd be more sympathetic."

"No, I didn't mean that."

"Yes, you did, and you're entitled. But I can tell you one thing. I don't have children, but once upon a time I *was* a child. I remember being frightened the first day of kindergarten. I remember being frightened when my mother— um—when my mother had a catastrophic major depression, actually. I was five. Anyway, I *was* a child, and Danni is a child, and I sympathize with her."

"I accept that, Polly."

"Tell me about Danni."

"She can do lots of things. She can ride a tricycle. She can put on her clothes, all except buttons in back and tying her shoelaces. She helps me bake cookies. Children her age can do most daily tasks. They're smart. Have you ever stopped to think, Polly, that little children, not much older than Danni, can pronounce one of the longest words in the English language, five syllables, and do it every day?"

"Well, no. What word?"

" 'Refrigerator.' We just don't give children enough credit. They have a lot to learn, but they're very, very smart. And much more alert than adults. Much quicker. Anyway— when Danni first said 'fish eraser' a few months ago, we couldn't understand what she meant. She kept saying it and saying it, and she got so frustrated finally that she burst into tears. So I said, 'Can you show me?' and she took me into the kitchen and pointed to the refrigerator. She's lacking one syllable and the 'g' and the 't' are both 's', but she's still saying a four-syllable word."

"Yes. I get it. I stand corrected."

Maggie sat back and became less fierce. Her eyes were

still on the television screen and her red hair haloed her face. "I'm sorry, Polly. I was lecturing you."

"No. I needed to know."

"I just get so tired of people acting as if children were stupid." She held up her hand. "Not you. Just people generally. Let's get back to the subject." She bit her lip, took a breath, and again successfully fought off tears.

She said, "Danni is telling us there's no refrigerator in that room."

"Oh. Now I understand."

"Polly, do you see any food there at all?"

seven

My office door opened fast, and a woman I didn't know marched in without knocking. She was short, had about as much meat on her as a sparrow in February, and her dark brown hair looked like it had been chewed off by a particularly angry pit bull.

"What do you want?" I snapped, irritated that she hadn't knocked.

"I'm Special Agent Hannah Khalid, FBI," she said, standing with her feet about twelve inches apart, her head raised. "I'm the agent-in-charge on the Gaston case."

Oh, shit, was in my mind, but I said, "Welcome to Chicago."

She had to be about forty-five or fifty, which put her about ten years older than me and meant that she either had gone into the FBI at a time when the agency would rather have warts than women, or she had risen in rank in some other police-related field, like Army Intelligence, and then taken the training and made the switch.

She said, "I've been here before. Greylord."

Greylord was a well-known federal investigation that had caught a raft of Cook County judges taking bribes for verdicts. So she'd helped clean up Chicago's dirty laundry, huh? And now she's back to fix things again? Dirty judges were no friends of mine, but I didn't exactly want Hannah "the Lone Ranger" Khalid hanging over my every move and dictating every decision.

Sam was on the phone, his eyes following the action in the room. He must have felt the tension.

To Khalid I said, "Sit down. We'll have to get everybody's roles straight—"

But Sam jumped to his feet. "They want us in room 223 this minute."

"Who does?"

"DiMaggio."

"That's Deputy Superintendent DiMaggio," I told Khalid, who was still standing. I scooped up the reports that Ainslie's men had made and tucked them under my arm. "Let's move!"

"Four hours and nothing!" Chief of Detectives Burkholder squawked. "What are we paying you for?"

He was yelling at me and Ainslie both, completely unconcerned that this new burst of bad temper was all being said in front of Agent Khalid, who was a feebie. With the long-standing competition between the FBI and local police agencies, it was a major breach of cop manners to hurl accusations in front of a fed. Far worse than in front of CPD people.

I said, "Commander Ainslie had a full account of the event in my hands in minutes. His people had written reports on my desk in an hour." I waved them in the air. Ainslie was a good cop, and I couldn't let Burkholder ream him out.

Ainslie jumped in. "Every step in the protocol went into play immediately. The parents had a photo on them and we faxed—"

"It's results that count! If you'd buttoned up the city of

Chicago the way you should have, we'd have the kid now. You let them get her away. We need somebody with more smarts than you and Kelly."

"Hold it, Chuck," Deputy Superintendent DiMaggio said. Chief Burkholder froze in midrant. DiMaggio, who was Burkholder's boss, added softly, "And, Chuck, sit down."

He did. DiMaggio went on. "I've never seen a kidnapping net go into place faster."

Burkholder said, "But if—"

"If nothing. We are all going to have to face the fact that whoever snatched Danni Gaston planned it superbly. He is extremely clever and we can see that he's extremely sophisticated technologically. Now let's all settle down."

I said, "Let me introduce FBI agent Hannah Khalid."

"Holy shit, two of them," Burkholder muttered, meaning he had two women on the case. DiMaggio froze him with a look that must've left Burkholder wishing he was camped out in a bunker somewhere.

"Let's *all* sit," DiMaggio repeated, cocking his head toward the table.

Room 223 is large, square, and featureless, except for the flag of the state of Illinois and the U.S. flag hanging like bookends for the wall-length blackboard. The long, oval dark veneer table in the middle is surrounded by plain metal chairs. With a great deal of scraping, everybody settled. Khalid took one of the two head ends of the oval. DiMaggio, glancing at her, took the other end. I stuck myself next to him.

DiMaggio said, "Anything you want to ask us right now, Agent Khalid?"

"We have our own protocol, of course," she said, "which we will put into effect immediately. First of all, we need complete monitoring of the senator's phones at the Knickerbocker Hotel. When the kidnap demand comes in, we need trace equipment in place, ideally in a room adjacent to the Gaston's suite."

DiMaggio glanced at me. "Been done," I said. "Three hours ago."

"And?"

"No demands at all. Lots of calls. Sympathy calls, wanting-to-help calls from their friends."

Khalid said, "But any one of those could be a gloating call. You need—"

"Been done. Every one traced, taped, logged, and also listened to by a real live human being."

She shot me a glance. "Good."

DiMaggio said, "All right. Kelly, you'd better tell us everything you know so far."

I stood up. I had not quite opened my mouth when the door burst open and the Superintendent of Police strode in. "What the hell have you all accomplished?" he barked.

"Deputy Chief Kelly was just about to tell us," DiMaggio said mildly. DiMaggio was known for speaking more and more softly as a crisis got more and more severe. He was a management genius, actually.

The superintendent nodded sharply, sat, and folded his arms.

I held Fetterman's initial report on the abduction and now read from it in detail. I picked up the detectives' prelims and read selectively from those. I described the Cook County–wide tight net, the looser Illinois state net, the national queries. When I finished, there was silence for a few seconds.

Then the door blammed open again. *It's a day for doors,* I thought. Two bodyguard-types entered, trailed by three extremely worried uniformed police officers who thought they should have somehow stopped what was happening and, oh yeah—wait for it!—the *mayor!*

I breathed, "Oh, hell."

Burkholder gasped.

"This makes Chicago look like shit!" the mayor yelled.

The superintendent bolted to his feet. "Mayor Wallace! Glad to see you, sir."

Like you'd be glad to see the Ebola virus.

DiMaggio said, "Mr. Mayor, this is the representative of the FBI, Special Agent Hannah Khalid."

Mayor Wallace waved his hand, dismissing Khalid. "I want this thing solved," he said.

"So do we all, sir," the superintendent said.

"I had a call from the president. He is a personal friend of Senator Gaston. He is deeply concerned."

I heard DiMaggio whisper, "He's deeply useless." DiMaggio was some distance away from the mayor and the superintendent, and nobody else would have heard him, but I smiled, then quickly killed the smile. Chief of Detectives Burkholder started to stammer pointless excuses. The mayor overrode him.

"Plus six other senators have called asking how this could have happened. They're scared for their own kids. Plus, do you people realize this is *on the net?* Everybody is gonna see it!"

The mayor and his entourage were still standing, which had forced all the rest of us, one after the other, to rise to our feet. There were plenty of chairs, but Mayor Wallace was enjoying our discomfort.

Wallace stepped toward the table, and it looked like he was going to sit. But instead, he slapped the tabletop.

"So who's in charge?" he demanded.

Silence everywhere. Crack! He slapped it again.

Burkholder said, "We're just about to form a task force, sir. The head of it will probably be Deputy Chief Polly Kelly, sir."

Probably? What was this all of a sudden? Did he want to take over himself? Very unlikely. Or did he prefer the FBI? How *could* a Chicago cop prefer the FBI?

"Her?" The mayor pointed at me. "And this is our FBI guy?" He pointed at Khalid. He smiled a death grin. "How nice. We're gonna have two girls in charge."

"We can supervise them, sir," Burkholder said, making things worse. "We're all in charge. There's a chain of command here."

"Actually, I'm in charge," Khalid said. "The Bureau is taking over."

The mayor looked at the superintendent and the superintendent looked at DiMaggio. DiMaggio got the message that the buck had gone up to the top, stopped, and had bounced two steps back down to him.

He laced his hands behind his back and faced Khalid. "I don't think that's quite the way it works, Agent Khalid."

"Yes, it is. There's a U.S. senator involved. We're assuming that the kidnapping is politically motivated."

"That could be. But it's a Chicago case as of now."

"We're taking it over."

"I don't think so. The agency has a mandate to come in if there's a ransom demand. That's a legal principle that goes back to the 1930s. We have not had a ransom demand."

She replied, "And also if twenty-four hours pass and the victim has not been found. At that point the presumption is made that the case has gone interstate. This is in 18 USCS Section 1201."

"Not exactly, Agent Khalid. You're thinking of 18 USCS Section 1201(b), which says, if I remember correctly, that 'failure to release the victim within twenty-four hours after he shall have been unlawfully seized, confined, inveigled, decoyed, kidnapped, abducted, or carried away shall create a *rebuttable presumption* that such a person has been transported in interstate or foreign commerce.' I might be off on a word or two. Up to 1956, the cut-off was seven days. Up until the act of August 6, 1956, in fact. You don't want to be too hasty about this. You can get into real trouble in court later on if you come in wrongly and the prosecutors try to prove on inadequate evidence that a specific kidnapping was a federal crime. You might want to take a look at *United States v. Moore*. It's a 1978 New York case. I think we've sealed Chicago enough to rebut the presumption."

Khalid fixed her gaze on him, her thin, leathery arms crossed. DiMaggio added, "Plus, it's only been four and a half hours."

Khalid was silent. The mayor looked on, bright-eyed. Burkholder miraculously managed to keep his mouth shut. Finally, Khalid said, "You hang around twenty-four hours with your thumb up your ass and she turns out to be in

Vernal, Utah, dead, you're gonna look like shit."

"Checking on leads outside the city of Chicago, if there are any, is your job. Chicago is our job. Danielle Gaston is probably in Chicago, and in Chicago Chief Polly Kelly's in charge."

The mayor said, "Has Kelly got any experience with a case this big?"

DiMaggio said, "Polly Kelly is the best we have. She handled the negotiations with the bombers in Daley Plaza last year."

The superintendent said, "Come to think of it, I'm not sure we've ever *had* a case this big."

"Well, I think you'd better pair her up with somebody— uh—else," the mayor said, not wanting to say male.

"If you wish, of course we can—" Burkholder began, forgetting in his excitement that there were two people in the room more highly placed in the CPD than he was.

"That's enough, Burkholder!" DiMaggio barked at him.

The mayor said, "And we need to develop a consistent story to tell the media."

"I'll talk with News Affairs when I leave here," the superintendent agreed. "I'll get right back to you."

"I'll have my press rep call your press rep," the mayor said.

"But wait," said Burkholder. The man still hadn't caught on. His basic problem, besides lack of guts, was he wasn't real bright. "How long will we give Kelly? Do you want me to partner her—"

I said, "Some one person has to be in charge. There has to be a center!"

"But the question is who?" said Burkholder. "The fact that you *want* it, doesn't mean you can do the job."

"Hold it!" I said, finally really pissed off. "There's a little girl out there someplace going into a long night all alone. She has no idea where she is or why Mommy doesn't come."

Mayor Wallace's brows drew down so far they hid his

eyes, but I was so mad I didn't care. Either I got the chance to do this right or screw it. Who needs this?

"I don't know that I do want it," I said. "I only *want* this if I can do it right, and it's going to take more than talk to do it right. It's gonna take resources.

"Now look," I went on fast, "let's not blow this. We haven't passed the point of no return. It's still way less than five hours since the kidnapping. But if we don't commit resources *now,* we're going to find by noon tomorrow that we've lost data—because we failed to gather it in time— data that we will never be able to get back again. Trace evidence gets stepped on. Memories grow dim. Or get falsely amplified by news reports. We need to commit manpower now, or yes, Chicago *is* gonna look like shit.

"First, I want at least another twenty detectives to canvass. Detailed to Ainslie from other areas. Area Three is stripped already. All apartments with sight lines to Holy Name need to be queried in the next few hours, by which I mean *tonight,* before people forget what they saw; and God grant we're lucky enough that somebody saw something."

"Amen," the mayor said.

"Then tomorrow the whole area around Holy Name needs a deep canvass. Ainslie has my directives on it. He's been doing a great job. But he needs *a lot* more personnel. Fifty or better even, a hundred more cops."

Nobody said yes or no, so I went on.

"Second, I want the city *scoured* for video experts. Somebody extremely sophisticated set up that surveillance camera in the room with Danni, and they've set up the server in a way that our cyber guys haven't been able to trace yet.

"Third, I want every rent-a-car place in the city and suburbs queried. Every single one. Tonight. For this I don't need detectives. District uniforms can do this. They all know their own districts. Whoever snatched Danni Gaston had a car. They didn't walk off with her, down State Street, hand-in-hand. And they sure don't seem to me dumb enough to have used their own car. They may have had to rent a car within walking distance of where they've hidden Danni, because if there's just one or two kidnappers, there may be nobody else to chauffeur them all over."

"But we don't know what kinds of people to ask the rental places about," Burkholder said.

"I realize that, sir. For now we'll have to fall back on the 'Did you notice anything or anybody strange?' line, but it's gotta be done. Nervousness, haste, a driver's license that didn't smell just right. Something that caught some rental agent's eye. Our guys know how to ask. We do have Maggie's description of the man. Maybe we'll get lucky and find out a man in a *priest's* outfit rented a car. The point is to get the data now while it's fresh to have it for later, to put together with the other info we're going to get.

"Fourth, I want the feds—Agent Khalid and her gang— to take over the technical search for the server. They have to trace back through the net to the service provider then to the person who paid for the service and find the videocamera in Danni's room, wherever that is. The feds've got a whole lot more expertise in that kind of tech stuff than the CPD has and much, much, more hardware." The superintendent drew a breath to object, but then thought better of it. Maybe he figured he could pass the buck easier if he could blame the feebies.

"You can do that, right?" I asked Khalid.

"Sure. We've got the tools."

"Although I assume Quantico started the search at noon, when I first queried them, and they haven't found it yet."

"It's just a matter of time," Khalid said firmly. "All they have to do is ask the service provider who the subscriber is. If they don't have an address, they'll have a charge card number. Then we trace back to the address and go in and pick up the child."

"If it's so easy, why haven't you got results already?"

"I'll find out," she said firmly.

I said to the mayor, "When I got back here today after talking with the parents, I called Motorola in Schaumburg. Just in case we don't find the source—" Khalid frowned at me "—so quickly." Schaumburg was at least thirty-five miles northwest of the Loop, but it was considered a suburb. "They're willing to give any high-tech help they can on identifying the type of hardware the kidnappers are using. They know this stuff cold. For that matter, they probably manufactured it, and they might be able to tell us where it was sold. I'm sure Agent Khalid will be eager to use them all she can."

I looked at her. Her dark brown eyes stared at me coolly for a second; then she said, "Sure. Fine with me. The more help the merrier."

"Fifth, I also want the FBI to deep-background Senator Gaston and Maggie McKittredge at the Missouri end. As you all know, the most likely kidnapper is always a family member or a close confederate. We think we know Maggie and the senator because we've seen them so much on TV. But in fact, we don't know them personally at all. Can you do that?" I asked Khalid. I knew what she'd say, of course.

"No problem."

"And in D.C., as well. Full data on the senator's committees and political stands and especially every enemy he's ever made. If I know politics, this will be a *huge* number."

The mayor laughed out loud.

"Sixth, Agent Khalid, we're going to need all the television footage of the senator and Maggie that we can get our hands on. His campaigns. Her television specials. Talk show appearances. News bits. I want it all scanned for the faces in the audience. I'm especially looking for anybody who keeps turning up whom we can't background and explain."

"Seventh, this is for the CPD. I want a major citywide search launched for that fake priest. I have a sketch artist working on it with Maggie and the Senator and Father Raymond, using the computer Identikit system. Also of the old man who collapsed. I want News Affairs to make sure both pictures run on all news programs—print media, TV, whatever—as soon as they're ready."

"Why the old man?" Burkholder asked.

"He disappeared. One minute he's deathly ill, distracting everybody, and the next minute he isn't there anymore."

DiMaggio said, "Right. Good."

I said, "Plus send the drawing of the priest to every church and religious order in the area. That priest outfit came from someplace.

"And last—" I said.

The mayor, happy now, said, "Whew."

"And last, I want twenty-four hour monitoring of the web site of Danni. I've already ordered continual taping with time tagging. But I want an informed human being, preferably a senior detective, physically watching at all times, so if there's any important development I can be flashed on it right away.

"That's it. So far."

There was a short period of silence. Then DiMaggio, taking the temperature of the room accurately, said, "Well, I think that covers it. Kelly, this will be the war room. Agent Khalid, do you want to operate out of here or the local FBI office?"

She glanced at me. "Here will be best."

"I'll have filing cabinets moved in immediately. Computer terminals, printers, phones. Shouldn't take half an hour. Electrical's all in place." He grinned. "And maybe a direct line to News Affairs?"

I rolled my eyes.

He said, "You got CNN continually running the site; it's on everybody's computers; every channel has Breaking News Bulletins; and two dozen reporters are already clogging up the lobby. If you think this is bad now, just wait until people go home for dinner and the whole world sees Danni on the evening news."

The mayor looked thoughtful. Or maybe worried, not thoughtful.

I said, "Okay."

We hit the hall, letting the mayor and superintendent go first, of course. I glanced at Khalid, wondering if I'd been too hard on her.

She said, "Hot damn! You gave it to 'em good!"

eight

Dinner for William Harper Jordan and his wife, Phoebe Jordan, was a simple affair. They ate it in the family room in front of the television set.

Bill and Phoebe lived in Winnetka, one the wealthiest suburbs in the United States. Their house, though substantial, was not by any means a mansion. There were plenty of mansions in Winnetka, hundred-room Tudor palaces on the lake, country French "cottages," formal white colonials, and antebellum southern mansions with grand pillared porches. The Jordan house had four bedrooms and three bathrooms. It was red brick, with a large terrace behind it where Bill and Phoebe used to entertain their friends and their children's friends. That was in the good old days, when the children were still living at home. The Jordans had three boys, all of whom were now married. Two lived in the Chicago area, and the other one, who lived in Sarasota, visited quite often, bringing his family, but it just wasn't the same anymore.

The house was quiet. The dining room was especially

quiet. It seemed almost hollow without the kids, as if it had some sort of negative echo of the voices that were no longer there. So Bill and Phoebe just didn't eat in the dining room much anymore.

Bill was senior vice president in charge of loan applications at the Copley Water Tower Bank in Water Tower Place, a huge, elegant, vertical mall on Michigan Avenue two blocks west of Lake Michigan. He kept banker's hours, in a sense, arriving at Water Tower by eighty-thirty and leaving work most days by four-thirty. He went into town every sixth Saturday also, since the bank was open until two in the afternoon and one bank officer had to be on hand any time the bank was open. Bill traveled each day by the Chicago & Northwestern commuter train, and on Saturdays went home on the one that arrived in Winnetka at 4:21. He always walked the five blocks to his house. Phoebe had their dinner ready at five-thirty, a salad, lean fish (today salmon) and a small glass of white wine each. They carried their dinners into the television room.

They sipped their wine without talking. Bill smiled at Phoebe and she smiled back and touched his hair. They were comfortable with each other, happy with each other in a quiet way, and the fact that they didn't talk much was the result of having lived together thirty-five years. They knew each other well and didn't need to fill silences out of nervousness.

The five-thirty national news came on as they sat down to eat.

"Our top story is a bizarre kidnapping in Chicago," said Lynne Lowery, her eyes wide. "The three-year-old daughter of popular country song stylist Maggie McKittredge and Missouri senator Neal Gaston has been abducted."

A view of Danni in her prison room appeared on screen. "In a bizarre twist, a picture of the child, Danielle, is being broadcast on the Internet, apparently live."

The picture of Danielle shrank to a box in the corner as the camera again showed Lowery. "The child was with her parents at a Saturday morning mass at Holy Name Cathedral in downtown Chicago when she vanished." Now the primary picture was the cathedral, with police cars in front and the sidewalk strung with yellow barrier tape. Danielle remained in the upper corner box.

"The Chicago Police Department is asking that anyone who has seen the child"—now a full-size studio portrait of Danni filled the screen—"contact the Chicago Police Department immediately. The number appears on your screen."

The focus shifted to Lynne's coanchor, Bret Kasmarczyk.

"The child was abducted during a morning service that began at eleven A.M. Police estimate that the child was removed from Holy Name at or near eleven forty-five. She is thought to have been abducted by a man dressed like a priest."

Lynne said, "Bret, the FBI entered the case immediately, and a top FBI kidnapping negotiator has been dispatched from Washington. NBC has learned that a task force consisting of Chicago Police Department members and FBI agents has been formed. Detectives in Jefferson City, Missouri, are probing for threats aimed at Senator Gaston."

Bret said, "The career of Maggie McKittredge spans fifteen years—"

As the pictures of Maggie came on screen, Phoebe Jordan said, "That poor woman! I can't stand to think of it!"

Bill said, "Mmmm," absently. They watched scenes from Maggie's career then Senator Gaston's career for a few minutes while they ate, the view of Danni still in the upper corner. Phoebe Jordan did not especially notice that Bill wasn't saying anything because silence was normal for them.

"Neither Maggie McKittredge nor the senator could be reached for comment. Calls to the senator's office in Jefferson City, Missouri, were answered by the request that people everywhere watch for Danni.

"In other news, the Chicago City Council today voted on a proposal to decentralize the Chicago school system—"

A few minutes later Phoebe said, "Would you like some dessert?" She smiled. "Remember the days when we could have ice cream? I have fresh pears or applesauce—" But Bill was shaking his head, so she stopped.

"I think I'll go out for a walk," he said.

"Really? Are you feeling okay?"

"Sure. I'm fine. I just want to think about something, that's all."

Phoebe put the dishes in the dishwasher. Then she ate one of the pears, thinking it was a little mushy. Where were the crisp pears she remembered from her childhood? The ones that snapped when you bit into them?

But finally it was an hour later and Bill still wasn't home. Taking a walk after dinner was unusual for him. Not unheard of. If there was a problem at work, he liked to walk and think.

When two hours had passed, she started to worry.

nine

Midnight.

The war room was relatively quiet. On the wall, a hanging twenty-seven-inch Sony television constantly ran CNN. This was much better TV equipment than Electrical Maintenance had sent to my office and much better than we usually were given in these days of budget constraints.

The <helpmeplease> net site itself ran on a monitor hooked into the building's T1 line, which gave it the bandwidth necessary for great clarity. A detective, this one from Area Two, watched the picture. He had replaced a man from Area One. We switched them frequently. After four hours of staring at Danni on the screen, they tended to space out. In front of the detective was a notepad where he would write down anything that worried him, and the time, and then he was to tell me—or page me if I wasn't in the room. This was a very low-tech approach as things go these days. But it is vital never to leave the human assessment out.

The page from the Netscape browser carried a record feature that downloaded the image and recorded it as a

QuickTime file with a time stamp. This way we would be able to look back to any day and time whenever we wanted and see exactly what the room looked like and what Danni had been doing.

Maintenance had done a flat-out great job with the war room. The table was gone, and the room was ringed with a variety of high-tech gear. In addition, we had six phone lines, not including the dedicated line to the FBI office in Chicago. We had three Dell computer workstations and two officers assigned to full-time data entry. They used a Microsoft-access data-management program called COPS that ran on Windows; a local consulting company had developed it for us a year ago. There were three file cabinets for what one of our data-entry people called "Stone Age files," files made out of paper. The other computer jockeys sneeringly called it "treeware."

Khalid and I each had a desk. Three other small, unassigned desks were for the occasional use of people like Ainslie, or the CPD attorney, various visiting experts, my aide, Sam, who worked back and forth between my real office and this place, or even Fetterman.

The wall behind me was completely covered with blow-ups of the evidence photog's pictures of Holy Name and the sidewalks, buildings, and shops around it. I'd ordered them mounted in a panoramic layout so that I could stand in front of them and almost feel I was on the steps of Holy Name seeing the north corner first on my right. Then, turning my head forward, I could look out west across State Street and the parking lot, and so on.

Another set was of the cathedral's interior.

A war room is actually a rare thing in police work. Ordinarily, if we have a barricade or hostage situation we send in the HBT people, hostage-barricade-terrorism. They take the mobile scene van, called the "kiddy car," as an on-site war room, park it as near as is safe, and that's the command scene. Most of us think the primary purpose of the van is as a place for the brass to do "photo ops" for the media, because the actual cops spend no time in it to speak of. In stranger-danger kidnappings, which are fairly rare here, we may set up in the victim's home. We don't often use a room in the CPD.

I flipped the report of Detective M. Bruce to my left and from a thick pile picked up the report of Detective J. Robinson.

Robinson had talked with twenty-two of the residents of the high-rise on the corner of State and Superior.

One tantalizing scrap was embedded in page seven of his report. A resident whose apartment faced State Street in roughly the middle of the block had been tending her house plants. The woman, a Mary Anne Mahoney, who gave her age as "over seventy, but it's none of your bloody business," had complained about the difficulty of growing plants in a west exposure. "Nothing much wants to bloom." Mahoney had been going back and forth to her front windows with a watering can and had noticed a car parked with its motor running next to the curb in front of her building. "Badly tuned. You could see the exhaust." This would have been a half block south of the cathedral's main doors.

I got up and walked closer to the photos. Her description of the street was accurate. Parking meters marched the whole length of the block. A car could wait unobtrusively a long time if there was a parking space. It was far enough away from the cathedral that a casual observer wouldn't think of it as waiting for somebody to come out of the church. And it was close enough so that the driver could easily see whoever emerged on the church porch, which was raised six steps above street level.

Robinson, of course, had asked Mahoney to describe the car. This was the bad news. She thought it was "ordinary." Color? Well, maybe dark. Green or dark blue or black, although probably not brown.

Two-door? Four-door?

She wasn't sure and how could she be expected to see car sides from way up here anyway, and besides she didn't know she was supposed to watch for cars, did she?

Still, it was a smidgen. She was sure it was a car, not a limo, not a truck, not a camper.

Of course, it also might not be a kidnapper.

I stretched and groaned just as Deputy Superintendent DiMaggio strode in. He looked as fresh as he had seven hours earlier.

"Why are you still here?" he demanded.

"Oh, boss, I couldn't let it go. Look at her."

He stopped and stared at the screen a few seconds then rubbed his hand over his face. Danni was sitting up, rubbing her eyes with her hands.

"I understand how you feel, Polly. But forcing yourself isn't going to help."

"I keep thinking I'll get some blinding, brilliant insight."

He patted my shoulder. "You may. Probably you will. But it won't come by forcing it. You'd do better sleeping on it. Insights come out of some deep subconscious place when you least expect them."

"Yeah, well, but they have to be fed with some data first."

DiMaggio was a great boss. Give us a hundred like him and the CPD would be heaven on earth.

"So go home," he said. "There'll be plenty of time to work. I want you ready for a long siege."

"Why? What do you mean?"

"Oh, just that I think this has been too well-planned to be solved in a matter of hours."

I looked squarely at him. All cops get feelings. Cops as good as he is get feelings that are very often right.

He said, "This is not gonna be easy."

Hannah Khalid was frustrated and angry. She had been sitting temporarily at a borrowed desk in the Chicago offices of the FBI at 219 South Dearborn, but she got so impatient with what she was hearing that she picked up the phone and walked around. It was not a cell phone, of course. It was a direct line to Quantico, both mechanically secure and garbled at this end, decrypted at the other end. "Like it matters," she grumbled to herself while the other voice droned

on. There wasn't enough goddamn good news to bother
keeping secret.

Finally, she said, "You *told* me it wouldn't be any problem. Piece of cake, right?"

The voice on the other end, belonging to George Stanton,
said, "If you're going to get huffy, I'd better pass you on
to Myron for a fuller explanation."

"You do that."

It took only thirty seconds to get Myron Kinnick on the
line, but by then she had paced to the left wall, to the right
wall, and back again three times.

"Stan said you wanted to talk to me."

"You bet I do! Myron, exactly why can't you find out
who's posting that fucking web page?"

"Well, I know I told you it would be easy—"

"Skip the bullshit and just *tell* me!"

"Okay. You understand that the Internet isn't a company
and it isn't a governmental agency."

"I know that, Myron."

"Well, a lot of people think it's governmental because the
NSF provided some of the original funding. Anyhow, it's
not exactly a single thing either. It's more like a fraternity.
Or a dog pack. All the commercial on-line service providers,
like AOL, Prodigy, et cetera, et cetera, are independent."

While computer crime and computer espionage wasn't her
department, Khalid had taken the basic courses and knew
this. She snorted. "Look, whoever is sending <**helpmeplease**>
is going through a service provider. They have to pay their
provider. These services aren't free. The provider knows
who they are. They even have their goddamn *credit card
numbers, for Chrissake!*"

"Right, right," Kinnick said in a soothing tone. "What I'm
trying to tell you is, there are large commercial providers,
huge providers in fact, like AOL. And there are smaller ones
like Genie and Delphi. And there are very small ones that
are sort of private. And really small ones. This page is going
on the net from a very small provider, almost, you might
say, a boutique provider. It's called Albionpic, located in

Albion, Michigan, and it specializes in advertising pages.
They help format and advise on color and placement and
fonts and so on."

"So?"

"Well, they don't have a whole lot of emergency problems."

"So?"

"So they're out of the office."

"You can't be telling me this."

"We can't get hold of them."

"Somebody has to be minding the store."

"No, it's pretty well automated. I mean you're probably
thinking of a staff of cute girls with sausage-roll curled hair
like in the twenties, plugging calls into holes in switch-
boards—"

"Myron, quit that!"

"It's Saturday night. The owner has gone canoeing somewhere north of Muskegon. Leaves Albion at noon on Fri-
days and camps someplace overnight. One of his friends
says he's on the Pere Marquette River and another friend
says he's definitely on the White River."

"You're making a joke."

"Listen, if this were AOL, there'd be somebody home. I
guess. I mean, AOL's even got a Vice President of Integrity
Assurance, if you can believe such a thing."

"This is a disaster."

"Why? The kid's not going anywhere and nothing's happening. These friends both say he always gets back Sunday
before noon because he has Sunday dinner with his mother,
and besides, he has to get ready to be at work at the crack
of eight Monday morning. They say he's very responsible."

"I want him *now*."

"We have two agents set up at the Best Western in Albion. One camps continually on Albionpic's doorstep, well,
in a car across the street actually, the other sleeps. They
trade off. They'll see the guy the minute he gets back. Trust
me on this. We've also located a federal circuit court mag-
istrate who will fax them a search warrant immediately if

the owner gets sticky about revealing his subscriber list. You don't want some sort of court challenge later, do you? Evidence thrown out because you didn't get a proper warrant?" She didn't answer. "It's all covered, Khalid. There's no reason to get your bra in a twist."

"This foot-dragging is making me look bad. I've made promises here!"

"Hannah, don't yell at me. I didn't make the world."

"I didn't either. I'd do a better job."

It was Myron's turn to reply with total silence.

Hannah said, "All right, all right, say he gets in tomorrow morning. How long to work back to the address?"

"Could be very fast. Could be a matter of minutes, if all goes well."

"Well, Myron, you just better make sure it does."

ten

I sat bolt upright in bed, drawing a breath to scream. Just in time I smothered my mouth with both hands and held myself that way a few seconds. My mother was in the house now. She didn't sleep well; most nights she only dozed off and on, and the last thing I needed on top of this crazy panic was for my mother to have one of her hand-wringing anxiety attacks.

My own hands were shaking. I had been dreaming that I was starving—no, that that tiny, lovely girl was starving, and it was all my fault. The child's little ribs stuck out, she was so thin. Her ribs looked like long, bony fingers clutching at her chest. And she wailed—she wailed quietly, softly, like the east wind wailing in a tree. She did not want to make a fuss, did not want to bother anybody; she was such a good little girl. But she couldn't help moaning because she was so hungry.

And what she said was, "Polly—help me, Polly. Why can't you help me, Polly? Polleeeeee!"

"God!" I said under my breath. Jumping out of bed, I

headed into the hall. I couldn't lie in bed hearing that child calling me.

As I put one foot into the dark hall, I remembered my mother again. Absolutely, she must not hear that I was awake, so I slowed down, placing my left foot forward, getting it flat on the floor before I shifted my weight off of my right foot. I moved this way, like a stork in a swamp, as I passed my mother's open door. Was there enough spill of streetlight for her to see me?

I peeked into my mother's room. The light from the street shone through the two front windows and lay across the bed. My mother's chest rose and fell evenly, and breath softly sighed in and out of her lungs.

Grateful, I went on to the head of the stairs. I descended them cautiously, stepping near the wall side of the treads. Not until I was crossing the dim living room toward the kitchen did I begin to walk normally, and even then I was careful not to bump into any furniture.

I've always done a lot of my paperwork at the kitchen table. That was going to have to stop now, I realized, seeing a teacup left there by my mother. The formsets and evidence documents I brought home were too confidential for my mother and Mrs. Drobney to read. Besides, I didn't really trust my mother. She could quite easily throw the papers out and say later, "Oh, were those important? They were just left lying around. I thought I'd clean up. I always try to help out wherever I can."

It was shameful to think that she meant to sabotage me, but it had happened with other sorts of things, childhood possessions at home, books that I had read and loved as a child and wanted to keep. My mother had "cleaned out." It had happened with my high school yearbook. I really did *not* believe that my mother did this intending to hurt, or at least not consciously, but she has always resented the evidences of other people's friendships or jobs or competence or self-confidence. A neighbor of ours decided, in her early seventies, to travel around the world. It was the trip of a lifetime. In Singapore she became horribly sick and spent three weeks in a hospital where she was diagnosed as having caught scrub typhus from a chigger bite. With tetracycline and chloramphenicol, she recovered. But my mother was grimly satisfied, repeatedly saying, "I told her not to try to take that awful trip at her age."

And I was quietly satisfied that our neighbor finished out her whole tour and told us when she got back that she'd go again tomorrow if only she had the money.

My mother is really a good person underneath. The problem is psychological, of course, but I think actually chemical and very basic. It's not her fault. She isn't trying to be negative; she really is negative, and she is sincerely baffled that anybody would even have the energy or desire to undertake a round-the-world tour, much less actually go and do it. She has an illness. Her Uncle Albert, her mother's brother, was depressive, and so was their grandmother. There are family stories of Grandmother Barclay staying in her room for a week at a time, living on trays of food left outside her door, refusing the family's constant pleas to come out.

I feel like I've dodged the genetic bullet in my family. I should be grateful—I *am* grateful. And I should be understanding.

I moved my mother's teacup to the sink and sank into a chair. There's a small television on the counter facing the table. Good for watching the morning news before forging out to attack the day. Should I turn on CNN?

My hand reached out and punched the on button, even as my mind said, *No, you need to rest.* That was the whole point of coming home when you really wanted to stay at work; you need to be fresh tomorrow.

Mrs. Drobney, bless her, had told me she didn't sleep much and would come back at dawn or any time I called her.

CNN had made a format change since I last looked. Their news anchor was talking of other events, not the kidnapping, unrest in China and preliminary test results on a new AIDS vaccine. But in the upper corner of the screen in a box was

Danni. She lay on a mat in her prison room. Her hands covered her face.

How can I sleep when that child is alone and frightened, God knows where? My mind said, *Hurry, hurry, don't rest a moment.*

There's been a revolution in the last ten years in police work. It's another good news/bad news kind of thing. When my father was a young cop, the job was fairly simple. Not *easy,* but simple. You walked your beat; you watched for evildoers; if you saw them, you whapped them with your club.

Probably corporal punishment never really worked. You don't turn a burglar into a church usher by whapping him. But the basic job was as simple as that. Say you had a run of burglaries in the neighborhood. You asked your snitches to keep an ear out. You questioned neighbors to find out if they'd seen anything. And yes, you fingerprinted, but fingerprints rarely solved a case in those days. If you caught your perp, you could match the prints, but you couldn't effectively search for him if you didn't have him.

Nowadays, it's not just a matter of searching fingerprints through AFIS, the Automated Fingerprint Identification System. The whole job is techy. From your first hour in the academy, you're taught DNA, AFIS, how to use NCIC, the National Crime Information Center, what accelerants are in arson cases, taggants in explosives. You might as well be in a science class.

Detectives need to know even more than patrol cops, naturally, and the detective's exam is heavy in tech questions.

In my job, I have to be a jack of all trades—chemistry, physics, pathology, computer science, you name it. And, of course, no one human being can possibly know all this stuff. Laymen think you can walk up to a murder scene and tell the technician, "Send it to the lab," but it's not that easy. There has to be a human being in charge thinking it through. Send what to the lab? Well, let's see. If the killer got in through this particular broken window, he must have climbed across on the gutters. Is it worth fingerprinting the gutters? Even though it has rained since? And how did he get to them? Shall we check the cigarette butts in the alley for saliva, and shall we do an expensive DNA on it, or is the fact that there's lipstick on the butts mean the cigarettes all belong to the victim?

Do you send cops rushing out immediately to look into every sewer within a mile of the murder for a blunt instrument before it gets washed away, or do you know that what looks like a purple bruise between the victim's eyes is a typical hypostatic effect from lying on his face after death, not from a blunt instrument?

So here I was, trying to assess how likely it was that Quantico could actually find that prison room of Danni's by tracing back where the video signal had come from. Or pull lots of cops off other cases as if the cybernetic trace would fail? The fact that the FBI said they could trace the signal meant nothing, or at least not enough. I didn't blame them for overstating their powers. The Bureau is like any other agency: It always says it can.

We probably would too in the same situation. Police agencies are like doctors. It's not good for the patient to tell them you haven't got a clue. Instead, you tell them you know exactly what you're doing; then you work your ass off trying to do it, and you hope it'll all turn out okay.

How can we find her? What else should I have done today?

What if I screwed up?

What have I missed? Think.

I had an idea. I could see a few spots on the floor where Danni had spilled a little water. We could learn something from them. I would get somebody to analyze those spots from the screen image, which was all we had, of course. Surely different fluids dry leaving different residues. Water would leave very little residue.

Nutritious fluids would leave more. Get a chemist to study the spots. Maybe those bottles contained Pedialyte, the infant supplement they gave my nephew when he had salmonella and couldn't take milk. If it was Pedialyte, at least that would keep the electrolytes in her blood within a normal range for a few days.

If so, we'd have a little more time.

Oh! Another idea. Contact costume shops. That priest outfit did not necessarily come from a religious source. I should have thought of it earlier.

For about a minute, I was pleased with myself. Then the doubts came back. I really *should* have thought of it earlier, shouldn't I? Oh, God.

What if I screwed up the rescue? What if this turned out to be the one case I failed miserably? I not only had to be good; this time I had to be good fast. A real, living, tiny human being was depending on me to save her. How could I be so arrogant as to think I knew how to do it? Or to think I should try instead of letting somebody else take over my role, maybe somebody better qualified?

But somebody has to do it. Isn't human responsibility always like this? Surgeons must feel the same sort of fears at times. Do they wonder how they can be so arrogant as to invade a human brain with a scalpel? Do they think, *Who am I to stop a heart and go inside and cut out a piece of muscle or valve and put in a piece of plastic?* They must decide that it has to be done, and they are as good as anyone.

Do I usually feel this uncertain? No, but I don't usually have this sort of case. There usually isn't the extreme urgency. Usually the death has already happened when I take the case.

What am I thinking—*death?* This child must not die!

Still, I've tracked serial killers we knew were out there somewhere, shopping for a fresh victim who fit their specifications. And I've tracked the human time bombs, spree killers who've killed when something set off their rage and would kill again and again until we caught them. I have had many cases of the most common of all child killers, parents. One child is suspiciously dead, and my job is to find out how, whether it's murder, and prove it if it is before it happens to the brother or sister.

So why am I having these self-doubts? I've been in the

business a long time. I believe in being humble enough to listen to subordinates' ideas, humble enough to learn. Even humble enough to listen to Burkholder's ideas, in the rare event when he has one. Humble enough to listen and assured enough to move ahead. When I have self-doubts, usually I just work harder.

Why now?

Slowly, my gaze rose to the ceiling above my head. In the room upstairs, my mother was sleeping.

You should let somebody do it who really knows what they're doing.

All my life, every time I wanted to take on a challenge, whether it was trigonometry or the police academy, or start some new project, like playing soccer or helping my friend Adelle cook for her church's annual picnic, my mother always had one of three reactions: It was too much work, it was too dangerous, or it would never turn out. Never, ever, "You can do it, Polly; go for it."

Living apart from her, I had been able to put the nagging voice of doom out of my head for long periods. It was going to be much harder now.

The vast crescent sweep of Lake Shore Drive glittered in the dark, sculptured buildings that had revolutionized the history of architecture—glass cubes, diamonds and tapered obelisks and nacreous crowns—and at their base, pearl necklaces of streetlights and the eternal river of red-and-yellow lights of cars, all of it cupped against the breast of jet dark lake. This view had been called the Rio de Janeiro of the north.

Sen. Neal Gaston stood in the darkened bedroom of his penthouse suite in the Knickerbocker and frowned at the sight before him.

Maggie was not in bed.

Sighing, rubbing his face with both hands, he turned from the window and pushed open the door to the sitting room. He saw exactly what he had expected.

Maggie sat on a sofa in the darkened space, lit only by

the television screen. Her hands were folded in front of her face as if she were praying. Bluish light played over her face, making her look old. Neal shook his head to clear it of a momentary anger. "You told me you'd go to bed," he said.

"Neal! I didn't hear you come in."

"Well, here I am. You told me you'd go to bed."

"I lay down on the sofa."

"Did you sleep?"

"Mm, no, not really. But how could I? Did you?"

How should he answer this? The question was impossible. "Yes, Maggie. I admit I fell asleep for a while—"

"It's all right. Please, Neal, don't apologize. Let's not wrangle over silly things. If you can sleep, you should."

Then, as one, they both turned and looked at the screen. In a box in the corner of the screen was the view of a room. On the floor was a kind of pallet or sleeping pad. The lighting was bright and flat. And on the sleeping pad, without pillow or blanket or her purple dinosaur bed pal, was Danni.

"You've been watching her sleep," Neal said, keeping any criticism out of his voice.

"Of course I have," Maggie said. "It's wonderful."

"What is?"

"Look really closely, Neal. See there? You can see that she's breathing."

Danni was lying still on the pad, but she was not asleep. She had her hands over her eyes and was wondering whether she was a bad girl. Several hours earlier she had realized she just couldn't wait any longer; she had to go potty. But there was no bathroom and nowhere to go and no way out of this room. She tried the doorknob again; she had no idea how many times she had tried it. Danni could count all the way to twenty, except for problems with the eleventies, like eleventy-seven, but she hadn't even bothered. The doorknob never turned. It would rattle, but not turn.

Mommy had been so proud of Danni. Of the three friends who lived near her and came over to play, one, Penny, still wore diapers and had to be changed, and the other, Georgie, had accidents. Mommy said Danni was a big girl. Danni never had accidents anymore. Ever. Danni's play school only allowed big children in it who were toilet trained. Danni was a big girl.

Until today. She waited and waited and nobody came. And she didn't know what to do. Finally, she took off her underwear and went over to the farthest corner of the room, away from her sleeping pad, and urinated, but she felt really bad about it.

Then again, just before bedtime, she went again.

Then she put herself methodically to bed, pretending to be her mommy singing her to sleep. She pretended to tuck sheets up to her chin. Pat. Pat. Pat. Then she said, "Night, night. Sleep tight," in her mommy's voice, and closed her eyes.

And now she lay there wondering if she was a bad girl. She thought maybe she was. And if she was a very bad girl, would her mommy ever come back and get her?

day one

helpmepleasehelpmepleasehelpmepleasehelpmeplease

sunday

twenty-four hours

eleven

State Street was impassable. I couldn't get to my office in the CPD building. Even though it was 6:30 A.M., the parking lot on South State was a gridlock of cars and people, and the street itself was clotted with media vans equipped with satellite guns. Fifteen uniforms in the street whistling and shouting and gesturing didn't move them. I saw four mounted officers on shiny brown horses. They shooed and pointed, and the cars still didn't move.

I could walk to the building, but the reporters would see me.

I phoned from a diner two blocks down and the department sent a black Lincoln Town Car out for me. These cars are ordinarily reserved for the Cook County judges who work in courts in the building—Branches Twenty-six, Twenty-seven, Thirty, and Branch Forty, Women's Court, familiarly called "hooker court." The car brought me up the rear alley off Holden Court and none of the media people paid any attention to it. Today nobody cared about judges.

Television coverage was a firestorm. The local early news

shows had nothing but Danni and her family. The 5:30 A.M.
Wall Street Journal Report and CNN's *Sunday Your Money*
talked about Danni. Channel Five and Seven's 6:00 A.M.
news and Channel Thirty-two's *This Week* were all Danni.
Even the *Early Morning Farm Report* talked about her. By
the time the major channels came on at seven, I was ready
for the intense concentration. The *Sunday Today* show spent
ten minutes—longer than they usually spent chatting with
presidential candidates—on selected segments of Danni in
her prison room. They showed her waking, singing, finger-
painting with imaginary paints, putting her ear to the floor,
apparently listening to something, and sleeping. A child psy-
chologist was interviewed, then on voice-over with Danni's
live video picture, he explained how the three-year-old was
coping psychologically with separation and isolation. How
long would the child stand it? What about permanent psychological damage?

"Well, of course, children are very resilient. But on the
other hand, any trauma would leave some psychological
trace. The important thing for her psychological health is to
end the ordeal as soon as possible."

Jack Ford manfully refrained from saying, "We all know
that." He replied quite simply, "We all hope Danni is rescued right away."

Channel Seven produced an extended special on Maggie
McKittredge and her singing career. In a particularly heart-
rending clip, she was shown singing "Hush, Little Baby."
There would have been more news programs if it had not
been Sunday, but the channels broke into everything possible—church services, golf, talking heads discussing the
world, cooking shows—with news of Danni. Between an-
nouncements, they bannered the bottom of the screen.

Fetterman arrived and told me it was the same on the
radio. He'd heard nothing but the Gaston kidnapping all the
way downtown in his car.

Virtually all the news shows, both network and local, de-
voted large sections to the career of Sen. Neal Gaston. The
twin themes were his relationship with his beautiful family

and his high position in the nation; chair of a Senate committee, friend and confidante of the president. And every program ended with the thought: If the kidnapping of a child can happen to a person this powerful, wealthy, and protected, it can happen to anybody.

Dateline NBC, 48 Hours, 60 Minutes, Hard Copy, 20/20, and God knows what-all else, all promised hour-long specials on the kidnapping of Danni Gaston, each one by its next air time.

"All right, where's she being held?" I demanded of my task force. Ainslie, Sam, Hannah Khalid, four senior CPD detectives, a fellow named Spencer Holcomb, and three FBI agents stared impassively back at me. Fetterman was less impassive. He looked ready to cry.

"If we knew that, we wouldn't have a problem," Ainslie finally said.

"I don't mean the address. I mean, have we narrowed it down at all? Is she in Chicago or Los Angeles or Mexico City? Khalid, how are your people doing at tracing the source?" She probably hoped it was LA. If Danni was not in Illinois, the whole case would become Khalid's.

She said, "As far as I know, the techies haven't found the source of the web page yet."

"You're very calm about it."

"They're getting closer fast."

"Can they tell us what part of the country the feed is coming from?"

Pause. Long pause. "Actually, no."

"Can they even tell whether it's coming from the United States?"

"Uh—no."

"You're saying that this, this *moving picture* is being beamed into everybody's home computer and nobody knows where it's coming from?"

"Well, it isn't really being beamed into them exactly. It's more that you can reach out and access it on the net if you want."

"Listen, Khalid, are you a cyber expert?"

"I'm relatively knowledgeable. But it's not my ticket."

She meant not her field of expertise. "I assume you have somebody *extremely* knowledgeable working on it."

"That's what I was about to say, Kelly. There's an entire staff in Quantico working full time and two very good people are coming here to work on-site. They're due into O'Hare at nine-thirty." She glanced at her watch. "A little less than an hour."

"Good. Then let's go at this from another direction. I asked Spencer Holcomb to come here today. Holcomb was a CPD officer for twenty years and for three years commander of the Traffic Division. He got so interested in the dynamics of populations in motion that he took night school courses, got a master's, and was hired by the Northwestern Traffic Institute. To put it another way, his specialty is how to get people from one place to another as fast as possible and, in our case of course, to tell us where these people could have gone from Holy Name in the time they had."

Spencer stood up and said, "Howdy." He talks like that.

I said, "The kidnappers had seventy-five minutes between the kidnapping and the appearance of Danni on the net. How far could they get?"

Spencer pushed a videotape into the VCR slot under our bigger monitor. When he activated it, the picture of Danni vanished and a map of the ten-block area surrounding Holy Name Cathedral came onscreen.

He said, "Chief Kelly, you told me there was no record of any ambulance or any squad car running lights and siren in the immediate Holy Name area yesterday at the operative time, except for three specific ambulances confirmed running to the Northwestern University medical complex right at the lake front. Five blocks away. That still true?"

"Still true. Double-checked. Not only no record; passersby don't remember seeing any, either."

"So, okay, eleven forty-five, earliest possible, our kidnappers're outta the church on foot. Three minutes is about minimum. State Street is two-way, but say they go north because if their car is stopped at the curb nearest the church, to attract the least attention, it's aimed northbound. Okay?" We all nodded. "Now, leaving this area by car. See the construction on Chicago Ave? If they take that to Lake Shore Drive, it's slow because of the road work. Pearson is one-way eastbound, but narrow. No less than seven minutes to get out of this area at noon on a Saturday."

Khalid said, "Probably the seven scariest minutes in their day."

"No lie." He clicked and an aerial view of a mile-wide square appeared, showing streets all the way to the lake on the east and the Kennedy Expressway on the west.

"Aw right," he said. "Do I go Lake Shore or highway? Highway at noon is iffy. Busy. Lake Shore less so. Plus, on the highway, if there's an accident the sheriffs can stop all lanes and you can't get to an exit to get off. I was a kidnapper, I'd be real nervous of the highway. Anyhow, once we get this far away from the church, we know for sure there were ambulances running around, squad cars—"

Khalid said, "You're supposing they could have used an ambulance?"

"Or something dressed up like a squad car? Yes, ma'am. Not 'cause I have any special reason to think they did. Sheerly for my purpose here, which is to tell you the fastest they could have made it out of town if they were going like billy-hell, or as much as you can go billy-hell in the middle of Chicago in the middle of the day. So I'm gonna add another eight-ten minutes to get them out of this grid."

He clicked again and all of metropolitan Chicago appeared.

"Now this here is what the statisticians think of as Chicago. It's just the city proper. We all know Chicago is a lot bigger, with all the suburbs, which we then call Chicagoland, ma'am," he added, addressing Khalid directly.

She turned a hand palm up, acquiescing.

"So now they got the option of the Kennedy north, then the Edens to the north suburbs or the Kennedy the rest of the way northwest out to O'Hare and what we call the Land

Beyond O'Hare. Or they take the Dan Ryan south. Or they get on the Eisenhower and go west. Once you get on Eighty-eight, you can go straight west without hardly a curve in the road till you hit the Rocky Mountains."

Ainslie said, "Shit."

"However, to get out of this grid here this time a' day you're adding another twenty minutes easy. Now we're at thirty-eight minutes and that's without any of the usual foul-ups you get on the roads here.

"Now—greater Chicagoland!" The whole area around the city appeared, with its hundred suburbs, its forest preserves, lakes, rivers, industrial parks, giant refuse and "sanitary landfill" blocks. I groaned out loud.

"Well, you might feel that way," Spencer agreed. "However, it's the fact and we gotta deal with it. You have to go this far out to get to any airports. Except Meigs. Which is too small, too personal, too much attention, too isolated on its little island, too much chance of somebody noticing. Plus Chief Kelly already checked Meigs. Mind you, I'm leaving out watercraft. If they took a boat in Lake Michigan and are heading for the Saint Lawrence Seaway, it's not my department."

"We'll cover that later," I said grimly.

"Hoo-kay. Trains?"

"Faxed the stations. They looked at every human body getting aboard anything. Buses, too."

"Any trains leave moments before you faxed?"

"We were very quick, Spence. Thanks to Fetterman and you, Ainslie. Anyway, as far as the ones that left just before? Knew where they were all going, naturally. Trains don't wander off course much. Had cops meet them at the first stop, watch anybody getting off, and hand faxes of the photo to the conductors. Cops checked every stop after that. Ditto the buses."

"Spiffy. Back to my pictures. In this grid, you have your airports. O'Hare, Midway, also Glenview Naval Air base, so on."

I said, "Every single one of them was notified within ten

minutes of the kidnapping. Individually, plus CAB, the City Aviation Board. Nobody fitting Danni's description—and we faxed them, too, of course, we didn't just tell them—nobody like her left on an aircraft."

"In luggage?" Khalid said. "Doped up?"

I said, "Luggage is X-rayed. If the child has bones, she wasn't flown out of here."

Spencer went on. "So if they haven't flown out of that grid, they've gone by ground transport, a car or truck or ambulance, whatever, and we charge them another twenty-five minutes."

"That makes sixty-three minutes," I said. "Out of seventy-five."

"And what," said Spencer, "if the camera was inside, say, a moving van? They could start the video as soon as she was inside and they were set up."

I said, "I know that. I have to say, to me it looks like a real room—"

"A good techie could fake that."

"Yes," I said. "But I don't see any vibrations, either, as if the room were moving. Danni herself doesn't lean this way and then that way, like countering the motion of a ship or truck. In any case, for that I have to get a specialist to look at the picture. For our purposes here, let's assume she's in a real room in a real building."

"Well, then, we go to my next grid," Spencer said. "They're still on the ground. If it was me, I'd wanta get inside a building quicker than this. I mean, every second they're on the road, all they need is a fender-bender or a flat tire or the transmission falls out and they're toast. But say they're still traveling. Kelly, you want to allow any time for getting the kid out of the car and into the place with the videocamera and all?"

"Sure. But not more than three minutes. I think they were as efficient as hell. And the videocam must have been already set up and tested ahead of time."

"Then this," he clicked again, showing us a still larger view that included northern Illinois, a slice of southern Wisconsin north of Illinois, and a slice of western Indiana south of Illinois, "is pretty much your target area. The red circle is as far as I think they could *possibly* have gone." There was a large circle with the area of Holy Name as approximately Ground Zero.

If Indiana and Wisconsin were possibilities, the case could be interstate.

Inside the red circle was a blue circle, only a little smaller. It took a tiny bite of Indiana, but no Wisconsin. "What's the blue circle?" I asked Spencer.

"Oh, that's what I call the most probable. It's roughly twenty-five hundred square miles and contains about six million people."

Khalid pulled me aside. "Hey, I'm not pleased about you taking me to task in front of the troops."

"Oh, you're not?"

"No."

"Well, number one, they're not 'the troops.' They're police officers; and if their rank is lower than mine or yours, that doesn't make them ciphers. Number two, while I'm in charge, I'll take you or anybody else to task if I need to. Like I said before, somebody's got to be the center. Number three, in fact, I wasn't. I asked reasonable questions, based on the fact that *you* said that tracing that server would be no problem."

"You're a great one for numbering things."

"Sure. Keep focused. Keep rational."

twelve

Khalid and an FBI techie named Hatch huddled over computer number one in the war room. Hatch was freshly arrived from Quantico. He was the least FBI-looking FBI agent I had ever seen. He was rumpled, lumpy, and dumpy. His eyebrows were hairy, like woolly bear caterpillars in autumn. He had a fuzzy beard. And even though he wore the FBI "uniform" of navy suit, shiny black shoes, white shirt, and red tie, the suit pants were two inches too long and bagged around his ankles. The shirt should have been made into cleaning rags a year ago and was also too tight, making triple wrinkles over his plump tummy. The tie wasn't worth talking about, except to say it showed evidence of a long, hard life, and if you were out of groceries you could boil it to make soup.

Hatch was at least ten years older than Khalid, even though his hair was mostly brown. But Khalid was his superior officer. She ordered him around, making her superior position entirely clear. Hatch showed no evidence of minding this. Or even being interested.

His appearance being what it was, anyone might have thought that Hatch's sartorial sloppiness had prevented him from advancing in the FBI hierarchy. But I didn't think so. Hatch was a techie. An older techie than most, but a real techie. You could see it in the dexterous way he caressed the keyboard and the blinding speed of his touch-typing. Before even sitting down, he had corrected some of the war room wiring.

Now Hatch had the FBI kidnapping profiler program up on the screen. The questionnaire consists of a couple of hundred multiple-choice items. Khalid hung over him. She wouldn't let him make a move without her methodically checking every single answer. The idea was to key in everything we knew about the kidnapping, which was precious little, and rotate that against the FBI data on thousands of kidnappings. Theoretically, this should give us an idea of the type of person we were dealing with. It might even give us some names—people at large who'd been suspected of similar kidnappings, or arrested, tried, and not convicted.

This worked very much like the serial killer profiling developed many years ago by VICAP and constantly updated as more killers were caught.

They had finished "description of the victim" and turned to Block Two.

"Place of abduction," Khalid said. "(a) In a public building." I read over her shoulder. The choices I could see before they went on to the next question were:

(b) victim's home
(c) another private residence not victim's home
(d) an outdoor open place
(e) secluded outdoor space
(f) woodland or forest
(g) on water
(h) on beach or near water
(i) on public transportation
(j) at school

(k) in a place of public entertainment such as theater,
    sporting arena—

By then Khalid was saying, " 'Persons in area at time
of abduction.' We can choose more than one response
here—".

Hatch sighed faintly.

I walked away and sat down at my stack of "canvass
reports." Each one was a sheet, called a formset, filled out
by a detective or patrol officer, and each one represented a
single "encounter," which is to say interview, with a single
individual. I had asked Ainslie to order the canvassers to
write down as much as possible of the actual words of the
"respondent," which officers usually do only minimally. As
a result, I had a grab bag, a stew, a veritable tossed salad
of human notions.

"I seen a priest," one elderly man had told the cop, "but
he was goin' in the church, not out. And no kid." Appear-
ance? "Kinda curly hair, blond maybe." Weight? "Chubby.
Not fat, though." Where was he coming from? "Don' know.
Walking up State Street." From the south, you mean?
"Yeah. From the south."

Not far off the description of the kidnapper. Not right on,
either, but very possible. He had seen him at 10:20, earlier
than I thought was likely. He was sure of the time. He knew
because he was late for a ten o'clock appointment.

Cars? Well, of course people had seen cars. They'd noticed a blue Toyota Tercel, a Jeep Cherokee, a Honda Ac-
cord: "I think it was blue or white, but I remembered it
because it was driving so slowly. Just cruising. Or it might
have been green."

A red Chevrolet Beretta: "A great bright red!" A white
Dodge Ram van. A Volvo 740GLE van: "I noticed because
I have one." A khaki Range Rover. A Checker cab "with
no passengers. Stopping in front of Holy Name, then going
away." A maroon Chevy Lumina. Buick LeSabre. Dark blue
Lincoln Town Car. Dodge Dynasty "in that nice champagne
color." Limo. A Jetta. Cadillac DeVille, "really really old."

A white Ameritech van. Toyota Camry. Gray Isuzu pickup "with a funny license plate, UCANT." Ford Aero Sport van. Dodge Intrepid "in a really dark purple, a really dark purple. They must have had it done specially." Cannonball delivery van. Plymouth Voyager, "the kind with wood-look sides." Bus. Green GMC Jimmy.

Some had paused "suspiciously" in front of the cathedral. Some had passengers who "looked funny." I flapped them in disgust.

Khalid's phone rang. She listened, said, "Yes," several times, then, "Right away." She listened some more, said, "Fifteen minutes," and hung up.

She got up rapidly and shrugged her arms into her coat.

"What about this?" Hatch asked, gesturing at the profiler on the screen.

"You finish it," she said. "Kelly has the details."

I said, "What's the deal?"

"I have to meet some out-of-state agents."

I said, "Oh, don't mind us," to her retreating back as she went out. I shook my head and chucked the reports still in my hand onto the table.

Hell, if there had been a standout in these reports, I would have been told about it already. Frustrated and dizzy with the variety, I took the pile to one of the data-entry people, a young woman named Sandie.

"What I need you to do is start an automobile file. Enter every detail in these reports. We need you to set up the fields so we can recover by make, general type of vehicle, specific type, what was it doing, in other words driving where or parked where, color, time, and place, and then I want you to see if one car turns up in more than one report.

"Why, sure!" she chirped. "Right away, Deputy Chief Kelly." Sandie was bright, young, slender, and had her hair in a pert little ponytail.

I said, "There are probably two hundred cars mentioned in these reports alone. We'll have a lot more by the end of the day. You'd better get all these entered before the next batch starts coming in."

"No prob!"

"And open data fields for vague words like 'dark' and 'light' and 'big' and 'small.' Any car somebody has described as a van another person might just call 'big.' So I want a generic entry for every reasonable variable, as well as specific variables. And be sure to enter any sighting in all possible categories. By this I mean duplicate as much as you need to. A lot of people don't know cars beyond dark and light."

"Yes, boss!"

"And then take the list the guy is going to bring you with the cars seen on the security cameras from the ATMs and the drive-throughs. They'll just say 'dark' or 'light' because there's no color. But they'll have the make and model, and in some cases even the license number."

"Ooh, my scrunch fell off."

"What?"

"My scrunch." She leaned over and picked up a ruffled blue fabric-covered elastic that had fallen to the floor. She pulled it over her ponytail. I gritted my teeth.

"This data won't wait."

"I'll start right now."

"Start sooner than that."

All this work and nothing! At least nothing that jumped out and said, "Here I am. I'm a clue."

I was getting more and more tense, close to the point where I might say something I regretted to somebody who was only trying to do his job. Nobody could do the job fast enough for me.

What was wrong with me, other than the obvious, a starving child and a stymied police force? One glance at the clock and I knew. It was 11:35. In ten minutes it would be twenty-four hours since Danni had been kidnapped.

They always tell you if a kidnapping isn't solved in twenty-four hours it's "gone bad." Of course, just like the rule that "you have two days to solve a murder or you never will," this is only an approximation. It's a probability statement. You could say twenty-three hours or twenty-five hours and it wouldn't make a damn bit of difference statistically. The likelihood of solving a crime tapers off more like the right half of a normal bell curve. Plenty of murders are solved a week later, and since we got AFIS, we've been solving crimes even twenty or thirty years after they occurred.

Besides, the pundits had never had a kidnapping like this. We could see her; we could hear her; we just couldn't touch her.

Well, I couldn't sit here in the war room any longer. I couldn't stand it. I jumped up and headed for the lab.

thirteen

"I know you don't feel like it, Maggie, but we have to do this," Neal Gaston said.

Maggie stood in the center of the entry hall of their suite at the Knickerbocker. Several mirrors in gilt frames lined the hall, each with a bowl of pink freesias on a half-table underneath. She turned around and around, first circling to her left, then to her right, not rapidly but desperately, as if something were chasing her.

Neal Gaston said, "Do you really want to wear that dress? It's very bright."

She didn't answer and he became aware of her turning slowly around.

"Maggie!" he said. "Are you all right?"

"No, of course not."

"I mean—Christ, Maggie, you aren't going crazy on me, are you?"

"I don't think so."

"What are you doing?"

"It's these mirrors. I don't want to see myself and I keep catching glimpses."

"I don't get it." He walked over and put his arm around her shoulders.

"It's because I look so—"

"You look lovely. It'll be all right."

"Oh, Neal, you idiot," she said, her voice kinder than the words, "I don't care how I *look*. What I mean is, when I see myself in the mirror and I look absolutely terrified, I realize it's all true. It makes it real. Danni's really gone. When I see myself I can't go inside myself and hide and pretend."

He stared into her face. "Shall we cover the mirrors, like the Jewish people do after a death?"

"Oh, no, no!" She cringed at the word "death."

"No. I'm sorry. Of course not. Tell you what we'll do. I'll walk on this side." He stood on her right. Then he put his left arm around her back, his left hand gently up to the left side of her face, blocking her view. "How's this?"

"Better, Neal. I know I'm being silly."

"Now, we really do have to go. Todd's outside."

"I don't know if I can do this."

"We have to."

"I think I have stage fright. I feel sick."

"Maggie, you've spent your whole life on stage. Audiences love you. You never have stage fright."

"It's never been this important before."

The inner lobby of the Knickerbocker was so packed with media that the temperature had risen fifteen degrees. The junior manager had made the decision to turn on the air-conditioning, but he didn't feel that it helped very much. Reporters continued to push in, and the temperature continued to rise.

Todd Haralson, who arranged all the details for Senator Gaston's travel, stood against the wall farthest from the door. The backdrop was dark, matte-finished wood paneling fronted by a matching lectern and dark red drapes on the

left. Todd nodded minutely. Good in television lights. No
reflective surfaces. He went to the lectern and stood there,
holding his position silently for a full minute, letting the
camera people get their range.

Then Todd said, "Quiet, please." The reporters near him
quieted. Those farther away kept talking, shouting, com-
plaining, and pushing for better positions. Bret Kasmarczyk,
from NBC in New York, shouted, "Let me through. I need
to get in front." Somebody muttered, "In your dreams." The
NBC affiliate Chicago anchor followed behind Bret Kasmarczyk, silently furious that he had been supplanted. He
could have reported this national story magnificently and
made national waves and maybe a big career doing it. He
was perversely happy when nobody moved for Kasmarczyk.

"Move!" Kasmarczyk said to a small woman from a local
magazine. His cameraman shouldered past her like a running
block, and Kasmarczyk slid ahead.

A bouquet of microphones topped the lectern. Neal Gaston, in the doorway, just outside the room, said to an aide,
"Tell Todd to lose the lectern."

The aide ran in and told Todd. A couple of minutes
passed while the lectern was removed and the mikes placed
on individual stands and hand-held poles.

"Why bother, Neal?" Maggie asked. "I want to get this
over with."

"You don't want to talk from behind a lectern. We can't
look formal. Okay?"

"Yes. Okay, anything. You're right."

And then it was time. Maggie and Neal walked into the
buzz and the blue-white lights. The lights bleached out colors, exaggerated shadows, turned every person into a flat
paper cut-out, and made the dust-mote-laden air look more
solid than the people.

Maggie held her head up. Neal's arm was around her
waist.

"Have you heard from the kidnappers?" someone shouted.

"Is there a ransom demand?"

"Have there been any threats—?"

"Are the FBI in charge?"

"What are the police doing?"

"Do you know where—?"

"How is Danni's health?"

Neal held up his free hand. "Please," he said. The room hushed.

"My wife and I want to make a statement. Afterward, we'll take as many questions—as many questions as we can stand."

Now there was no sound but breathing and the rustle of clothing and the sighing of air-conditioning.

"Our daughter has been stolen from us. I won't make any effort to describe how horrible that is. If you can imagine it, please sympathize with us and pray for us."

Maggie said, "Pray for Danni."

Neal said, "Exactly. We have two things to ask all of you, everybody. First, if you have seen Danni, call the police. *Any* police number, or nine-one-one. They'll pass it on to the right people. Call even if you just *think* you've seen a child who looks a little bit like her. Nobody will blame you if you're wrong. Even if you saw her yesterday, saw her with the counterfeit priest, or whatever, and didn't think to come forward or didn't want to get involved, everybody understands that. Nobody will blame you for waiting. I promise you.

"Be our eyes and ears now. We can't be everywhere. The police and FBI can't be everywhere. But somebody watching this broadcast is near Danni. She's in a room in a building somewhere on this earth. You may hear her cry. You may realize that there is no family living in an apartment where you hear a child crying, or you may know that a child arrived there only yesterday. You won't know it's her, I realize, but *please report it.*"

He paused a few seconds. "You could save her life."

His tone changed. "Next, I want to speak to the kidnappers. I can't promise to make this go away or to hold you blameless. It's a police matter now, out of my hands. I can't promise if you let her go the police won't still be looking

for you. But I can say this: Don't make it worse. The longer
you hold her, the worse it will be for you in court. And if
she doesn't—uh—and if you get her back to us alive, the
courts will look kinder at you. Please let her go. Drop her
at a school or a hospital or a church. Anywhere. Let her go
and help yourselves."

"Senator!" a reporter yelled.

Another said, "Maggie, tell us how—"

Paying no attention, Maggie began to speak. Neal stepped
back a little.

"Danni, honey," she said, "I hope you're watching. We
can't tell. We don't see television coming into your room,
but I hope there is one. We haven't found you yet, Lady
Bug, but we will." She swallowed painfully and said, "I
promise, honey. I want you to be brave if you want to be,
but if you feel like being really sad, that's okay, too. You
see my dress, Lady Bug? I wore the one you said looks like
a garden. Just for you. I hope you're watching."

Tears ran slowly down her face, but she only blinked
once, then opened her eyes, which looked directly into the
camera in front of her. "I will not sleep until we get you
back. You rest as much as you can. Keep strong. You try
to sleep because you can be sure we aren't sleeping."

A few reporters wiped tears. Maggie said, "I can see you,
you know, Danni. You're on television. So I'm watching
over you. I'll always watch over you."

But Danni did not see her mother. There was no television in Danni's room. She had noticed a gray box up on the
wall, in the corner where two walls met the ceiling, and she
had even noticed the shiny lens of the videocamera, though
she did not know what it was. Since it never changed and
did not light up or make any sound, she lost interest in it.

Instead, she thought about a peanut butter and jelly sandwich. She was just so hungry.

fourteen

"I need you to find me an acoustic engineer and a video analyst."

The director of the Crime Laboratory Division was an intense man named Ernest Fowler. He had been listening to the feed from Danni's prison room from the beginning.

"There's virtually no street sound," he said. "That faint rushing noise is a white-noise generator."

I said, "They're covering any chance of us hearing something that places her."

He nodded at me.

"So I need an expert."

"Shouldn't be a problem. I have to go outside the CPD for them though. They'll charge a fee. Okay?"

"Absolutely. I think the FBI and the army call them 'signal engineers' or 'signal analysts.' Get the best. We need to look for traffic noises, el trains, aircraft, manufacturing noises, heavy trucking, whatever."

I ought to have started this yesterday instead of just having our own techies do it. But I didn't say that to Fowler.

I kicked myself, thinking if it hadn't been for Khalid's certainty that she would find the source of the feed right away, plus the fact that there was so little background sound anyhow—

Damn! Blaming her wouldn't help, and anyhow the buck stopped with me. It was my fault.

Fowler said, "We have good tape of the web site for the full—what is it?—twenty-eight hours now. And sixteen-bit sound? An engineer will have plenty to work with."

"My impression is the room the child's in is soundproofed."

"It is. Must be. But not fully. There's almost no such thing in the real world as total one-hundred-percent soundproofing."

And the video expert: "I've had a CPD tech studying the feed, but we need an expert. We need to know whether it's possible that Danni's being held in a boat or a moving truck. You should be able to tell from vibrations in the picture, shouldn't you?"

"Probably. Or if at any point she was held briefly in a moving truck or boat."

"Yes, but they haven't changed her from one place to another," I said. "There hasn't been any interruption in the broadcast. There hasn't been any time they could have changed her from a boat to a truck or to a room."

"They could have if her room is a shipping container."

My blood went cold. He added, "They could have just put the box on a truck and taken it off at the other end of the trip."

"Oh, my God." I shivered.

"I'm gonna let you talk with Perry Orloff, who's pretty good. And she's got industry contacts."

"Just hurry."

I shivered again and while he paged Orloff, I concentrated on not letting Fowler see how terrified I was.

I was back at the war room, waiting for one of Fowler's contacts to call. Had I eaten any lunch? Or breakfast, for that matter? Couldn't remember any. It was now two o'clock.

"Fetterman, could you go out and get me a Big Mac and a Coke? No, get two of each so you can have one. More than one if you need it."

"Will do, boss."

I got the call promptly, thank God. A senior acoustics engineer with a background of CIA and McDonnell Douglas, now in private consulting, was willing to help us. Free, no less. I ordered a copy of the tapes from the beginning to this moment, twenty-eight hours of recording, to be hand carried to him. "Right now," I told Sam. "Have the courier report to me when he or she gets back. I want to make sure there's no delay."

Also, our video guy sent word that he was on his way to give the tapes to a woman from the Northwestern University Technical Institute who consulted for CBS, Channel Two, in Chicago. Okay so far.

By then Fetterman was back and I settled down with a sigh. I unwrapped the burger and took a breath of the aroma. Meat, cheese, fat, salt—oh, my!

I took a big bite, chewed happily, and glanced up at the wall. Danni lay on her sleeping mat, legs pulled toward her chest, sucking two fingers of her right hand.

I swallowed. The mouthful of cheeseburger went down like a lump of wood. The rest of it fell from my hand onto the desk.

"Oh, true utter damn, damn, damn, and shit," I said.

Danni had now been twenty-nine hours without food.

I held my head in my hands and stared at her, feeling suffused with gloom. On our net site feed, the one monitored by a detective, Danni sat up and looked around herself. Maybe she had been dreaming of home because her expression changed from dazed to infinitely, shockingly sad. She gazed around the room in a 180 degree sweep of the head. Then tears rolled down her cheeks.

And the screen went dead.

No, not the screen, the system lights were still on. The site went dead.

I gasped and jumped to my feet. So did the cop. I reached out to the screen, stupidly trying to bring Danni back, suddenly aware how much just seeing that she was alive had meant to me.

"Look!" Fetterman said. "Quick! Boss, quick!"

Fetterman pointed to the CNN channel running on the Sony.

You always recognize it when you see a portion of your hometown on the news, even if it's a part of town you don't know well. Maybe it's the types of streetlights and the types of curbs and road paving, or the trees. In any case, I knew instantly this was Chicago, even before the voiceover sank into my brain.

"—just minutes ago. The FBI tells CNN that the location was traced by FBI net specialists."

Now a different view showed a reporter standing in front of a four-story brick building. He said, "The building on North Sedgwick, said to be low-cost housing for the elderly, is completely surrounded; and as the agents close in, we are told that the video of little Danni Gaston in her prison room has gone off."

I saw Hannah Khalid, wearing a navy blue vest with big yellow letters reading FBI on the back, standing crisply erect and caucusing with four other agents on the sidewalk, flanked by several black agency cars, red lights flashing on their interior dashboards. Then the five walked toward the central doors of the building. The reporter said, "This will bring to a close the long ordeal of the little girl and her family, an ordeal that has captured the sympathy of the nation and, indeed, the world."

fifteen

The tiny old woman spoke in a mountain twang that Khalid could hardly understand.

"He don't like them channels," she said.

"So he—let me get this straight," Khalid said. "He gave you a brand-new television set and a modem and an extra phone line—"

" 'N some wahrs."

"Wires. Yes. I see."

"Mm-mm."

"And told you he wanted to get even with the television channels?"

"Didn't like them channels."

"Did he say how he'd get even?" As the old woman shook her head, Khalid said, "Never mind. Is this everything he gave you?" Khalid gestured at the TV and some anonymous equipment on the little plastic table. And a lot of wires.

"Nope. Give me a letter."

"I need that letter."

The old woman stared hard at Khalid. She was a tough little old woman, though her hair was so thin on top that the freckled scalp showed through and her forearms were so thin they were smaller around than her wrists. She'd survived the deaths of four children and the disappearance of two husbands and three other children, including the boy who had brought her up to Chicago from a failing farm outside Balcom, Illinois, which was south of Carbondale and south of the Kentucky border.

The old woman didn't like Khalid, and she was really mad at the way these other feds—and she knew they were feds, goddamn white shirts, blue suits, red ties, shiny black shoes—had pushed her and the tenants on her floor around. "You'd think we're Bonnie and Clyde," she said to a neighbor, while the feds rampaged through her place. All one-and-a-half rooms of it. And two adjacent apartments and the ones right above and below hers.

She was also a canny little old woman. The man who had given her the TV and all had told her to give the letter to whoever came, even though he hadn't said it would be feds.

"If the channels get mad at me, it'll let you off the hook," he said.

But she figured to make them think she was doing it just to be helpful. Public spirited. Goodness of her heart. Couldn't hurt; might help.

"Prob'ly shouldn't do this," she said. "But seein' you're police. Here."

She pulled a three-by-five file card out of her pocket. Khalid said, "Wait! Don't touch it!"

"Been in my pocket a whole week," the old lady said. "Touched it a lot."

"Just drop it on the table."

The old woman dropped it with two fingers, like she might have dropped a dead mouse she had by the tail. It lay there, face up.

There was just one hand-printed line:

YOU THINK YOU'RE SO SMART

sixteen

Two blocks away a very tall man wearing a navy blue uniform, creased pants, and a short, belted jacket bearing the logo ILLINOIS BELL stood in the window of a small room and rolled up the last part of four hundred yards of phone cord. His gray work gloves looked natural with the uniform. His baseball cap was incongruous, but it shaded his eyes, enough so that when he left this place most people passing him on the street would barely notice the sharp beak of his nose and pointed chin.

He watched impassively as another FBI car with a flashing red dashboard light sped up the street. That made seven. All of them, he reflected, with a slight smile, seriously pissed off.

The various phone boxes his colleague had left in the old woman's apartment were mostly window dressing. The nice, new, free TV had secured her cooperation, although he wasn't sure it had been necessary. He thought the old woman had a bit of the rebel in her nature anyhow.

Strictly speaking, the old woman herself was not needed.

He could have simply tapped into her phone line on the exterior of her building and sent the signal. Or he could have sniffed a credit card number somewhere along the net line when a customer was ordering a product and paid Albionpic with it. Or he could have gone low-tech no-brainer and bought a stolen credit card and paid Albionpic with that. Which would eventually have sent the feds to a wrong address. That would have been mildly amusing. But it carried its own risks of the feed being cut off before he wanted it cut off, and he needed to teach the FBI techies a lesson right at the outset.

He had also considered the possibility of ticket sniffing. Some states now allowed automobile drivers to pay their speeding tickets through the World Wide Web. They actually believed this was a secure system because the numbers were encrypted when entered and not decrypted until they reached the state computer acting as server. But this was like phoning somebody on a scrambled line. If you intercepted the message on the way from caller to callee, of course you wouldn't understand it. But bug the room where the call was being made, before it was encrypted, or the other end where it was being responded to, and you understood every word. Given enough time, he believed he could have invaded the state server and captured credit card numbers after decryption. Then he could have used one of those card numbers. The FBI, tracking back, would have found a cardholder who hadn't a hint until then that anything was wrong.

But this certainly would have been less satisfying than installing that wonderful Rube Goldberg patch-and-paste in the old woman's room.

It was possible that the FBI, if it tried hard enough, with enough people, could locate this rented room where the feed had been relayed from. Not likely though. It was two blocks away from the old woman's and faced onto a different street; and only one of hundreds, maybe thousands of cheap rooms within a few blocks in any direction. It would take hundreds of man hours. And even if they found the room, there was no way for them to retrace a multiple call for-warding on a pirated phone line that physically no longer existed. The tap was gone, the phone was gone, the wire he had strung from this window to the woman's apartment was gone, he'd be long gone, and where the signal had originated from no one would know.

And all those wires! He smiled. Line cords, coaxial cable, T1 line, and all of it used stock, with a smorgasbord of trace evidence. Fibers, animal hair, paint, plasterboard, human hair. The one from the hair-styling salon should give the FBI lab weeks and weeks of nerdy fun. Also the piece from the lumber yard. He still wished he could have taken the connector from that fabric store to crimp onto the line cord he used, but there was so much to do, so little time.

The man placed the coil of phone wire carefully into a blue bag labeled CBC CABLE next to several other pieces of hardware. He zipped the bag. He adjusted the cap with the bill farther down over his face.

Then he walked out of the room and down the stairs.

seventeen

No Danni! They had not found Danni!

In the car going back to the CPD, I couldn't speak I was so sad. Fetterman, bless him, was quiet too, either sensing my mood or saddened himself. I was so desolate it swamped my fury at Khalid and her treachery.

No Danni. No Danni. No Danni in the old woman's apartment. No Danni on television either. I felt so desolate it put me back into the emotions I had had when my dad died. Bereft.

My dad had been the mainstay of my family, the light, the sanity. He'd kept my mother afloat many years; and if he had not been around when my sister and I were little, I cannot imagine what life would have been like. It's difficult enough being under the influence of a madwoman. It must be terrible being under the total, sole control of a madwoman. My dad was there to say, "No, Lorna, don't pick at her. Polly can do this. It's all right. Don't stop her."

Danni, of course, was still *somewhere*. But I needed to see her and see for myself that she was all right. I understood now why Maggie wouldn't take her eyes off the television screen.

What would Maggie be feeling now?

I said to the driver, "I changed my mind. Go to the Knickerbocker before we go back to the office."

Outside the Knickerbocker, I jumped from the squad car. My foot had just touched the curb when I saw Khalid being spun out through the revolving door. She stopped and stood still on the sidewalk.

For half a second, I was going to yell at her. But she spoke first. "I was under orders," she said.

"That's not good enough."

"You know how organizations like yours and mine work. There's a hierarchy. It's like the army. I'm not my own boss."

"Bunk. You're the AIC."

"I'm still not the boss."

Very slowly and low I said, "As the AIC you can tell them what will work. If you had talked to me, I could have told you that the address you had was just about the *last* place in Chicago to hide a child. That building is low-rise subsidized housing for the elderly. It's not like other apartment buildings or even other public housing. Other public housing has screaming kids everywhere and people who don't know each other and don't want to know each other. But those old people do nothing but visit in and out of each other's apartments all day long. They know each other's business down to whether they dusted the coffee table yesterday. How many doughnuts they bought at the local grocery. Plus, there are *no* kids. A crying child would be noticed. Plus the fact that the units aren't soundproofed and you couldn't go in there to soundproof one without everybody in the building talking about it."

"We didn't know that."

"Damned right you didn't. *We do.* You didn't ask. That's why you people do better working *with* the local law enforcement instead of trying to scoop them. Sneaking around hiding what leads you have so you can scarf up all the credit for yourselves! You have your ass in a sling right now, and the way you acted, by God, you deserve it!"

I walked around her and into the building.

eighteen

"Well!" the superintendent said, slapping his hands together in a mock jovial salute to the group. "I imagine we can all agree that *this* little showboating project didn't work out at all well."

He rocked back on his heels and fixed his angry gaze on the clump of people standing uneasily in his office. Some shifted from foot to foot. A few cleared their throats. I stood rigid, still very angry.

The big boss had a particularly flexible voice and was not above using its full range. Building up a head of steam, he growled, "I want you to know this: Channel Seven interrupted the Bulls game with a breaking news bulletin. The Bulls game! 'Raid on old folks home!' Isn't that a fine thing? Pictures of *you people*"—he pointed at Khalid— "coming out of the building. Empty-handed. Empty-handed! And half a dozen fragile, elderly people standing around looking dazed. And one of them saying *you people* pushed him! Isn't that a fine thing?

"Plus two channels interrupted the Sunday afternoon

movie and two interrupted golf. If it's possible to interrupt something as glacially slow as golf. I suppose we should count ourselves lucky that none of the local papers puts out a Sunday afternoon edition. Let alone the *Reader* and *Chicago Times*. But just wait. Wait for tomorrow!

"The only reason Mayor Wallace isn't here right now is that he has laryngitis. He has laryngitis *from yelling at me!* It seems quite likely that he also yelled at your director at the Bureau," he said grimly to Khalid and the head of the Chicago FBI office. The superintendent added, "I fervently hope he did. I'd consider that a *truly fine thing.*"

The local head honcho for the Bureau flinched slightly. Khalid stood stolid, but rigid. Ainslie hadn't been called to the reaming out because the "event" had not happened in Area Three. The rest of the audience for the superintendent consisted of Deputy Superintendent DiMaggio, Chief of Detectives Burkholder, me, the area commander from Area Six, and an attorney for the FBI, apparently imported from Washington in less time than it took to tell about it. What had they done? Modem him in? I mean, it was now three in the afternoon, just two hours since the fiasco.

Chief of Detectives Burkholder said, "Well, at least we've found out the child is really in Chicago."

The superintendent wheeled on him. "No, we haven't, you hairball. We've been well and truly fooled, and we don't know whether she's here or in Puerto Vallarta. I say 'we,' but it's the feds who were handling the tech side."

The boss shifted into four-wheel drive.

"Plus, the mayor wasn't the only person who called," he snarled. There were times you suddenly remembered, in spite of the excellent suits and ties, that he had once been a Chicago patrol cop out on the streets all day. "The governor. Both senators, our Republican and our Democrat, total nonpartisan agreement here. Also the governor of Missouri. Let me put it this way. They are all well aware we have overlapping federal and state justice systems." His voice got even harsher. "What they don't want to hear is that one of them damages a case and jeopardizes a child just to get the glory. That's, of course, if there had been any glory to get. Instead of *fanloads of shit*."

Gordon West, the attorney for the Bureau, cleared his throat. The superintendent said, "You got a cold, or does that mean you want to talk?"

"The FBI policy in recent years has been one of full co-operation with local law enforcement across the nation," said Gordon West. He looked like he had a sea urchin up his ass.

"Then what went wrong here?"

"Uh, we realize that local law enforcement has the best knowledge of local conditions and suspects. We are uncertain of how this authorized entry came to deviate from our previously stated policy."

I looked at Deputy Superintendent DiMaggio and found him staring back at me. Just for a split second, he crossed his eyes.

Four P.M.

The monitor screen in the war room stared blindly, empty of Danni. On the television, CNN was running news, without the corner box of the child. I was trying to concentrate on writing a list of priorities when the in-house phone rang and Sam picked up.

"Yes?" he said. "Oh! Sure!"

He plunked the phone down and said, "Polly!" pointing to CNN. Then he said to Hatch, "Grab the E-mail."

CNN abruptly changed to a full-screen still picture of Danni. She lay curled up on the floor pad, sucking her thumb. I said, "So?"

Hatch punched some keys and our monitor began a slow scan, developing a picture slowly from the top down. It was Danni, but it was a still picture, like CNN.

"Why is a still photo any use?" I asked.

Sam said, "Apparently the CPD E-mail got a message to check this site. Obviously CNN did, too. It's been on a while."

"But what good is an old, still picture of Danni?"

"It's not an old picture," Hatch said. "Look."

A new scan had begun at the top of the screen. As it worked its way down, overlapping the existing picture, it arrived at the center of the image, where Danni lay.

She had turned her head and pulled her thumb out of her mouth.

nineteen

"E-mail is slow," Hatch said, shifting his shoulders in his baggy suit. His tie was pulled down and the knot hung at the middle of his chest. "What it is—they can only transmit enough bits to put out a picture at most every thirty seconds. Nowhere near sixteen or thirty-two pictures per second, which would give the illusion of motion. Like movies."

"Hatch," I said softly, so as to catch his attention fully, "Khalid isn't here right now. Whether she was or not, you realize I'm in charge?"

"Yes, I do."

"I get told *everything,* right?"

"Right."

"This is E-mail, right?"

"Yes. Basically."

"Basically? Explain that."

"It's coming in from an anonymous remailer."

I groaned. I knew nothing about what that was, but I knew what it sounded like.

"Which is?"

"They're Internet sites that forward E-mail to recipients without identifying the sender."

"Hatch, do these anonymous remailer companies know who the sender is?"

"Sure. They have to be paid. Plus, most of them take replies from the addressee and mail them back to the sender."

"In this case, they don't need that feature."

"Right. But they know who's paying them."

"Then find that anonymous remailer, Hatch. We have to force them to turn over the sender."

"I know, Chief Kelly. I've already sent a message to Quantico. They'll come down on them like a ton of bricks."

The screen continued to change, slowly, so slowly. The scan was so slow it was agonizing. You kept staring at the new image as it developed, worrying about what had happened to Danni in the meantime.

But at least it was an image. I telephoned the Gaston suite at the Knickerbocker to tell Maggie it was on.

"She already knows about the goddamned picture!" Senator Gaston barked at me. "Just do your fucking job. Go and find Danni!"

The kidnappers were teasing us, of course. Exactly like they had teased us by intentionally picking a web service provider who would be away on Saturday and who would lead us to a dummy address on Sunday. They were playing with us; and for all the data we had now, they would go on playing with us.

And with Danni's life.

I told Sam to call Ainslie's beeper. When Ainslie phoned back, I said, "We've got to get proactive."

A moment of silence while, no doubt, he thought *no kidding.* "How?"

"I want you to sit down with all your Eighteenth District crime reports beginning Friday, twenty-four hours *before* Danni was kidnapped, and continuing through to today. I want you to pull anything unusual and bring it to me. Any anomaly at all. Anything that catches your eye."

There was another job I'd been forgetting to do, and leaving it undone wasn't fair.

I said, "Fetterman, I've got good news and bad news."

His weather-barometer ears turned pink, and he smiled. He only heard the good news part. Unlike my mother, I think Fetterman is the sort of person to whom the glass really is half-full.

"Yes, ma'am," he said.

"On the whole, Fetterman, I would rather you called me 'boss.' "

"Yes, boss."

"The good news is that I was very pleased with the level of detail in your report yesterday, the fact that you let 'downtown' know instantly about the kidnapping, and I've been further pleased with the quick and apt way you execute orders."

His ears turned the color of good borscht. "Thank you, boss."

"You may think that just about any young officer will pretty much fulfill the orders he or she is given and take appropriate actions and decent notes of events."

"Uh—"

"Don't I wish."

"Yes, boss."

"So I'm going to ask to have you seconded to me for the rest of the Danni Gaston case." His smile stretched from one red ear to the other. "That means you report here, not to the district. And as you well know, doing a good job on an assignment like this looks great in your personnel jacket."

"Yes, sir, boss."

"And there's the added bonus that if I'm happy with your work, I will put in an excellent 'attaboy' letter."

I shifted to a more serious mode. "The bad news is this: You will put in long hours."

"Yes, boss!"

"Not too fast, Fetterman. You will not only follow me around all the time I'm here, which is a lot more than a twelve-hour day, and take notes on all interviews so as to keep me from dropping a stitch later; but also when I leave work for the day I may give you extra assignments to go find something, like that child-care book, or take messages to somebody, or pick up video or audio tapes, or whatever. And this leads me to the final bad news. What you will be is a gofer. Underpaid, underappreciated, with no special title, and very overworked."

"Oh, *yes,* boss!" Fetterman said.

Up in Winnetka, Phoebe Jordan was terrified. William Harper Jordan had never come home from his after-dinner walk. On Saturday evening she had begun to pace around the living room at 8:00 P.M. and by 9:00 P.M. she couldn't stand it any longer. Needing to do something, she put on a light jacket and walked around the block, then down toward Lake Michigan and the beach park, especially checking in the shadows under bushes along the road. People in Winnetka liked thick plantings around their houses. They liked the feeling of privacy provided by stands of juniper, yew, privet, or azaleas between the houses and the road. Phoebe Jordan pictured Bill crossing the street, being struck by a car—it was driven by a teenager most of the times she pictured it, but by a drunken middle-aged man at times, too—then staggering into some thick bushes and collapsing there. If he had collapsed on the sidewalk or roadway, almost anyone passing would have called the paramedics. Winnetka was that kind of suburb.

But by ten o'clock she realized she was being foolish just wandering around. Maybe she was even risking Bill's life. She couldn't find him. She had no idea in which direction he had walked.

She went home and called the Winnetka police, and while she waited for them to arrive, she called Bill Junior, in Highland Park, then Teddy downtown, and finally, even though he couldn't really help, Brandon in Sarasota. Bill Junior said he'd be at her house in ten minutes. Teddy said he'd be there in forty-five. Brandon said he'd call back in two hours and was sure Dad would be home by then.

She spent only a minute or two talking with each child. By the time she hung up with Brandon, the police were ringing her doorbell. Winnetka was that kind of suburb.

That was last night.

Brandon and his wife were due in at O'Hare today, just a few minutes from now. Bill Junior was picking them up. Teddy was making coffee in the kitchen.

Not finding Bill last night had been frightening enough. But she had kept telling herself that he was lying unconscious in the dark somewhere, and as soon as the sun came up somebody would see him. By now the police all knew Bill's description; they had a photo of him, and they'd had a full day of clear sunlight to look. And Winnetka householders had been out and around all day, a pleasant Sunday to be outdoors gardening. Children had played all day in all the parks. Dogs, on leashes and loose, had run all over the grass and woods. Still, nobody anywhere had found Bill.

twenty

Khalid entered the war room. Four of us, Sam, Sandie, Hatch, and I, swung away from our work to look at her. Of the four, only Hatch, who of course was a fellow FBI agent, nodded at her.

Dead silence. So we were going to go on as if nothing had happened?

Beyond the tiny window, a mist was forming. It had been a warm, sunny Sunday, and warm, sunny days in spring bring the moisture up out of the ground. When evening cools the air, the moisture turns to mist.

"Okay, you're angry," Khalid said.

No answer. We waited.

She didn't cringe or back down, but she said, "I'm sorry. Let's hope the bigwigs have learned their lesson."

Well, you had to admire her. She was toughing it out. She wasn't going to take responsibility, but then again, maybe she was justified. For all I knew, she had fought the decision to circumvent the local police and the raid had been forced on her.

I said, "We've gotta go on from here. There's a little child who needs us."

"Right."

"She's going into her second night alone. And hungry."

We all, of course, swung around to see what Danni was doing. The slow scan was as frustrating as ever. Danni was seen in a still picture, one of the water bottles to her lips. The scan line moved down across the screen, taking about thirty seconds to produce a new picture. The water bottle was now in Danni's lap. Her face was sad.

The scan line moved down again. Danni was crying.

"Well, it won't be long," Khalid said.

"What's happened?"

"That's what I came in to tell you. The company that does the anonymous remailing is located in Kansas City. The Bureau is getting a court order to force them to open their files. We'll know in an hour or less who's sending the E-mail."

"Great." I had my doubts that it would be as easy as they thought.

"And, Polly," Khalid said, "I am authorized to tell you that if Danni is in the Chicago area, the raid to rescue her will be run by you."

"Thanks a whole lot."

"We know we don't have the number of officers on the scene that you can call up."

"No kidding! You must think I don't know shit, Khalid. The FBI has 11,500 agents. Nationwide. For the whole country. Plus, unknown to the general public, they do send them abroad."

"True."

"Eleven thousand, five hundred agents. The Chicago Police Department has 11,800 officers. All right here and ready to go."

"Point taken."

"Good. Working together is all I want." I felt much more skeptical than I sounded.

"It shouldn't be long now."

And right then the video screen went dark.

Twenty minutes later, still no picture. The mayor called to yell at us, like we'd intentionally turned it off just to bother him! Burkholder called to yell at us—three times. What an idiot he was! Several aldermen called. How had they gotten the war room number? One senator called, six state reps, and the fire commissioner. I was exhausted and not from getting any work done.

Fetterman had come in with messages and had been sent out again for coffee. Even Sandie had lost her perkiness.

"Well, they can still trace where it was coming from," Khalid said.

"Oh, sure," said Hatch. He was more upset than anyone else. "They'll find that somebody paid by stolen credit card. Or paid in a check for a month of service. They'll go to the bank and find that the account was opened a couple of weeks ago with several small deposits of cash—everybody knows anything over $9,999 triggers an investigation because of the drug business. And that'll be a dead end."

I was surprised how harsh Hatch's voice was. And the content of what he said was a direct challenge to Khalid. She was his superior officer. Maybe he didn't like the way she'd handled the raid on the old people's home. Maybe he didn't like her.

She didn't respond.

"See, this isn't how we usually work cybercrime," Hatch said.

"What do you mean?"

"This is backward. Usually, what we are tracing is theft of services or cybertheft of money. Once in a while we trace assholes who like to break into the Pentagon or stuff like that, or theft of info, but not mostly."

"So what does that have to do with this?"

"This: Most hackers and crackers are into getting something for nothing, like the phone phreaks in the 1970s, who worked out all kinds of ways of getting free telephone service. Like they had a box that would duplicate the sounds, the exact tones, of the long-distance dialing codes. Called them blue boxes. Right now they exchange theft methods on E-mail or the net about, say, how to get DSS service for nothing. DSS is the television service provided by a satellite to your home dish. It's scrambled so that you have to pay for the service in order to get the unscrambler. The hackers trade notes on how to unscramble the signal without paying for it. And they still try to get free phone service, even though it's gotten a lot more difficult to steal phone service. And free net service. There are whole *books* written on these things. And vee haf ways of tracing them."

"Right. But?"

"But, see, that isn't what our kidnappers want to do. They don't want to get free service off the net. They might pay with a sniffed credit card number. But they want to put something—Danni—*onto* the net. They'd even be willing to pay for it. They just don't want anybody to be able to backtrack to where she is."

"Are you saying you can't deal with this?"

"I'm just saying it's harder."

I said, "Well, right now the remailer is what we've got. Go after it."

"Oh, we are. We're way into the search." He thought a few seconds. "And really, they've got to slip up eventually."

The phone rang. Hatch's phone.

"Oh," he said, after listening and nodding. "Man, oh man! I can believe that. Well, beam us up, Scottie."

And a moving picture of Danni just like before, rocking back and forth, her arms around her stomach, appeared on both screens.

day two

helpmepleasehelpmepleasehelpmepleasehelpmeplease

monday

forty-eight hours

twenty-one

"It looks like the el train did this woman a favor," Dr. Balthasar said.

The body that lay on the autopsy table only appeared human if you reconstructed it in your mind's eye. Parnella Grant had been a big woman. She now looked as if the creature from *Alien* had clawed its way out of her belly.

I hate autopsies. And as a big enchilada in the CPD, I no longer have to attend them the way I had to as a young detective. But this was the first of the "anomalies" Ainslie had found for me, and it could be important.

It was seven forty-five Monday morning.

Last night I had cried myself to sleep. I know, I'm a grown-up, and I shouldn't be giving way like that. But I was so frustrated that everything we did was a dead end, and so frantic to help Maggie, and just so damn *sad!*

I didn't even remember falling asleep. I just cried and cried; and when I woke up, which was before the sun had even risen, there were dried, salty tear tracks down my cheeks.

The hell with techie stuff. The hell with cybersearching the source of the web page or whatever they do. The case would be solved by good police work—look for motives, opportunity, trace back every whiff of a (pardon the old-fashioned word) clue.

And Ainslie's choice of anomaly was one such clue. He had said, "The Eighteenth isn't a high murder-rate district, Polly. It's a high white-collar-crime district. Plus a high pickpocket district and a very, very, *extremely* high shop-lifting district."

With all the pricey stores in the area, this was no surprise.

"Parnella Grant's death was made to look like an accident," he said. "Very few killers get cute like that. What makes this stranger is that she has no estate for anybody to inherit, and as far as we know she hasn't stolen anybody's boyfriend."

So here I was at the autopsy of Parnella Grant.

Parnella was thirty-three. She worked at the coffee bar in the mezzanine at Water Tower Place, probably the most popular coffee shop in the Gold Coast. On Saturday, on her way home from work in the late afternoon, four hours after Danni was kidnapped, she had fallen in front of an el train. Fallen—except that one of the few witnesses willing to stay and talk to the responding officers said a man had pushed her.

What did he look like?

"Oh, real average."

"White? Black? Old? Young?"

"White. Kind of sandy hair. Maybe forty. Not skinny. Ordinary. Very ordinary. I really don't remember anything else."

What made him think the man pushed her?

"He was just standing real close to her. I mean she's a black lady and he's a white guy and they don't look like they know each other; and he's standing too close, like not exactly behind but behind-next-to, if you know what I mean. And then she falls and he yells, 'Call nine-one-one' as if he wants to help; but the next thing you know, he's gone."

Dr. Balthasar had completed the destruction of Parnella Grant that the el train had begun. At this moment he was lifting the lower lobe of her right lung onto a scale.

"What do you mean the el train did her a favor?" I asked.

"See this?" He prodded a large area in the lobe that even to my eye looked wrong. The tissue was grainy and dimpled and the color was speckled.

"She probably didn't know about this yet. Twelve, maybe fifteen centimeters in diameter. It's amazing how big a thing like this can get before it really causes symptoms."

"And it's—"

"This is lung cancer," he said.

twenty-two

"**You go first,**" I told Khalid at the noon brain-storming session. "Let's get all the facts we have so far on the table, and then we can talk about what happens next."

"Of course, it's a waste," Burkholder said.

I looked blankly at him. What now?

At this data-pooling meeting were Commander Ainslie, Chief Burkholder, Deputy Superintendent DiMaggio, Agent Hatch, Agent Khalid, my assistant, Sam, to act as executive secretary moving documents and displays, Fetterman to take notes, and me. I had just sent off another twelve teams of canvassers after a thorough debriefing and rebriefing. They needed to know what to do, but they did not need to sit in on top-level discussions. Let alone hear idiots like Burkholder.

"In what way, Chief Burkholder?" I asked.

"Well, after all, it's only one kid."

"What is?"

"The child. Danielle Gaston. Aren't you listening? We have a whole city to protect and serve, and here we're tying up twenty top people and a hundred detectives and God knows how many other guys for just one child."

I held my breath for a second or two. Only one child? Even from here, we could hear reverberations of the television crews clamoring, honking, and jockeying for position down on State Street. Shouts echoed through even our tiny window. And in my mind's ear I could hear the tumult across the world.

"Are you n——?" I stopped myself. I could hardly ask my direct superior if he was nuts. Even as I caught myself, he rose from his chair. I said, "You're wrong. What we do for one child, we do for everybody. We show possible future kidnappers they can't get away with it."

"Bullshit."

"And Danni needs us. She's alive, and we can save her."

"One child. That's what I call waste. And I, for one, don't have time for this," he said. "I've got work to do."

I jumped up too, but DiMaggio beat me to it.

"Carry on, Chief Kelly," DiMaggio said, following Burkholder out of the room.

That left six of us.

Either Burkholder was losing it, or he thought we were going to fail. He thought the world was going to see Danni starve to death on live television. And he was distancing himself.

Ainslie said, "Chief Kelly, how long does Danni have?"

"I've been over this with three different specialists," I said. "One was a survivalist, a man who advises backpackers and wilderness explorers and mountain climbers on what survival gear to carry and goes out with rescue teams to rehydrate victims of various disasters when they find them. One was a consultant to the U.N. on the effects of famine. And one was a pediatrician specializing in nutrition. Apparently there are two kinds of starvation. The one they call 'natural starvation' is like the results of famine. The person is getting something to eat but not enough, and what they eat may have serious nutritional deficiencies."

"Like kwashiorkor," Khalid said. "Protein deficiency. The little children with distended bellies you see on news reports."

"Right. The other is 'total starvation.' That's what we have here."

"So how long can Danni last?" Ainslie repeated.

"She has water. Without any water, she might be dead by now. With water, they weren't sure. An adult with no water or food will die in ten to twelve days. There have been quite a few university experiments on starvation in adults, but never in children. With water alone, adequate water, an adult can live several weeks, depending on how fat they were to begin with."

Ainslie said, "That's amazing. I would have thought a lot less."

"Right. Me, too. But remember that that several weeks' figure is only for an adult. All the experts say a child can't live nearly as long. They just don't have the reserves. Their total bulk is too small."

Sam, who hadn't said anything yet, asked, "Does that mean days?"

"If nothing worse happens to stress her, like heat or extreme cold or an infection, the consensus is she might die in five to seven days."

"What will we see happening to her?" Khalid asked. "What symptoms will she have?"

Sighing, I slipped my notes out of the folder. At this point DiMaggio reentered, saying nothing about Burkholder, and sank back into his chair. He said, "I should interject something here."

"Go ahead," I said.

"This has become a special type of kidnapping. There are levels of seriousness in kidnapping children. Technically, in sentencing, the severity of the offense is increased by what's called 'four levels' if the child is denied nourishment to a life-threatening degree. Even sexual exploitation only ups the ante three levels. My point is that our kidnappers are taking a real risk already."

"Which will make them harder to find."

"I would think so."

I nodded grimly. "All right. Back to Danni's symptoms. She'll feel cold. If you touched her, her skin would feel cold to you, too. She'll be very hungry the first couple of days, but in total starvation the hunger goes away. Not in natural starvation; in famine conditions the person is constantly hungry.

"All the experts were careful to say they had almost no experience of total starvation in children. Nobody does starvation experiments on children, of course. But they think in children the symptoms would be more severe and come on sooner. So—mild cyanosis. Her skin will look bluish. That and the cold feeling is caused by reduced peripheral circulation. The body reduces circulation to the extremities to try to save itself. There will be increased thirst and an increased desire for salt. Starving people drink three or four or five times the amount of water they'd drink normally."

"We've seen that already," Khalid said.

"Yes. We see her drinking frequently. Also, the heart rate slows down at first. It's called sinus bradycardia. The low heart rate appears early on in the starvation process, the experts say, when the body weight loss is only fifteen percent or so. After a while the heart rate goes back up."

Ainslie said, "Is that good?"

"No, the heart is conserving itself at first. After more weight loss, the heart can't cope so well because it's undergoing degeneration itself."

There was depressed silence.

"A starving person," I went on, determined now to get it all out, "acts as if she is mentally dulled, unaware of her surroundings, and not feeling the ordinary stimuli like sight, sound, or touch. But apparently there have been a lot of controlled experiments on starvation in university settings that show the dulling is only apparent. Vision stays as acute as before and hearing appears to become more acute."

"That could be important at some point," Ainslie said.

"Yes." That was a fact to remember. "Respiratory efficiency declines," I said. "There is usually diarrhea. The cardiovascular effects of changes in posture increase. This means she would feel dizzy. She might faint if she stood up suddenly. She might black out or grab at something to support herself."

"Isn't anything in that room to grab onto," Khalid said.

Sadly, I said, "I know." I read the rest of the page of notes fast and angrily. " 'She will be lethargic, fatigued, nauseated, have abdominal pains, cramps, and maybe shortness of breath. Eyes glazed and lusterless. Skin dry, inelastic, cold, and pale. At the time of day when she normally would eat, there will be discomfort and restlessness. She may develop an infection. Death may occur after one-third to one-half the body weight is lost."

twenty-three

I said to the group, "I was hoping that those bottles in Danni's room had something more nutritious in them than water. Something like Pedialyte. I called a chemist in to try to find out."

My consulting chemist, Professor Heisenberg, had looked exactly like a chemist, or at least he looked like he'd been hanging around too many chemicals. His fingertips were stained a yellow-brown and the ends of his nails were black. His face was leathery, and while his hair was brown, flecked gray, his eyebrows were yellow. I had had a college buddy who'd tried to make some explosive from picric acid. The whole batch exploded too soon and his eyebrows had looked exactly like this.

I had said to Heisenberg, "Let me explain what I want. You see the bottles the child, Danni, is drinking from?"

"Yes, of course."

"You see that she has spilled a few drops?"

"Certainly."

"I'm wondering whether you can look at those dried

drops and get an idea of whether that's water or a more nutritious substance."

"Well, of course." He shrugged.

"Great!"

"Within reason. I can tell you whether it has rather completely evaporated, like water does. Or whether it's left more residue, like sugar water would."

"Could you tell whether it was something like Pedialyte? Or even uncolored Gatorade?"

"Probably not. If it actually crystallized when it dried, we might theorize that it had salt in it."

"They wouldn't give her saltwater, would they?" I asked, more to myself than to him. "It would kill her."

"Might. A very dilute saltwater might keep her alive longer than plain H_2O."

"I see."

"But sugars and proteins ordinarily would dry sticky, not crystalline. They might be impossible to distinguish from each other. This is just a TV picture, after all."

"But you can give me something to go on?"

"Yes. Of course. Not from just looking at the screen here though."

"Well, then how would you?"

"If you're serious about this—?"

"I am so serious."

"Well, then, let me go back to the lab. I'll get the best resolution I can on a screen there, freeze a few frames, and see what I can see."

"How soon can you let me know?"

"I'll see."

"Professor Heisenberg, you have the skills to tell me how long this child might be able to live if we don't find her fast."

"All right." He got up to leave.

"Professor Heisenberg? By noon tomorrow? Okay?"

And at noon he had called.

I told the group, "It's nothing but water. Evaporates like Chicago tap water. Leaves only a slight residue on surfaces, like Chicago tap water. Not as pure as Evian, not quite as cruddy as New Orleans water. Tap water."

"That's too bad," Khalid said, after a few seconds. "Nothing is going right."

"Well, actually one thing is."

"Oh?"

They all brightened up a bit.

"My video expert, a woman who consults for two major networks troubleshooting their tech problems, took a look at our video. The whole tape from the very beginning. Forty-four hours of tapes, including the still frames. The question was: Is Danni at any time in a moving vehicle?"

I saw Ainslie's hands clench. What a nice man he was. He feared for Danni; to him she was more than just another case in a lifetime of cases.

"Vibration is very important to control in any video production. They have moving cameras in television dramas all the time, of course, and they deal with the problems of filming on location with the camera in cars and boats and aircraft. The smallest vibration can be annoying to a viewer. So—this is something she really knows about. We were afraid Danni could have been loaded into a truck or a boat or a shipping container. If so, the kidnappers could have started filming right away while they were still moving her. That would have made us *think* they couldn't have gone far, probably not farther than the outlying Chicago suburbs, when actually they could have been flying her to Timbuktu."

Everybody nodded.

"Ms. Schaeffer says no." I saw Ainslie's hands unclench. "Not enough vibration. She also looked at the water in the bottles. Thank goodness they're clear. The water doesn't slosh. And she looked for what she calls an acoustooptic effect. Sound waves apparently produce photoelastic changes in materials that you can see with instruments. Anyway, there's no vibration that would suggest a shipping container.

"And Danni's body language confirms it. As a matter of fact, there is so little vibration that Ms. Schaeffer believes

Danni is in a well-constructed building. Something solid. And since all buildings sway, and taller buildings sway more, as anybody who has been ninety floors up in the John Hancock can tell you, Danni is most likely on a lower floor."

"Yes!" said Ainslie, pumping his fist at the ceiling.

"Right. Two more facts we can use. You realize that Danni *could* have been moved during the blackout times. But there's no particular reason to think she was. They were very short up to this one. Everything in the picture is utterly unchanged. This one today was the longest, twenty-two minutes, but I doubt that they'd move her now that there's so much public attention. There was no blackout during the crucial first twenty-four hours. So our belief that she is in the greater Chicago tristate area is now much stronger."

twenty-four

"Sorry, Khalid," I told her after I finished. "I was going to start with your report when we got off track."

"No prob."

"What have you got?"

"Actually, some interesting material."

I held my breath a few seconds, then exhaled. Please, let it be good.

"I'll give you the data from D.C. first. Sen. Neal Gaston may have some very interesting enemies. Turns out that for the last five years he has chaired the Senate subcommittee on hate groups."

Ainslie said, "Ahhhhh."

"Ah is right. Nazis, 'citizens' militias, white supremacists, the Ku Klux Klan. His committee has been investigating some of the most serious nasties in the country. Even as we speak, Washington is E-mailing me a list of all Chicago and northern Illinois area groups and all hate groups that have associates living in the northern Illinois area, even if the group itself isn't officially based here. In other words, very soon we ought to have the names of people around here who loathe Senator Gaston."

"Any idea how many people we're talking about?"

"In greater Chicago? They figure maybe two, three hundred. But that's a guess until they actually run the data."

"There's no guarantee our kidnappers are homegrown in Illinois."

"No. They could have come in from outside. His home state is second most likely. The office is going to pull up the Missouri militias and hate groups next, after they do Illinois."

DiMaggio said, "I like it."

I said, "We need more detail than just names and addresses. We need to know which groups the subcommittee has only studied and which groups they've had real effects on."

"I know. They're getting it."

"Couldn't we have had this yesterday?"

"Well, they did have it yesterday."

"But you thought you knew where she was." I knew I was being confrontational. Khalid said nothing. Telling myself not to antagonize her, I added, "Oh, well. I gotta say it sounds promising."

"Okay. Second. About Maggie and the senator's home front—" Khalid paused for dramatic effect. Well, I figured, let her take credit. If she had the material, she had a right to be proud of it.

"On *her* home front we have one real possibility. He's a man named Oscar Czielski. Czielski is Maggie Mc-Kittredge's arranger. He and Maggie had a serious falling out five years ago."

"What about?"

"Czielski, on his own time, is a composer. He writes songs. Maggie writes many of her own songs, as I'm sure you know."

"Pretty much everybody knows," Ainslie said.

"Five years ago, during a rehearsal, Czielski flew into a fury and accused Maggie of stealing one of his songs, one he called 'Angel in the Sky.' Everybody in the studio that day heard him yelling about it. Musicians, technicians, even the janitor. He was actually violent. Although he didn't attack people, he attacked objects. He threw somebody's snare drum through a speaker cover, stamped on a couple of string instruments, threw a chair into the glass window between the studio and the sound booth. I mean, big-time fury."

"What happened?"

"Well, first everybody wrestled him to the ground. Then he got free and ran out of the studio. A few days later Maggie got a letter from a lawyer. Czielski was suing her."

"So then what happened?"

"The usual exchange of accusations and challenges. The case wasn't settled, like so many. It went to trial. To make a long story short, Maggie's song, which was called 'West Wind,' and Czielski's were very similar, but they were both derived from an old Appalachian lullaby. And in fact, Maggie had referred to the lullaby several times when she sang the song at concerts. Not taking personal credit, see?"

"Well, but why didn't Czielski realize this? If they told him that during pretrial skirmishing, why did he sue?"

"Beats me. But he calmed down after the verdict. I guess the fact that all the jurors heard the similarities the same way woke him up to reality."

"Hmm. So is he in Chicago?"

"In Chicago, yes. That's not all. He's come back to work for Maggie. The person who replaced him apparently wasn't as good."

"But what's he doing here? She's not singing on this trip."

"No, but she's planning to sing at the Chicago Theater in September. *Was* planning to before this happened anyhow. They say he's here looking at the acoustics."

"And they're all friends now?"

"That's what I wonder. He came back to work for her. But maybe he's still carrying a grudge."

Ainslie said, "Yeah. He doesn't sound too stable."

I said, "What about Maggie herself? I like her a lot, but

we have to be hardheaded. Is there anything nasty in her background?"

"Well, I have to admit they haven't come up with any dirt. Of all of them, near as anybody can figure out, she's clean."

Fetterman spoke, for the first time. "Gee, even in this world, *somebody's* got to be clean, don't they?"

Every single eye swiveled and looked at him. Not a word was spoken.

Khalid shuffled one page to the bottom of her pile and studied the one that was now on top. I said, "There's more? Go ahead."

"I don't know whether you've run into Todd Haralson. Todd is an arranger in a different sense. He's the senator's events arranger. He sets up everything for the senator—hotel accommodations, airline reservations, dinner reservations, political speaking tours, and he takes care of making sure everything is kosher when the senator is on television. You know, the lights, sound system, who's going to ask questions, which questions the senator won't answer so don't even ask, all the details. When I say he's an arranger, I mean exactly that. He's not a secretary. He tells the secretaries to actually *make* the airline reservations or the dinner reservations. Whatever. But he arranges it. He's also not the senator's press secretary. She's back in Missouri right now. Didn't come on this trip, although they tell me she's flying up tonight."

I said, "What about Haralson?" I wanted all the detail we could get, on anybody, but the suspense was killing me, and Khalid's one-nugget-at-a-time narration was driving me nuts.

"Right. He belongs to a fundamentalist church called the Redeemer Returns."

DiMaggio said, "Oh."

"You've heard of it, Deputy Superintendent?" Khalid asked.

"I certainly have. They have a few churches in southern Illinois."

"Then you know they are quite strict about certain things. Oddly, they don't forbid alcohol, or dancing, or a lot of the other things that some fundamentalist churches do. Their focus is the human body, specifically the continuity of the human genome, the human germ plasm from the time of its gift from God, as they put it. From the Creation. And so they oppose gene therapy, of course."

I said, "Of course."

"They oppose surrogate motherhood, artificial insemination, even of the husband's sperm, artificial insemination by donor, which they say is adultery, surgery in the womb, prenatal testing, chorionic villi sampling, which is some sort of testing of the placenta to detect defects, ultrasound in pregnancy, fertility drugs, and artificial insemination."

"I'm surprised they don't disapprove of surgery," Ainslie grumbled.

"I suppose that would be consistent. They claim these practices are against the word of God. And they claim no good comes of these things."

I said, "And I suppose the senator is on a committee to promote medical intervention techniques."

"No, it's more than that."

"What is it then?"

DiMaggio said, "Get to the point, Khalid."

"Maggie conceived Danni at a fertility clinic here at Northwestern University after years of trying to get pregnant. Danni's very existence is a result of medical technology that violates Todd Haralson's idea of what's morally permissible."

twenty-five

The knock sounded on the anteroom door of the Gastons' suite in the Knickerbocker. From the living room Sen. Neal Gaston heard Todd Haralson ask who was there. The two Chicago cops slid up next to Todd to check the visitor. These two cops seemed to live permanently in the anteroom. Two other cops and two FBI agents lived in the extra bedroom, staffing their wiretaps and recording devices.

Finally Neal heard the door open and the clinking of glassware. A wheeled cart entered the living room of the suite, propelled by a waiter in white jacket, black pants, and black bow tie.

"Lunch, Maggie," Neal said, with forced enthusiasm.

"Oh, that's nice. Thanks," Maggie said in a monotone. Not once did she take her eyes off the television screen.

There were several covered dishes on the cart, two ceramic coffee pots, regular and decaf, two bowls of fruit, and a variety of condiments. Gaston signed the chit, adding a tip. The waiter shuffled his feet, stared away from Neal, pained and embarrassed, as the staff all were, and he turned and left hurriedly as soon as the check was signed.

"You'd think misery was catching," Gaston mumbled angrily. Maggie had mentioned this behavior, too; she said the hotel people were just uncomfortable because they didn't know what to say. She was kinder than he was, Neal had said.

And she was probably right.

Neal picked up a small salad plate. He took the covers off the serving dishes and found a variety of triangularly cut sandwiches under one, a dish of hot scallops under another. He placed one small sandwich and a small scoop of scallops on a plate, added sliced strawberries from the fruit selection, and picked up a fork.

He placed the plate in Maggie's lap and handed her the fork. Absently, she said, "Thank you."

Neal poured two cups of coffee and put one on the table next to Maggie.

Neal served himself two sandwich wedges and sat in the middle of the sofa, near Maggie. He watched her, not the television.

After several minutes had passed, she became aware that he was staring.

"Neal, what is it?"

"You aren't eating."

"Yes, I am."

She picked up the coffee cup and sipped.

"Maggie, you can't fool me. I noticed this morning at breakfast. You don't eat. Think back. I don't think you've eaten since—uh—since Saturday."

"But I have."

"No, you haven't. You'll drink things. Coke last night. Tea in the middle of the night. Coffee. You think nobody will notice if you drink things. But *I've* noticed. Maggie, it won't help Danni if you get sick. You apparently believe if Danni can't eat, you won't either. But there's no sense to that."

Maggie looked at the plate of food in her lap. Tears pooled in her eyes and spilled over to run down her cheeks.

She held the plate in two hands and pushed it a few inches farther away.

"Please," Neal said.

Maggie picked up the sandwich as if she didn't know what to do with it, as if it were some strange machine she didn't know how to turn on. After a few seconds, she leaned toward it as a child might and took a bite.

She swallowed, took another bite. Maggie began to choke. She coughed, inhaled, coughed again, and jumped up. The plate spilled from her lap as she ran, gagging, to the bathroom.

Danni's skin felt funny. She wasn't sure why; Danni had never gone two full days without a bath and never even half a day without washing her hands, but she didn't realize that was why her skin felt strange, not exactly sticky, sort of greasy, not quite right. Her face felt as if it had a thin layer of butter on it. She didn't like feeling this way.

Her blue-and-white dress was all funny, too. Dirty and stiff.

And there were pains in her stomach. She understood this perfectly well. She was hungry, and she knew she was hungry; and while the hunger went away sometimes for a few hours, it came back at certain times too, even stronger. She thought about a nice cool glass of milk. Peanut butter and jelly. She thought of the peanut butter melting in her mouth and the jelly making that tart-sweet feeling on the sides of her tongue. She could almost taste it.

Danni had decided this morning that she was not a bad girl. Mommy would never think she had been bad just because she had to use the end of the room as a bathroom. Her mommy never blamed her for things that weren't her fault.

But what she had decided had really happened was worse. She was sure Mommy and Daddy had been taken away.

During her short life, Danni had sometimes overheard her parents talking with her father's security people. But just in the last few months she had begun to understand what they were saying.

Danni called him the " 'curity" man, on the theory that they were saying they would "see curity man." She paid close attention to the "curity man" precisely because she sensed that Mommy and Daddy tried not to talk with him when she was around. Or they talked softly and walked away with him into another room.

. But she knew it all had to do with people who might attack them.

Daddy was a very important man, which was very dangerous, and Mommy had lots of "fans," and sometimes there were "rabid fans" whatever they were. It sounded bad. And sometimes there were "loons." Loons, she had overheard, were people who you "never knew what they might do."

So they may have taken Daddy and Mommy away. And if they didn't let Daddy and Mommy go, what would happen?

Or what if they had shot Daddy and Mommy? People sometimes got shot. Danni knew that for sure; she'd seen it on television.

Maybe they were killed. Danni shivered. She felt so cold all the time. She began to cry. She loved Mommy and Daddy so much. Killed was very bad. Danni thought killed dead meant forever. She was sure it meant never coming back.

If Daddy and Mommy were hurt and killed, then nobody would ever come for her.

twenty-six

The man with the hawk nose spoke to a confederate over a secure line. "He says to give this twelve hours; then I'm supposed to switch to the dark fiber."

"I bet you could stretch it to twenty-four."

"Probably. But why push it? As somebody—was it Jimmy Durante?—said, 'I got a million of 'em.'"

"Okay. I got the WGN end in place. It's in the ceiling over the third floor, where their T1 line runs."

"They won't see where you went in?"

"Oh, please! There's a dropped ceiling. You just take a panel out and climb in. Put it back when you leave."

Dark fiber was the unused part of fiberoptic cabling. The phone companies had found that the physical installation of cable, digging the trenches or stringing lines on poles, tearing out walls and ceilings of buildings to run cable, was far more expensive than the cable material itself. So these days when they laid new, high-bandwidth cable they usually included a large amount of extra fiberoptic cable material that was unused and might remain unused for years—hence, dark fiber. The difficulty in pirate use of dark fiber wasn't finding it, since it was almost everywhere new cable ran. Even oil and gas utilities were stringing it in pipes they laid, on spec that it would be extremely valuable some day. Nor was there any problem getting a signal into it. That technology had been around for decades. The hard part was figuring out where it went and therefore how to get the signal out at the far end. The ability to get a signal into WGN in the Tribune Building was a real technological coup, and the man with the hawk nose was justifiably pleased with himself. He said, "With the T1 line, they'll get superb picture detail."

"But will they be grateful?" The other man laughed. "Oh, no."

He had it all ready to go. The joke of it was you could just go buy a kit almost anyplace. Called a "fiber optic breakout kit," it was actually rather inexpensive, considering that twenty years ago it would have been almost as exotic as television to George Washington.

What a wonderful world we live in, the man thought.

The kit contained everything you needed, including an outer jacket for the fiberoptics made of aramid, a synthetic yarn developed for its great strength. Besides its use in cable work, it was used in applications where strength was important, such as ripcords on life jackets.

The kit also contained premade and preset loose-buffer tubes into which he placed ends of the two fibers he was splicing—his incoming signal that would carry the video of Danni—and the existing outgoing fiber that ran three circuitous miles to WGN. The tubes received connections and positioned the splices without actual pigtail splicing. Much faster than doing it manually. Then he slipped the jacketing sleeve made of aramid yarn over the tube that had the splice inside. At that point the spliced cable became the equivalent of an intact fiberoptic cable.

Over the whole splice, he pulled a plastic boot. He focused a heat lamp on it for a few seconds, effectively shrink-wrapping the whole splice, giving it additional strength.

twenty-seven

Fog shrouded the small window. Night had fallen on the city, but not darkness. Chicago is never dark. The Loop is multicolored all night, with hotel signs, advertising neon, beacons, the lights of cars and store windows and apartments. Here at the police department, the salmon-colored streetlights stained the heavy mist. Looking out the window, one would think some dirty bilious amoeboid creature had pressed itself up against the building.

I love Chicago. Despite the crime I see, Chicago is vigorous and livable. And it has a history to love. Just a few blocks from where I sat in the CPD Building was the red light district of the 1890s. But it was not all tawdry. The Everleigh sisters ran a whorehouse in the 2100 block of South Dearborn that was as flamboyant as any of the hotels on Michigan Avenue. It had six pianos, including gilded miniatures. There were three four-piece orchestras playing every night. Twelve soundproof "reception parlors" each had its theme—Moorish, Japanese, silver, gold, copper, rose, blue-green. There were thirty boudoirs with gold bath-

tubs. And as if that wasn't enough, each evening hundreds
of butterflies were released to fly about the room and settle
on the ladies and sporting gentlemen. Is this a great city or
what?

I stared out the window into fog, wishing I had X-ray
vision like Superman, wishing Chicago would tell me where
it was hiding Danni.

Everyone had left the war room except for me and the
First District officer, who was watching the screen for us.

Danni slept, I hoped. Earlier she had cried for an entire
hour, pressing both hands to her tiny body.

I thought about a question I had asked Maggie Mc-
Kittredge at our first meeting.

The first day, while I was talking with Maggie about what
Danni could do and understand, I had said, very reluctantly,
"Maggie, will it hurt you too much if I ask you more details
about Danni?"

"I don't know. Probably. Let's just go ahead anyway."

"I want to know what she would normally eat in a day."

"For breakfast, maybe applesauce. She's going through
an applesauce phase. I think she likes the sound of the word.
She calls it 'awfulsauce.' I don't think she realizes how
funny that is. Um—and oatmeal. She's on an I-don't-drink-
orange-juice rebellion right now. A small cup of milk.
That's about it for breakfast. She doesn't have a morning
nap anymore, but she has a snack break in the middle of
the morning. Milk and a graham cracker or Fig Newton.
She calls Fig Newtons 'figgeroons.'

"For lunch, spinach or peas. Egg salad sandwich or macaroni with ground beef, or something like that. Different
every day. She loves green peas and eats them one at a time.
Banana for dessert. We don't give her much sugary stuff.
Dinner is chicken or pizza and a hard-boiled egg, or spa-
ghetti and meat balls. Carrots. Cheese. She loves cheese.
And milk."

By the time she finished this, Maggie was white-faced
with her effort at control.

"Moving on," I said. "What does she play with?"

"Her favorite toy currently is a broom; she loves what she calls 'brooming.' She's more into blocks, plastic color forms, crayons, her easel and water colors, and things like that, rather than dolls and toy dishes or that sort of 'girl stuff.' "

"What about games and sports?"

"Well, she and I have been going to a 'tot swim' group. She can swim pretty well actually. And she pretends to play golf."

"Does she go on hikes with you? Or camping trips?"

"We walk. She's too little to camp, although I have friends who go camping with children that age. Why do you ask?"

"Bicycle trips?"

"She rides a tricycle. But not on trips. Why?"

"Because of the bottles. The ones in the room with her. Like bicyclists use to drink from while they're riding. How would she know how to use them?"

Just for an instant, Maggie smiled. "Oh! That's easy! Neal and I both work out. And we drink out of bottles like that when we do the treadmill and stairs and so on."

"Okay. Who would be aware that Danni knew that?"

That had stopped her cold. She thought carefully for several seconds. "Uh—actually, I think CBS or NBC did a segment on Neal a few months ago, and at one point we were exercising. I guess just about anybody could have seen it."

"Oh." I made a note to check the segment to be certain.

I watched Danni on the screen. Right now I wanted so terribly just to give Danni a dish of awfulsauce. It wasn't much to ask. Just one dish, why not?

The video picture of Danni tormented me. She might be close to me right now, a block away, or miles off. How could we tell? I studied the lights. Fluorescent lights, according to our analyst. Now did that mean that Danni was in a store or a converted warehouse or some such commercial place, or a school, possibly? Or had her kidnappers installed fluorescent lights intentionally to make us believe it was a commercial space? I made a note: Get detectives to call contractors who install fluorescent lighting. Or had the kidnappers simply wanted a flavorless, flat light? Did the floorboards, which looked like old wood, tell me anything? What about that strange, square-cornered white patch on the floor in the foreground? It looked like it had been intentionally painted there. But so little of it was visible that it was just tantalizing, not helpful.

Talk to me, Danni. Tell me something. Where are you?

She mumbled, but nothing I could understand, and then turned over.

Despite the fog I heard a plane roar over the CPD Building—actually not despite the fog, but because of it. Most flights into O'Hare come in from the northeast. The glide path is over Glencoe and the northern suburbs. There must be denser fog at that end of the airport tonight, forcing them to use this runway.

There was a faint sound on the screen, too. Muffled, distant, a ghost of a sound, but it seemed like an airplane engine.

Was it possible that it was the same plane? Danni's room was so soundproofed that I quickly lost it.

Planes land at O'Hare every forty-five seconds during peak periods.

"Hatch! Turn off the printer!" I yelled. "Boyce, don't make a sound. Hatch, turn the TV sound up!" He did.

Wait. Wait.

And then I heard an incoming plane overhead, outside our office. On the TV, Danni groaned and it sounded like the roar of a lion, we had the sound up so far. Then she quieted.

And on the television we heard a plane.

I had narrowed the search from twenty-five hundred square miles and six million people to two hundred square miles and two million people.

And then I got a really major idea.

day three

helpmepleasehelpmepleasehelpmepleasehelpmeplease

tuesday

seventy-two hours

twenty-eight

Dawn.

The Huey transport helicopter appeared as a dot near the rising sun, half a mile out over Lake Michigan, its thundering engine audible despite the distance. The dot grew and turned into a huge olive green, slashing, thumping machine, the chopper the troops had called the Jolly Green Giant during the Vietnam war. It snarled toward the sandy shoreline at an altitude of one thousand feet. The angry bird stormed closer, heading for Chicago to make a run due west directly over the Eisenhower Expressway.

Meanwhile, on the Meigs's radar, I could see the other three copters paralleling the Huey's path. Five miles north a Coast Guard Bell moved east-to-west over Lawrence Avenue. Two miles south of the Huey, a Sikorsky flew east-to-west above 43rd Street. Five miles south of the Huey, an A-Star two-seater flew east-to-west over 87th Street.

It was just first light, the sun rising out of Lake Michigan a little north of east, where the Huey had come from. The day would be clear, the cool air that had caused last night's fog having settled and stabilized over the whole region.

The Huey passed overhead. Its whump-whump-whump shook the ground. The lake water showed huge cat's-paw depressions, now boiling back toward their centers, where the downdraft of the rotors had blasted it. To my eye helicopters are ugly, insectile, and clumsy, unlike fixed-wing aircraft, which look graceful. But I'd met the Sikorsky's pilot, and to him his plane was a beauty. He came with it. Nobody else was allowed to fly it.

Chicago is thirty miles north to south. With only four helicopters, even at a distance apart of five miles, we'd have to make two or three east-west sweeps to narrow down where Danni was. Then we'd go north-south and try to pinpoint her.

I hoped to be able to narrow it down, close in, and grab Danni before the kidnappers knew what was going on. And before they could move her someplace else.

Every police district in the city was on alert. We have twenty-five districts, each of which has thirty or forty squad cars. In an ideal world, we would use full intersection control, a squad car at every intersection, but that many thousands of police cars did not exist. One square mile of city blocks will have, on the average, 120 intersections. So I'd mounted a loose perimeter of eighty-five cars and two hundred foot patrols. As the area narrowed, I would collapse the perimeter.

I said into my cell phone, "You're getting this, aren't you, Dr. Friesland?"

"Oh, yes. Taping it here and I have a backup taping the feed at Northwestern."

"And you have the grid readout?"

"Yes, Chief Kelly. We have the radar and a time stamp and a tape of the radar, and a physical plan and backup observers marking the physical map with real live pencils. I assure you, Chief, I know this is important, and I know what I'm doing."

"Dr. Friesland, I never meant to imply you didn't!"

"I know. Don't sweat it, girl. I have a granddaughter Danni's age."

I exhaled, some of the worry leaving me.

The Huey was from Glenview Naval Air Base. The A-Star was city equipment. The Bell, of course, was from the Coast Guard, and DiMaggio had got the Sikorsky at the last minute, around midnight, with his vast powers of persuasion. I don't know from whom.

I would have liked twenty, but I had four. I'd been up all night collecting them.

Once I had the helicopters, I lined up the patrol officers and squad cars, which required cajoling from me plus help from DiMaggio, all of it made more difficult because most district commanders go home at night, like normal people. But by God, finally it had all come together.

I had caught two hours of sleep on a sofa next to the war room.

"We could have waited, Maggie," I said. "We didn't want to wake you up."

"I don't sleep," she said simply. And from the pallor of her face and her sunken eyes, I believed her. She had great dignity.

Khalid, who had come with me to the Knickerbocker, had insisted that we tell the Gastons what was going on. She was obviously suffering from the humiliation of having raided the housing for the elderly and found nothing to show for it. I was furious with her, but I agreed with her that we had a duty to keep Maggie and the senator informed about what we were doing. Not every detail, of course, but sheer humanity argued that we keep reminding them that serious efforts were going on.

The Monday papers had been cruel to the FBI.

The *Tribune* said rather cautiously: "FBI RAID FAILS TO YIELD DANNI GASTON," but the story itself quoted three elderly residents who said they had been pushed around.

The *Chicago Today* head was: "FBI ERROR IN JUDGMENT?"

The *Sun-Times*: "FBI RAIDS OLD FOLKS HOME."

And a tabloid, a local muckraker, said: "ANOTHER WACO?" Which, of course, it wasn't.

A picture tabloid carried just one big, full-front-page shot of the old lady, thin hair showing the freckled scalp beneath, one bony hand clutching her skimpy blouse to her caved chest, the other hand holding open the door to her barren room. Above the photo was one word: "DESPERADO?"

Well, the feds deserved it.

"Senator Gaston, Maggie," I said. "First, I want you to know that Danni is definitely in Chicago."

"You've heard from the kidnappers?" Maggie asked, grabbing my hand.

"No, not yet. I'm sorry."

"So what have you found? How do you know that?" Gaston said.

"Last night O'Hare was rerouting planes over Chicago. I heard one pass overhead, and I heard it simultaneously on the sound from Danni's room."

"Are you certain? It's not coincidence?"

"I waited and heard another one."

Maggie said, "Thank God!"

"At least it's narrowed the search," I said. "But there's a lot of Chicago out there."

"What now?" Gaston asked. His anger of the first two days had lessened. Maybe he was starting to trust me. Or maybe he was exhausted.

"You probably are hearing helicopters this morning. I have four different types of helicopters with four different engine sounds flying across Chicago in a grid pattern. I have an acoustics engineer taping all the sounds that come in on the television feed from Danni's room. They're muffled, of course. The room is soundproofed and there's a white-noise generator, but we certainly can tell when an engine gets louder and then fades away. And we'll know which helicopter was where at that moment. We'll plot the engine sounds on a grid of the city, and we should be able to get a real idea of where she is." ·

Khalid broke in. "You need to know that Chief Kelly made the initial observation herself and thought of this test entirely herself. She's doing a fine job."

Mmmm, I thought. *Olive branch time.*

She went farther. "And it was the CPD that took her idea and made it happen."

In a very cool voice, I said, "Thanks. Now—the copters did a slow run from east to west. They're just finishing a second run one mile north, which was west to east. Then they'll all move another mile north and do it again east to west. Then they'll head to the north suburbs, over Evanston, spread out two miles apart, and do the same thing north to south, then south to north. If we get really lucky and pinpoint an area, then we can talk directly to one of the copters and have it do localized fly-arounds for us. We may be able to get *very* close." I didn't tell her that we had cops out, hoping to draw a net tighter and tighter until we had her.

"With luck," Khalid said, "it's possible we could narrow it down to two or three city blocks."

twenty-nine

Dr. Friesland and I watched the screen. Little Danni was sitting holding her knees with both arms, rocking back and forth and singing "This Old Man."

"Will her singing make it harder to hear the engine sounds?" I asked.

"No. To you and me, yes. But not for our analysis. Completely different frequencies."

"Well, it's making *me* confused."

Friesland was keeping notes on a laptop, which had a street map of the city in white against a blue background overlaid with the paths of the helicopters. The first run, east to west, was represented by green lines, the west to east by yellow-green lines, the third, east to west, by yellow lines. The dots, signifying helicopters hovering in place and waiting for word to start a north to south run, were red.

"We'll have to analyze the engine sounds more closely," he said, "to narrow things down. But even from what we have so far, we know Danni is somewhere along this path." He punched a few keys and a shaded gray area came up. It was an elongated oval running east-to-west across the center of Chicago, with the brightest part of the gray a big egg shape in the middle.

I keyed my radio. "Sam, pull everybody down from Evanston to about Diversey. No, make it Belmont to be on the safe side. Pull everybody up out of south Chicago to Pershing. Leave the east and west perimeters where they are."

"Will do."

The effect of pulling in would be to tighten up the line. So far so good.

"This next run will cross the center of the area right here," he said, circling the egg shape with his index finger. "This will be the first run *crossing* the area that we've defined."

"So how many runs before we narrow the east-to-west axis?"

"Each one will narrow it somewhat. Four or five more permutations, and I'd bet we could almost pinpoint her."

"God, I surely hope so."

"In this run, I bet she's going to be directly under the path of the Sikorsky."

To the north, the signal had gone out. The four copters were beginning their run, which would be north to south, with the Bell at the edge of the lake and the other three, the Sikorsky, Huey, and A-Star, at one-mile intervals inland of it. The squad cars would be in place. The foot patrol would be moving in the direction of the center of the target area and would soon be fully in place. We were closing the net.

Even listening very closely, I could not hear a distant buzz yet. The origin of the run now appeared as four red dots on the screen.

The red dots began to move, forming short red lines.

Come on! I thought. She couldn't be north of Armitage, and she couldn't be south of the Eisenhower. She couldn't be east of Navy Pier, of course, because there was nothing east of it but water. And she probably wasn't west of Pulaski. This oval was about six miles long and three miles wide at the widest part.

Let's shave it down! Tighten it up. Pull the noose!

The red dots moved farther south, now just beginning to approach the area of probability and still no helicopter sound on the video of Danni. "So she can't be anywhere north of this line?" I said to Friesland.

"Right."

I keyed the radio again.

"Ainslie, pull the northern group all the way down to Fullerton."

"You got it."

I held my breath. And even though Dr. Friesland had just told me it didn't matter acoustically, I thought, *Danni, I love you for keeping cheerful, but just for a little while, don't sing.*

Amazingly, she stopped singing. Great! But then I looked more closely and realized that her mouth was still moving.

Dr. Friesland said, "What the hell!"

We still had the picture, but the sound feed had been cut.

thirty

I slid into my own office, not the war room. I needed a few minutes without any people around. After being awake most of the night, and with my hopes "sky high" as I had punned last night, when I was so pleased with myself, I now felt plunged into despair.

As soon as I got the door closed behind me, I kicked the desk, nearly breaking my toe. "Damn! Damn! Damn!" I stamped on the floor like a little kid, over and over and over again. Exhausted, I finally burst into tears. Kicking the chair away from the desk, I flopped down in it and sobbed.

So near and yet so far.

This was Tuesday. Tuesday noon, three days since Danni had been kidnapped, seventy-two hours that Danni had been without food.

The door opened.

"Dammit! Don't you know enough to knock?" I shouted, turning to see who it was.

It was Deputy Superintendent DiMaggio.

I said, "Oh, hell." Conscious that there were still tears on my cheeks, I swiped at them with my sleeve. Then I felt about eight years old, sniffling in front of my boss.

"It's not quite that bad, you know," he said.

"It's very bad."

"Not really."

"I had her *this close*," I said, holding my hands like two claws as if they were clutched around a softball. "This close! I could almost feel her."

"Polly, you *are* closing in. It'll narrow down even farther when your acoustic expert analyzes his final results."

"That's just the problem. It's not narrow enough. *One building* in that area, the John Hancock, contains eight to ten thousand people! We've managed to narrow it down to a large portion of the most densely populated part of Chicago."

I grabbed a city map and flapped it angrily in the air. "Look at this! Just look! The search area contains the entire financial district, the whole central downtown area, a zillion luxury hotels, transient hotels, seedy hotels, and a huge number of public housing units. It contains the Northwestern University Chicago campus, including the law school, medical school, and dental school and ten enormous Northwestern-associated hospital buildings covering a dozen square blocks. Speaking of hospitals, it contains the VA research hospital, Rush-Presbyterian-St. Luke's, and the University of Illinois Medical Center. Colleges? Loyola University, Columbia College, De Paul University, Roosevelt University, Illinois Institute of Technology, U of I Chicago, and Chicago Kent. Also, dozens of grade schools and dozens of high schools. It contains the Sun-Times Building and the Tribune Tower, and the CBS studios. It contains totally unique places, which'll be uniquely difficult to search, like Meigs Field; the Adler Planetarium; the Civic Opera House; the Art Institute; Navy Pier and the Navy Pier tourist attractions; the Museum of Contemporary Art; Marshall Field; Carson, Pirie, Scott; and the Shedd Aquarium! I can see telling the guys to search an aquarium. They must have storerooms galore!" I was shouting.

"Good God, look at all this!" I said, staring at the map. "The Chicago Board of Trade, the Midwest Stock Exchange, the Chicago Board Options Exchange, the Federal Building, the City–County Building, the post office, which is not only gigantic, but also is a huge maze of small rooms packed with every kind of junk on earth. Been there. Also the CAN Plaza, the Borg-Warner Building, the Equitable Building, the Inland Steel Building, the Exchange National Bank, the Continental Illinois Bank, the Harris Bank and Harris Bank East, Northern Trust, LaSalle National Bank, a couple of dozen other banks, Hartford Insurance, Union Carbide, the Wrigley Building, the Xerox Building, and Illinois Bell Telephone. And the Playboy Building. And the Merchandise Mart.

"Can you imagine searching the Merchandise Mart? They call it 'the world's largest building,' and it's chock full of wholesale stores and display rooms and storage bunkers and shipping boxes and old-fashioned heating and cooling and water piping and electrical rooms and basements. When I was working in the First District, somebody told me once it had so much floor space that if you spread it out it would cover the entire Loop! It would take a hundred police officers a month to do it right, assuming you actually wanted to *look into* every storeroom and crevice, not just take people's word for it that they weren't hiding Danni." I stopped, embarrassed.

"Kelly! That's enough! For God's sake, I don't know whether to laugh or yell at you."

"Sorry, boss." I drew a breath. I felt dizzy and sick.

"Let's take this in proportion," DiMaggio said. "You told me last night that just by hearing the plane, you got the target area down from twenty-five hundred square miles and six million people to two hundred square miles and two million people. Today's results must have narrowed that to maybe fifteen square miles and—"

"And half a million people!

Hatch was in the war room when I got there a few minutes later. He seemed to have spilled Coke on his pants and must have patted himself down with paper towels. He looked sticky.

"Good going," he said.

"Oh, sure." I was over the worst of the shock that they were one step ahead of us again. Now I was angry.

"No, I mean it, Chief Kelly. So okay, maybe they heard the helicopters and got suspicious. You made some real progress before they caught on."

"I guess."

"And now for more good news."

"What?"

"We've just located the signal."

"What does that mean?"

"They were call-forwarding like a Ping-Pong ball. Like a Pachinko game. Bangor, Maine. San Diego. Dresden. Tokyo. Reykjavik! Canberra! But call-forwarding is an old hacker identity-hiding scheme. It's antique. We're all over that kind of thing like white on rice."

"And?"

"The ball bounced right back here to Chicago."

"And?"

"It's a new credit card charge, a week and a half old, to a major, and therefore accessible, service provider. Unlike Albionpic."

"Excellent! What's the bottom line?"

"We have a name. And an address."

"Where?"

"Right in your target area. A building on LaSalle and Chicago Ave."

"That's just a couple of blocks from Holy Name!"

"What better? Grab her; hide her immediately. Minimal car trip; minimal risk."

"Move! Move!" I said. "They could take Danni someplace else at any moment!"

"You said you buttoned up the area." Khalid was pocketing her cell phone, while walking fast out the door. Not fast enough for me. Three FBI agents and eight CPD plain-clothes officers trailed us.

"Yes, of course I did. But they've fooled us before."

I had immediately ordered four beat cars from the Eigh-teenth to surround the building at Chicago and LaSalle. Then I beeped Ainslie, and when he called back seconds later, gave him the details.

The CPD HBT team was on the way. This is the hostage-barricade-terrorist guys, all top pro specialists.

Khalid had triggered the FBI's Hostage Rescue Team, and they were going to meet us there. "Under *my* command, Khalid," I said.

"Of course."

The building was twenty-six floors. Wide tinted plate-glass windows, steel verticals, and copper-look floor dividers. We stood half a block from the front door, out of sight of our target apartment.

I keyed the location on my laptop, then toggled down the maps to get smaller and smaller areas, and finally this very intersection. A detailed compilation of zoning information that included such items as fire protection and structural de-tails of this building, my maps also had water mains, gas lines, electrical service, and security info. Overlaid on the streets were bus routes, el or subway routes, police jurisdic-tions, and, if I wanted to pull it up, estimates of automobile and pedestrian traffic at each hour of the day and for dif-ferent days of the week.

"No nearby subway," I said to Khalid and Hatch. "That's a break."

I called over the HBT team leader, Sergeant Corvallis. He was a black guy, about thirty-five, and looked very solid.

"You place eight men out here, four at the rear door, and tell them don't move unless I call. You come with me with two men."

"Yes, boss. Check my team's radios with yours?"

"Sure." We did. We could all talk to each other. He was right; you never know.

He said, "And what do I do about them?"

"Them" were the FBI's HRT, Hostage Rescue Team. Corvallis slid up closer to me. He said in my ear, "Aren't these the guys who brought us Waco and Ruby Ridge?"

"Them and the ATF," I said. "Come with me." Corvallis followed, and so did Hatch and Khalid.

The HRT team leader was a slender white guy wearing what looked like L. L. Bean hunting duds. His name tag read "Glover."

"Agent Glover?"

"Yes?"

He should have said, "Yes, ma'am," to be on the safe side.

"Glover, I'm Deputy Chief Kelly. You will wait right here. You will listen to your radio for instructions. You will do nothing whatsoever, unless specifically ordered to do something by me."

"Yes, ma'am."

"By me by radio, or by Corvallis here as my agent. Not by anybody else. Do you have that?"

"Yes, ma'am."

"Nobody."

"Yes, ma'am."

"Check your radio with Sergeant Corvallis."

"Bertholt Lund?" the building manager said. "Sure, Thirteen-D."

I asked, "How long has he lived here?"

"Well, I think those records are kept in the managing company's central office."

"We don't have time for—"

"But I've been here six years, and he was here when I moved in."

"All right. We need the key to his place. I want you to ride up with us. Is there any vacant apartment on his floor? Or directly above him or below?"

"Yes, Thirteen-C is vacant."

"Bring that key, too. Nothing empty above or below?"

"No."

The manager said, "But I think I should tell you—"

At that instant, Commander Ainslie ran in with one of his detectives. "Here's your warrant," Ainslie said.

Khalid said, "I told you that you don't need one if you have evidence of imminent danger!"

I said, "Never mind. We have it now and it hasn't slowed us down."

I waved the warrant at the manager, who pushed it away and said, "I been trying to tell you Mr. Lund is out of the country."

"Why am I not surprised?"

"But his nephew is there."

"How long has Lund been away?"

"Six weeks or so. The nephew is perfectly legitimate. He came with a letter from Mr. Lund."

"You're saying Mr. Lund himself didn't tell you about the nephew before he left?"

"No."

"When did the nephew arrive?"

"May third or fourth or so. About a week ago."

I turned to Khalid, Hatch, and Ainslie. "I think we've got a live one."

I ordered Corvallis and his people to move in behind me. "If I get any feeling that the kidnappers would rather kill Danni than have us save her, then you need to take them out."

"On your order or on my assessment?"

"My order unless I'm unconscious or dead."

"And then?"

"Then it's save the child first. Catch the kidnappers second. Save the evidence third."

"We always save the victim first."

"Great. Then you shouldn't have any problem."

———

My heart was beating so fast I felt faint. But I was doing the commanding-officer-being-like-a-rock thing and walked steadily to the door of 13D.

I gestured at Gavin Morrison. He knelt at the door and placed the mouth of his "sniffer" at the crack under the door's bottom. The equipment is battery operated and when he turned the switch to "on" it made no sound but the slight sigh of air being taken in.

A wide range of explosives give off detectable vapors. If there were any booby trap bombs in Apartment 13D, I hoped they were the detectable type. The last thing we wanted was for Danni to be blown up on the point of being rescued.

There was silence for several minutes. Sometimes there is absolutely nothing you can do but wait for events to develop.

Finally, Morrison shook his head.

Two techies now attached listening cups to the wall, one to the right and one to the left of the door. Again, we waited.

Again, nothing. The techie on the right said quietly, "Refrigerator compressor sound. Otherwise, nothing special."

"No breathing sounds?"

"No."

I knocked. There was no answer. All right. We'd given them a chance.

I took the key and gestured to the building manager to leave. When he had reached the elevator, I nodded again, waving him away, and he stepped into the elevator. If things went really bad, we sure didn't need him caught in the crossfire.

Hatch was at my elbow and I moved him back, too. Inserting the key, I felt hope and just a stab of doubt. Suddenly, this seemed too easy.

I turned the key. It worked. I turned the knob. The door opened. Too easy?

I stepped in quickly to the right; Hatch jumped in to the left.

A large living room with blue-gray carpet and white furniture lay in front of us.

By now, with no shots fired or detonations or screams, Khalid and three members of the team jumped in behind us, the first to the right, second to the left, third right, fourth left, and fanned out along the wall.

Wide picture windows filled the whole of the north wall on our left. Sheer gray drapes were pulled over them, but the daylight filtered through. Next to the drapes were two philodendrons, a six-foot rubber plant, and a four-foot dracaena, all drooping, brown and dead. The bland interior and the total abandonment of plants that were surely several years old gave me a hollow feeling. No sign of the "nephew."

Ahead of us were two doors in the east wall of the living room and to our right an arch into a dining room, with a set of swinging barroom doors beyond that must lead into a kitchen. I gestured at two cops to check the kitchen while we stood guard here. But I didn't think there was anybody in the kitchen. I could see reflected outdoor light on the ceiling from the kitchen window, and no shadows had moved against it.

"Nobody, boss," the team leader said.

So we had in front of us two closed doors. Bathroom and bedroom, for sure. I gestured for everybody to stay put while the team checked the door on the right.

They pushed it open with no response. They jumped in. In a second I heard the clatter of shower curtain rings as they pushed it back. They came out shaking their heads.

"Khalid, you and me," I said, as I started to the bedroom door. I felt like being generous to her. If Danni was in there, let Khalid be in on the rescue.

The others fanned out farther, silent, tense, and watchful.

I stood to the left of the door hinge and swept the door open, away from us into the room. No motion, no sound.

And where I hoped to find Danni, no Danni.

Khalid and I stepped in, separating instantly. Just a room.

I opened the closet door. Nothing. Gray wall-to-wall carpeting. A king-size bed.

I said, "Okay. Dammit! Nobody here."

Hatch entered first and went directly to the floor-to-ceiling windows, which faced east.

Hatch screamed, "Fuck! Fuck! Fuckfuckfuck!" and smashed his fist into the wall.

I don't know what made him so furious. All I saw was a bunch of electric gadgetry on a table at the window.

But then again, what I saw was a bunch of electric gadgetry on a table at the window.

thirty-one

And yes, the goddamn web site of Danni had disappeared from screens all over the entire world at the moment we entered the apartment. We had tripped a power disconnect under the rug when we crossed the living room floor.

And to add insult to injury, it now took the kidnappers all of thirty seconds to resume transmission, silent of course, using another new method. Obviously, once again they were ready for us.

Not just ready. Way ahead.

An hour later, back in the war room, we reviewed the blacking out of the picture and the re-up. It was seamless; Danni in her prison room simply reappeared, and according to CNN the feed was going directly to WGN in Chicago. This was a totally new method.

The video was real and live, too, not a loop. And not a copy of part of yesterday's. Danni's dress was just a little bit more bedraggled, her face just a little thinner and sadder all the time.

Hatch sat slumped in his chair, nursing a sore, swelling hand and a bruised ego. Half an hour after that, Hatch was in the Northwestern University Medical Center Emergency Room, getting a splint on one finger, broken when he slammed his hand into the wall.

The evidence techies were going over 13D with all the firepower they had: tiny vacuums, fingerprint crap, Superglue fumes for latents on metal and glass, paper bags to be filled with every damn piece of fluff and stuff in that apartment that wasn't part of the original furnishings—lint, hair, food crumbs, flecks of shed skin, flecks of paint, dirt from the bottoms of shoes. And we just hoped they weren't all left there by Lund. I mean, I have every respect for the techies; I don't mean to sound dubious. They had measured the walls, just to be sure there was no false wall anywhere, with Danni behind it. We knew from the video that Danni was in a fairly large room, so this was unlikely. But better safe than sorry. But the kidnappers were ahead of us at every single goddamn step.

Mr. Lund was provably in China. And Mr. Lund's "new" charge card had indeed racked up a web service provider charge. But only in the last nine days. No, the company told us, the charge would not yet have appeared on Mr. Lund's monthly statement. The first bill had not yet been mailed.

And Mr. Lund, reached in the middle of the night in Quanzhou was astonished. No, he had no nephews. Two nieces. Even in China, he had heard about Danni's kidnapping. He was amazed to have been swept up in the crisis. But he said, "That company had better not charge me for the services."

"I'm sure they won't, Mr. Lund," I said. I slammed the phone down, angry at him for his selfishness. Unfair of me. None of this was Lund's fault.

"Hatch," I said, "since Danni wasn't at Lund's, the picture feed was coming in from someplace else. Where? And how? Did it come by wire, like the one in the housing for the elderly?"

"Infrared laser."

"What?"

"The data was directly beamed by infrared laser to a receiver in Lund's window and converted there. Then the web site signal went out by telephone wire from Lund's bedroom telephone to the service provider. So when we traced back from the service provider to the subscriber's address, we got Lund."

"But the laser beam came from somewhere?"

"Of course!"

"In a straight line, I mean, right? Light moves in a straight line."

"Oh, I see what you're getting at. Naturally we thought of all that. You want to draw a line from Lund's window to all the windows in Chicago that look directly at it."

"Right. It looks east. I know there are a lot of windows in line. A lot of high-rises. A lot of hotels, too. I looked out. A lot, but at least a finite number. Trace them all, and in one of those rooms we find Danni."

"I hate to harsh your wave here, but it's just no good. You think Danni's at the other end of the beam. Suppose you're the kidnapper. You video Danni and convert your signal to a laser beam, beam it out a window to another window. There it's reflected or rebroadcast, say at a ninety-degree angle, to still another window. And another. Do that often enough and you could zigzag all over town. Or with a little planning, around to the back of those very same buildings that from Lund's window you can only see from the front. It could even be coming from the *other side of Lund's own building.*"

"Shit. How far can it be sent?"

"Miles. You could transmit it from Gary, Indiana."

"Oh. Wouldn't somebody have seen the actual beam? In the air?"

"No. It's mostly IR—infrared—which isn't visible. Plus, laser light is highly collimated. Means all the rays are parallel; there's almost no divergence. There might be some visible red. I suppose some of it might hit water droplets in the air and scatter a little, but you certainly wouldn't see it in daylight; and even at night Chicago is so brightly lighted that I just don't think you'd notice it at all. After all, the United States sent a laser beam to the moon, and it scattered so little that the red spot where it hit was visible from Earth."

And still no ransom demand. No word from the kidnappers. Not a peep! What did they want?

I stared at Danni, thinking, "Talk to me, honey. Tell me where you are." She seemed to nod at me, in silence of course. She made little forward pecks with her head, as if she were nodding "yes, yes."

Her blue-and-white dress was bedraggled now, stained with yellow around the hem, and stiff, probably stiffened with sweat, urine, and tears.

Still no ransom demand. No word at all from the kidnappers. Could they possibly intend to just leave her there and let her die?

The district cops were going door to door in our target oval, talking with the owners or supers, but no real lead had panned out. The room around her, even the little that was visible, should tell me more than it had. My techie architect analyst had confirmed that the floor was old, varnished wood. Just what it looked like. That was way short of being helpful. The squarish white patch that we saw in the foreground of the television picture was fresh paint, he said. But that didn't help much either. Danni was finger-painting squarish shapes on the floor at her feet with drops of water from her water bottles. Was she copying the white shape, beyond what we saw of it? If so, it was nothing more than a tallish rectangle.

And what could that mean?

Occasionally, she put her good ear to the floor and listened for a while, as if she heard something interesting from downstairs.

By now, after watching Danni climb onto the sleeping pad and trip over the corner of it several times, I realized that it was glued in place. So the kidnappers wanted to keep her in front of the camera, at least when she was lying down. They wanted to be sure she was visible to the camera most of the time. They'd thought of everything.

Come on, sweetheart, talk to me.

Danni had been using some far corner of the room as her bathroom area. It was just chance, I supposed, that this corner was out of camera range. Or really, the reason was that Danni wanted to get as far away from her bed and water bottles as possible.

There was something dignified and gentle about Danni, like her mother. I thought, *I love you, sweetheart.*

thirty-two

Hatch said, "Got them!"

For a moment I was encouraged again, but I said, "Got them how?"

"Holy shit! Can you believe this? They're feeding into the *WGN studios* on dark fiber."

"Oh." I'd heard about dark fiber. "But where is the feed from?"

"Well, dark fiber is difficult. Because it's all unused capacity; you don't have any history of what feeds to where. And a lot of it wasn't well charted in the first place. In other words, you know where the cables were laid, but not what connects to what. We have to work back along the line, and at every diversion point we'll have to test to find out where our signal comes from. It's like looking at a leaf in a huge oak tree and tracing all the way down the trunk to the roots that fan out from the trunk, to the rootlets that fan out from the roots, to the tiny little root hairs to find where one minuscule drop of water that went to that leaf is coming from."

From her desk, Khalid said, "That's very well put."

I said, "Well put, my ass! It's discouragingly put. This could take you *weeks*."

"Not that long."

"Days?"

Hatch hesitated. "Uhhhh. Well, yeah. A couple. Three or four maybe, if we're unlucky."

"You have to physically find and test every place this dark fiber diverges?"

"Well, yes."

"And physically test it even in spots where the cable is buried, or walled in, or even *under the Chicago River?*"

"Uh—not impossible. You don't have to go under the river though. You can test where it comes out."

"Wonderful. And when you finally find it, they'll switch to another transmission mode! This is absolutely, utterly hopeless!"

"I don't think so," he said stiffly. He was hurt; he'd been working hard. And I remembered how much I liked him. He was a sort of big, shaggy, sandy-haired bear, who just happened to have a major talent for cybertech.

"Listen, Hatch, I'm not criticizing you. You *have* to follow the lead of the video signal. I'm just saying these guys are always two jumps ahead, not because you're not great at what you do. As far as I can see, you're the best."

"But."

"Right. But. But. But. But, they'll *always* be two jumps ahead, because they're leading and we're following. They can plant false leads, two false leads, ten false leads, and walk away from them, but you have to follow them all up. We'll never find her this way."

Khalid interrupted. She may have been trying to get Hatch out of the line of fire, but I doubt it. She wasn't the type who protected her subordinates. She had pulled a stack of papers out of the fax.

"These are copies of the data they've been modeming," she said.

"Who? What data?"

"The agency. Data on the terrorist groups with a history

of kidnapping and ties to the Chicago area. They're now listed in order of descending probability."

I was still in a negative mood. "That isn't going to tell us the psychology of the groups. It's mechanical. It's like these computer programs for diagnosing illnesses. Punch in the symptoms and it's supposed to tell you what's wrong."

"Are you aware that most of the time those programs are more accurate than a live doctor?" Khalid demanded.

"I don't think—"

"They are, and the reason is that no human mind can hold all the possible permutations and subpermutations of all the things we now know can go wrong with the human body. Where a hundred years ago there was just the family doctor and his black bag, now we have subspecialties and subsubspecialties."

"If you'd let me talk for half a second, I'll respond to that."

"Yeah. Sure, Kelly."

"I don't think we're talking about the same thing. I know I—my *human mind* as you put it—is no match for any computer in searching millions of entries about hundreds and thousands of people and organizations and pulling the ones that have some connection to what we know now about this particular kidnapping. All I'm saying is that's mechanical. Useful, but not anything more than sorting data. What the human mind is supposed to do is get the feel of the crime. And back up from the behavior of the kidnappers on the scene to what sort of people they were and what they might have done next. Where they might have gone. And look at Danni and say, 'What is she doing now, and what does that tell us about the place she's being held?' Like her putting her ear to the floor. Maybe she hears a child crying downstairs."

"And maybe she hears somebody downstairs playing one of her mother's songs. You can't tell anything from that touchy-feeley stuff," Khalid sneered. "Means nothing. As far as analyzing the crime scene and figuring out what the criminal is like, we have programs that do that."

"No, you have programs that tell you what criminals have behaved in that way in the past. And—okay, don't jump on me—what sorts of people usually commit a given type of crime. I don't have a problem with that."

"Well, thanks a lot!"

"Say somebody knocks over a liquor store on the near North side and flees on foot. I key in my COPS program and download everybody who's not in jail. Who lives within, say, three miles of the incident, since he's on foot. With a history of knocking over liquor stores. I get a list. Send out my guys to interview all of them. Sure, nine times out of ten I get my man. I do this all the time. What I'm saying is that there's always the tenth case that's really different, where you've got to use your brain. Like did the owner rob his own liquor store for the insurance? And Danni isn't even a one-in-ten case; it's a case in a million. The mechanicals have to be supplemented by smart, thinking, and *sensitive* police work, using a human brain."

"Okay. You go ahead and use your brain. Personally, I'm using my data banks."

I stomped out of the office and instead of waiting for the CPD Building elevators, which are as slow as watching blood clot, trotted fast down the stairs. I shoved angrily out the front doors that opened onto State Street.

Coming into the building was Commander Ainslie, looking natty and freshly shaved, as usual. Did the man carry a razor in his briefcase?

Ainslie said, "I was on my way to see you."

"You've got something?"

"Maybe. Maybe not. I thought I'd check around a little farther afield. You wanted anything that seemed odd."

"Right."

"There was a drive-by shooting on West Jackson Street Saturday night, maybe six hours after Danni was kidnapped."

"But that's not so unusual is it? That's a high-crime area."

"No, not unusual. Unfortunately."

"Plus, that's the First District. What does that have to do with us?"

"The man shot was an Edwin Carter—"

"So? Never heard of him."

"He worked in a high-priced cigar store."

"Yes?"

"In Water Tower Place."

thirty-three

I stood on the steps of Holy Name Cathedral. From this vantage point I watched two of Ainslie's detectives leave the Burger King and hang a left to the McDonald's that's next to it on the east. From where I stood, they looked grim and worried. On the one hand, that probably meant they had not found any particularly exciting witnesses. On the other hand, it meant they felt involved. I've always noticed how little joking around there is when a child is injured or missing. Detectives, emergency room physicians, and morgue workers have the blackest senses of humor of any human beings on this planet. But not when the victim is a child.

I opened the cathedral doors. They were banded iron and so heavy that they moved with mechanical assistance from levers.

Golden light spilled down. I smelled candles and dust. And stone. Stone has a cold, clean odor. Stone pillars vaulted from the floor like the trunks of granite elm trees, fanning out a hundred feet above to hold the groined ceiling.

Somewhere a man mumbled and a child spoke and was shushed.

I walked down the aisle to the spot where Danni, Maggie, and Neal Gaston had sat.

To myself I thought, *I am a very smart kidnapper. I've timed this crime to perfection. At the precise instant I've told him to, my confederate has collapsed, gasping. People are rushing to help.*

Now, dressed as a priest, I approach the child and tell her the man is sick. I'm fortunate to find her dancing in the aisle, but if I hadn't I would ask the Gastons to leave their seats while I looked at the sick man.

Do I tell Danni there's danger? She might catch an illness? Or that Mommy and Daddy are going to help the man and we'll wait in the back of the church? Something like that.

So I carry her to the back. She is a happy child and that makes her trusting, no matter how much Mommy has said, "Watch out for strangers." She's seen priests all her life. A priest isn't a stranger.

I walked to the street doors. When I first arrived at Holy Name on Saturday after Danni disappeared, I had done this same tour, but I hadn't known as much then as I knew now. Besides, I thought I hadn't done it *right*.

Now I tell Danni we have to go back to the hotel and wait. At this point, Danni may say that she wants Mommy and Daddy to go along. I tell her they're coming soon, but she is getting suspicious.

But I've planned this well, and my confederate has seen me come out on the steps. He has pulled up in our car, right on time. He didn't hang around out here for fear of being observed. Had he been parked up the street?

I walked down the wide cathedral steps.

As the kidnapper, I lift Danni into the car, jump in next to her, slam the door behind us.

The car starts up. Okay, where do we go?

Straight ahead on State Street? Well, not far, if I don't

have to. I want to get into a different sort of neighborhood pretty fast, don't I?

I can go left or right, east or west, on Chicago Avenue. It's two ways, unlike a lot of these streets.

I walked to Chicago Avenue and stood at the corner. The school attached to Holy Name was on my right. Across the street was the Burger King.

Chicago Avenue was totally torn up. Sewer repair had left piles of gravel in the street along the north side, and deep holes guarded by yellow sawhorses pocked the length of the block. Traffic was moving in both directions, but very slowly; and the lanes were so narrowed that when anything large passed, like a truck, traffic in the other direction had to pull over and wait.

I made a cell phone call to Ainslie's voice mail: "Have detectives thoroughly reinterview the workmen doing the sewer repairs along Chicago Ave. Were they working Saturday?"

If I had just kidnapped a child, I wouldn't want to be held up by traffic. What if a pedestrian happened to glance into the car?

Of course, if I go west on Chicago Ave, I can turn south, pick up Ontario Street, and take it to the Kennedy Expressway. That might be good.

I walked one block farther north on State to Pearson Street. Pearson is one-way eastbound. It is clear; no construction.

Pearson is not a good street for casual witnesses. There is a Starbucks on the farthest corner from me, the northwest, but that is also the corner farthest away from a car turning east. And worse, from my point of view but better for the kidnappers, Starbucks has no tables on the street, few windows, and the windows have awnings that come halfway down over them.

The south side of Pearson as you go east is almost all Loyola University buildings. None of them have large windows providing views onto the street; in fact, by and large they appear designed to create as much interior wall space as possible.

On the north side of Pearson, the buildings are mostly old and were built in the old stoop-fashion style, like a lot of Chicago houses and stores from the late 1800s. This means that from the sidewalk you have to climb six or seven steps to the front door. So the few stores and one hair stylist along here have their first-floor windows half a story above street level. Their windows are rather small. The basement units are four or five feet below grade, and from their windows you could hardly even see a car go by.

As a cop, I'd better not expect witnesses here. But good God, this street was surely made for quick, unobserved getaways!

If I'm a kidnapper and I've really done my homework, this is the way I'd go. Five blocks ahead—east—on Pearson, I'd reach the lake. Lake Shore Drive would take me north or south. Most of the way Lake Shore is posted at forty-five miles an hour. And while it is limited-access, exits are frequent, unlike the highways. Perfect for a kidnapper. I took out my cell phone and left another voice mail message for Ainslie: "Canvass the businesses along Pearson east of State, too. In depth."

I'd take Pearson if I were leaving the area in a hurry. Unless there was some major reason I had to go west and get on the expressway.

But which had it actually been?

I paced slowly eastward on Pearson. Passing a restaurant, then Ghiradelli Chocolates, and then a large Borders Books on the corner, I reached Michigan Avenue. Lake Michigan was three blocks beyond.

In front of me was the old Water Tower, probably the best-known landmark in all of Chicago. One of the few buildings to survive the great Chicago fire of 1871, it looks like a giant yellowish chess rook and had been built to decoratively house a 138-foot standpipe that equalized water pressure from the pumping station building to its east. Oscar

Wilde called it a "castellated monstrosity," but he had to admit that it was an engineering marvel. The yellow stone was local Joliet Lemont limestone, very much prized in its time for its yellow color. It stood on an island built into the west side of Michigan Avenue.

The Water Tower no longer held water in its standpipe. It was now just decorative; an artifact of the late 1800s, an old cast-iron fountain, an iron horse waterer, and an old hand pump graced a tiny park that surrounded it.

Across the street was the gray-and-white marble vertical mall named after the tower: Water Tower Place.

Wait a minute. Water Tower Place?

thirty-four

By now the entire Jordan family was camped out at the house in Winnetka. Brandon and his wife, Anne, and their baby, plus Teddy and his wife, Kathy. Teddy and Kathy had slept overnight in a twin bed that had been Teddy's all through grade school and high school.

Bill Junior lived only six miles away in Highland Park, so his wife and children had gone home; but Bill had slept over on the sofa.

With forty-eight hours now passed, the Winnetka police had listed William Harper Jordan as officially missing. This meant that not only were they now more actively looking for him, but his specs had gone out to all northern Illinois police agencies and the Illinois State Police. The all-call included his name, address, age, and photo, as well as verbal description, last-seen, clothing-worn, medical problems (hypertension, early stage cataract, left eye, hyperlipoproteinemia) and his employer, the Copley Water Tower Bank.

The Winnetka police had queried the bank by telephone, learning only that Jordan had come to work for his short

day Saturday, a job all the vice presidents took in rotation.
This was his regular rotation day; nothing out of the ordinary there. Mrs. Jordan had already told the police the same
thing. And as Mrs. Jordan had told them, he'd arrived home
at the usual Saturday time. One of the bank vice presidents
had talked with the tellers and security people on duty that
Saturday, who said that Jordan had behaved much as usual,
had talked about no problems, personal or otherwise, had
not looked worried, had eaten yogurt and an apple for lunch,
much as usual, and had left work neither earlier nor later
than usual.

Since he had gone missing in Winnetka, not Chicago,
there was no reason to consider the bank involved, no particular flag to draw attention to the fact that his employer
was located in Water Tower Place.

Nobody sent a query about him specifically to the Eighteenth District.

thirty-five

"If we don't ask the public for help when we can and the little girl dies, we'll look like shit," the superintendent said.

DiMaggio said, "You have to consider the downside."

"You're telling me we know the kid is somewhere between Pulaski on the west, the lake on the east, the Eisenhower Expressway on the south—" He held up his hand as DiMaggio drew a breath. "Okay, a block or two south of the Eisenhower on the south, and Armitage on the north."

DiMaggio said, "Yes."

"Then I say let's tell the public this," the superintendent said. "We ask them by every means possible, and that includes radio, television, handbills posted everyplace in the area, churches, plus talks at any public meetings in the area, to be our eyes and ears. Did they see a kid being moved in on Saturday? Have they heard a kid crying since Saturday where there wasn't any kid before? Have them *call the police.*"

"Yeah," said Burkholder.

Khalid listened but said nothing.

The fact that Burkholder agreed made me even more certain I was right to disagree.

"Wait. Just let me restate," I said.

"Sure. Go ahead." The superintendent intended at least to look like he was giving both sides a chance.

"The kidnappers turned the sound feed off because they heard the helicopters and realized after a while that they were flying a pattern. That's very good thinking. So—these are smart people, and they are able to react quickly."

"Agreed."

"What they can't know is how far we got in our helicopter trials. Since we haven't burst in on them, they know we didn't pinpoint her. In fact, our busting into Mr. Lund's apartment tells them pretty clearly we *don't* know exactly where she is."

"Of course."

"But I hope we narrowed it down more than they *think* we did by the helicopter trial. They may figure our target area is twice what it really is. Now I say again, these are smart people. They plan ahead. This may be our one trump card—that we know more than they think we know."

"Agreed."

"They probably have a very specific plan as to how close they'll let us get before they move her. If we tell them what we have, they could dope her up, pop her in a car, and be out of there in a matter of minutes. And *then* we will have lost everything we've gained. They could take her anywhere! Iowa! California! Calgary!"

"Right," the Superintendent said.

"Or kill her."

"I suppose."

"What I have put in motion," I said, "is this. I have cops in the districts in the target area going door to door. They are talking to every building super or manager, asking him who lives there and asking our relevant questions: Who's new? Who has a child? Who doesn't let anybody in? We're making up a data management file. We're doing it more extensively in the target area, but to a lesser extent across the whole city, partly to confuse the kidnappers, who probably know what we do, and partly because we can't be a hundred percent sure."

Silence. The superintendent was thinking. This was good, although it gave me time for misgivings. Was I right or wrong? I was holding Danni's life in my hands.

"What is her condition?" the superintendent asked.

"Not good, but not terrible yet."

"Do we have days or hours?"

"A couple of days, I think." I hoped.

"And how close are you to her?"

"We aren't there yet."

After a few more seconds of silence, DiMaggio said, "I know it's a tough decision to make, but I tend to agree with Kelly."

The superintendent, who had the good sense to value DiMaggio's opinion, said, "All right. For now. But we'll reevaluate this in twenty-four hours."

thirty-six

"**Mr. Czielski,**" I said, "I know you've spoken with one of our senior detectives. But in a situation this desperate, we often have to go over things more than once."

"Why me? I'm busy."

"It's a missing little girl. We all should want to do what we can."

"Easy for you to say. It's your job. Not mine."

Czielski, Maggie's music arranger, was one of those fuzzy people. All the hair on his head seemed to be different lengths. His ears were fuzzy. His beard stubble was blond, so it didn't look like a five o'clock shadow; it was more like tiny pale cactus thorns. He wore a wool jacket so fuzzy that it must have prickled his skin.

"Yes, it is my job, Mr. Czielski."

"Plus, you're not asking me to help you think this through. You're scamming me. You think I'm a suspect."

"Well, suppose you were? You can help us by eliminating yourself as a suspect."

"How'm I supposed to do that?"

"Are you still angry at Maggie? Do you still think she stole your song?"

"I'm not angry. I wouldn't work with her if I was."

"For money you might."

"I'm not rich, but I'm not hurting. I don't need Maggie."

That was roughly true. He'd made some good money on other songs he'd written. But he was nothing like as well off as Senator Gaston. And he might be envious.

I said, "You didn't answer the second part of my question. Do you still think she stole your song?"

"Yes, I do. She got the idea from me. I was humming mine around the studio."

"But if it was from an Appalachian ballad—"

"There are hundreds, maybe thousands of Appalachian ballads. The idea to update it was mine. However, I couldn't persuade a jury, could I? What do they know about the value of ideas?"

"Sounds like you're still mad."

"No, and I'll tell you why. I think it was inadvertent. I've decided Maggie is not a thief. Frankly, stupid as it sounds, she's just too nice. She heard me humming, and it triggered memories of the song in her own mind. And she just plain never remembered later where she got the idea. Inspiration is like that. I can live with that."

"I see."

"I learned something though."

"What?"

"Keep every single thought to yourself until you're ready to publish."

"Mr. Haralson," I said, "you've spoken with one of our senior detectives, but in a case like this we have to go over everything more than once."

"Well, of *course* you do."

He was slick. He dealt with the media all the time; he would have to be slick. Looked slick, too. Slender, nice pinstripe navy blue suit, silk shirt, silk tie. Must have his hair trimmed once a week. Certainly he had shaved a second time today. Not only shaved and splashed on shaving lotion, which smelled like an herbal mix, but had lightly powdered his cheeks afterward. Maybe a professional barbershop job.

While Czielski's whereabouts at the time of the kidnapping were unknown—he said he was in a diner near the Chicago Theater, eating lunch—Haralson had provably been at the Knickerbocker Hotel arranging the Gastons' return schedule to Missouri, which was to have been today. All right, so he wasn't in the kidnap car. But we were convinced that more than one person was involved in the kidnapping. Certainly a second person, in addition to the priest, had to be involved. There had to have been a car waiting with a driver inside. And if there were two conspirators, why not three or four? I was pretty sure the old man in the church was a third. If Haralson was involved, it would have been to make an example of Danni. There was no other personal animosity between Senator Gaston and Haralson that we could find.

"You understand, Mr. Haralson, that we have to suspect people around the senator."

"Certainly. Most crimes are committed by people close to the victim."

"Yes."

"Most murders are committed by friends or relatives. Most kidnappings are by spouses. Most assaults are by so-called friends."

"Are you trying to tell me that Maggie or the senator kidnapped their own child?"

"Oh, no. Not at all. They certainly did not, in my estimation. I'm simply agreeing with you that you have to spread your net to include them and what you might call their entourage."

"Well, Mr. Haralson, help me out here. Convince me that you weren't involved."

He crossed one tailored leg over the other and gave himself up to half a minute of thought. People believe they can tell when a person is lying. They believe cops especially can tell when a person is lying. Well, I'm here to tell you that's total bunk. There are some obvious cases, of course, but when a thinking, calm person wants to put one over on you, you can't tell a damn thing. One of the wisest judges in Chicago once told me that it took her years to realize she *could not tell* when a witness was lying. She became aware of it after additional facts came out on some of her old cases. A nervous or shy person can appear to be lying when they're not. And a good liar can fool you as easily as a good actor.

What you do find out in an interview, though, is what sort of person this is. Is he proud of his intellect? Physically vain? Proud of his strength? Macho? Shy? Angry? Self-important? You can be sure of most of these things in a matter of a minute. Physical vanity, for example, is almost impossible to hide.

Todd Haralson had it. He thought he looked just wonderful. I watched him talk. He had another trait; he was the lecturer type, the teacher, the know-it-all.

Whether perceiving this told me that he could have kidnapped Danni, I did not yet know. But human characteristics can help you decide whether a particular person might commit a particular type of crime.

"Mr. Haralson, my detectives did not ask you much about your church."

"They asked whether we take violent action against people who don't believe as we do. The answer is absolutely not."

"Well, let's leave that aside for a moment. Have you any objection to any behavior of the Gastons, from the point of view of your church?" Maggie and the senator had not made her fertility treatments public. No reason why they should. It wasn't anybody's business but their own. So I did not know how much Haralson knew about it.

"You mean whatever treatment Maggie had at North-western?"

"Yes."

"I don't know exactly what was done. I arranged her transportation and lodging here several times. And I know our accountant paid her bills. But I don't know what procedure was done."

"And so?"

"And so what do I think? I think she couldn't get pregnant for a long time, and she must have had some sort of fertility treatment."

"Which you disapprove of."

"Understand my beliefs, Chief Kelly. My church, the Redeemer Returns, believes that humankind is a miracle, categorically different from the animals, and that the nature of humanity is a gift from God. Our genetic heritage has been handed down from the time of Adam and Eve. It is not the right of some doctors to alter it."

"But suppose you had a genetic disease, like Tay-Sachs. Wouldn't you want to spare your children from it?"

"I would hope it would miss them, but I wouldn't alter them. The human genome is a gift from God."

"Even diseases? God has created diseases? Genetic diseases?"

"Of course. Hasn't God created earthquakes and tornadoes and volcanic eruptions?"

"But suppose somebody just wanted to get pregnant? How could it be wrong to help her? Sometimes there are procedures to concentrate the father's sperm. Sometimes the woman's egg is removed surgically, fertilized, and replaced. That doesn't alter the genetic material."

"Removing it from the body is wrong. There's no telling what damage you do to the genes by taking the material into a foreign environment. We should not be playing God. Look what happened to Danni."

I felt chilled. "What do you mean? What happened to Danni?"

"She's deaf in one ear. Would that have happened if they had left it to nature to take its course?"

I met Ainslie in the CPD lobby as I was returning. "Any ransom demands?" I asked.

"I'd have paged you."

I told him where I'd been and how little I had learned.

Ainslie said, "Haralson and Czielski can't be the only people Maggie and the senator ever offended."

"Well, as far as the senator is concerned, I'm told the enemies are as numerous as the birds in the trees. Every person he ever beat in an election, all that person's staff and campaign fund donors and whatnot. Everybody whose pet bill he ever spoke against in Congress—"

"Spare me."

"Anyhow, the FBI is looking into all that. But Maggie— she has very few enemies. There are a couple of maids she let go for one reason or another. One stole stuff. One dropped and broke stuff. Although Maggie found them jobs other places. One nanny didn't watch Danni and let her wander off once out the back door of the house. I guess Maggie didn't recommend her to anybody. On the senator's home front, there was a gardener Gaston fired. But the problem with all these people is they don't have money."

"You're right about that. This crime took more than just malice."

"Exactly. This thing has planning and resources. And expertise. I can't imagine somebody like Czielski bringing it off. To do this one, you need one of two things: big money or a *lot* of people to help."

I got back to the war room feeling drained and worried. Fetterman said, "Dr. Abelson wants you to call him back."

"Okay."

Dr. Abelson was actually waiting at his desk for my call. Sometimes things work that way. "Is there a problem?" I asked, watching Danni on the silent screen.

"I'm afraid so. Have you noticed Danni making small head and neck motions?"

"As if she's nodding her head? Yes, I have."

"Not as if she's nodding her head. As if she's coughing."

My blood ran cold. I must have turned color because I saw Fetterman stare harder at me. "Coughing?"

"I think she has a respiratory infection."

"I just don't know why you won't have dinner with me. I suppose you're sorry you ever invited me to live with you."

"Mom, you know that's not it. It's the job."

"That's not true, Polly. Everybody eats. You can't tell me you go all day at work and don't eat anything."

"Lately, that's pretty close."

"I know I'm just a burden to you."

"No, Mom."

"But I have an idea. You come home for dinner tonight and I'll cook."

What was this? She hated to cook. "Uh, you don't have to do that. Where would you get ingredients? Do you and Mrs. Drobney want to go to the market?"

"No, no. You have lots of things in your freezer. You just come home. I'll make dinner. What time?"

I was in for it now. Not only would I have to take time for dinner, I would have to be there at exactly the time she wanted, regardless of what was happening to Danni. My mother was not exactly flexible.

"Okay. Well, let's say seven."

"Wouldn't six be just as nice? If I go too long between lunch and dinner, I get a little faint."

"Six is fine."

"Fetterman," I said. "I need you to go to Water Tower Place."

"Yes, boss."

"Find out whatever you can about the Water Tower Place building. How big is it? How many stores? What else besides stores? I think there are doctor's offices above the merchandise floors. Are there apartments? Part of it is a hotel, the Ritz Carlton. How much?"

"Yes, boss. Will they talk to me?"

"Probably. A lot of it will be public information. Puff stuff. Advertising flyers. Brochures for prospective renters. Get all of that kind of thing, all the printed material you can. If they seem really cooperative, try to get floor plans, but we can get them later from zoning if we have to."

"Sure, boss."

I was out of the war room at five-thirty and on my way to the car. I had shrouded myself in a ratty, hooded raincoat that I keep around for emergencies. In this case, the emergency was the media. With the hood pulled well over my head, reporters would overlook me, I hoped. But as luck would have it, I ran into Burkholder in the elevator. He curled one lip at the sight of my raincoat.

"You know, Kelly, I'm keeping an eye on you."

"Yes, sir. As well you should, sir."

He frowned. My remark was very close to rudeness, maybe even insubordination, even though it would never sound that way if it were quoted.

"You think you're protected by DiMaggio. But you're not really. I'm your boss, Kelly. And unless you get real lucky with this case, luckier than I think you will, you're history. I can have you back as a detective running down hooker ODs in less time than it takes to say 'shit.' "

thirty-seven

I was on the street as fast as possible, Burkholder leaving me scared, despite what an idiot he was. He could do me harm, no two ways about it.

Sneaking out the back door, I was able to get to the parking lot without being seen. I turned onto State Street a block down from the worst of the media circus. The TV vans with their satellite guns on top could have convinced anybody we were in a war, and the scud missile launchers were ranged in our street.

My mother was waiting when I got home ten minutes early, the slightly burned aroma in the air telling me the meal was more than ready to go. "Dinner's getting cold," she said reprovingly as she shooed me into a chair.

"And I made coffee," she said.

"Oh, great!" But as I watched, she poured boiling water into two mugs, one for her and one for me, then handed me a jar of instant.

"Now take exactly a rounded spoonful," she said. I did

so. It's far easier to go along with her. She said, watching me, "Now stir it briskly."

I did, then I put the spoon down.

"No, no, stir it *briskly*," she said. "If you stir it really well, it tastes just as good as fresh-brewed coffee."

"Okay." I stirred.

So many memories crowded back. One day after school my mother had allowed me to go over to Annalise's house to play. And Annalise's mother had made peanut butter cookies with us. When I got home I said it was so much fun. "Can we do that some time, Mom?"

She said, "We'll see." A couple of weeks later, while opening a package of Oreos, she said, "You don't have to bake cookies at home. They know how to make them much better than we could."

I felt rebuffed and didn't know why. She was right in a way; Oreos were nice. I must have been wrong; where was the fun in making cookies if you could buy them?

Now she brought in two plates. On each were four food items: a square of macaroni and cheese, a square of spinach soufflé, a square of some sort of pasta with tomato sauce, and a scoop of apple crisp.

I knew she hadn't actually *made* these dishes. I had bought them frozen and squirreled them away in the freezer. My job often keeps me at work twenty hours straight, and being able to nuke a dinner at any time can be a life saver. Still, my mother was a woman who hated to cook, and I was touched by her gesture. She had taken the time to microwave, or bake, these in order to eat dinner with me.

"Well, this certainly is nice," I said.

"Did you really stir your coffee? I notice you aren't drinking it."

I sipped the coffee, then dug into dinner.

The macaroni and cheese was oddly resistant. And it made a crunching noise as my fork pierced it. I cut a chunk off and put it in my mouth. The top was warm, the bottom was hot and tough, and the middle was filled with ice crystals. I swallowed cautiously and cut another piece, turning it over on the plate before I ate it. The bottom was black.

"How did you heat these, Mom?"

"I broiled them. I always broiled those beef patties your father liked so much."

A tolerant person, my father, willing to eat unspiced hunks of chopped beef, black on the outside and raw inside, and a dish of canned applesauce, and say it was good. What Mom had done tonight, I'd bet, was to run the four frozen foods under the broiler, right in their packaging trays. Broiling is the hottest setting on an oven. The tops burned, the bottoms got barely warmed, and the middle was still frozen. Then she flipped the contents over to hide the burned part, cut them in half and served them.

So what was this? A valiant effort to be helpful, handicapped by her chronic lack of energy? Or a subtle piece of sabotage? The mixed message: I love you, but I resent you, and I'm going to get even by making you just a little bit unhappy.

No, I had to assume she meant well. "It's nice to have dinner with you. I appreciate it, Mom."

I chewed the ice, made bitter by the underlayment of blackened carbos. It tasted awful, the icy part crunching and then turning watery as it melted in my mouth, the blackened part chemical in flavor, rubbery in texture.

But in a perverse way it was okay. Whatever my mother's motives, it was the kind of dinner I didn't feel bad about eating while Danni was starving.

I had never been able to eat *in front of Danni,* so to speak, to eat in the war room while I watched her on the television screen. But even away from the vision of her, I hadn't been able to eat heartily since the siege began. I had begun to see food everywhere. On the news, there would be a story about Danni, with pictures of her in her lonely cell, and then the ads would come on for Whoppers, Quarter Pounders, Hot Pockets oozing with ham and cheese, Oncor frozen dinners with more food than two people could possibly eat, Wendy's burgers with bacon, cookies bursting with chocolate chips.

In the case of this particular dinner, I finished everything on my plate.

"I'll let you do the dishes," my mother said, as if conferring a boon.

I took the two plates and two cups to the kitchen in one trip and put them in the dishwasher. There wasn't anything to it, a couple of minutes at most, but it was beyond my mother's energy level.

She couldn't help it.

She can't help it, she can't help it, she can't help it.

The trash can held four empty frozen food packages, Stouffer's Macaroni and Cheese, an Oncor pasta tray, and a couple of others. Two were aluminum foil trays, two were that tan stuff intended for either the microwave or the oven. The tan stuff was brownish black at the edges, the aluminum trays gray and buckled, confirming my theory about how she had cooked.

Sighing, I clicked on the dishwasher, just as my beeper buzzed.

It was the war room number.

thirty-eight

"**My God,** what are they doing?"

"It's been like this for"—Hatch looked at the digital timer—"twenty-two minutes now."

The picture of Danni's room was slowly getting larger. I don't mean actually larger on screen. Obviously our monitor was still the same size. But the picture looked as if the camera was dollying back slowly, or as if the lens were reverse-zooming, revealing a little bit more and more of the room every minute.

"If you want, we can show you what it looked like from the beginning," Hatch said. "We're already taping a separate loop of this. But it's all the same, a very slow zoom out. I'd been watching Danni continuously for several minutes, and when it first started, it was so slow, I didn't notice the zoom; I just felt like I was dizzy and falling backward."

The white corner painted on the floor was being revealed as part of a word.

It was the top of the capital letter **F**. The entire message

was written diagonally to the front plane of the picture. The
slope was shallow so that the words were easily readable
but were revealed very, very slowly. It now read:

FREE J

We were mesmerized. I could tell that people were coming into the room behind me. Word must have gone out that
something major was happening. I could actually feel the
war room warm up as more and more bodies entered; but I
didn't turn around to see who had arrived, and nobody made
a sound.

Ten more slow minutes went by. Now the words could
be seen as:

FREE JOHNNIE RA

I could hear breathing in the room. Frustrated, somebody
said, "Shit." After another couple of minutes, Hatch said,
"Bastards."

On the monitor screen, Danni went about her sad, lonely
evening, clearly unaware that anything different was happening. That told me at least that the camera was remote-
controlled. If there had been another person in the room with
her, she would have reacted. There had never, in all the time
she had been captive, been any sign that there was another
human being in that room.

Finally, the camera stopped moving. The message was:

FREE JOHNNIE RAFT

"Oh, God!" I heard Khalid's voice. "Bandwidth!"
The room erupted in noise.
"Who's Johnnie Raft?"
"I think I've heard—"
"Isn't he—"
"The bomber? Is he the—"

Cutting across the questions, I asked, "Why did they zoom out so slowly?"

Hatch said, "To tease us. They're teasing us again! They just do whatever they goddamn fucking well want to! God *damn* them!"

"And to get attention," I said, quietly. "Look how fast word went out around here. By the time the message finally became readable, probably one out of every two people on earth was watching."

I spun around and yelled, "Khalid!"

The crowd near the second TV monitor parted, revealing Khalid. She came over to me.

I said, "Is this Johnnie Raft on your terrorist list?"

"Um, you mean of Illinois area groups? No."

"Is he on your Missouri list?"

She hesitated. I said, "Khalid?"

"No."

"Then who is Johnnie Raft?"

Khalid said, "Oh, shit, Kelly. He's very bad news. He's the leader of Bandwidth—"

"And did you have Bandwidth, whatever that is, on your list?"

"No, but—"

Hatch, who had immediately gone to his terminal, yelled, "I got him right here."

"Okay, great! Let's go! If we're supposed to free him, he's penned up someplace. Where does he hang out?"

"Well, actually, in the Illinois State Correctional Center in Hillsboro, Illinois."

John Karrs Raft. Male white. DOB 10-1-64. Parents John Edward Raft (dec.) and Helen Chessman Raft (dec.). Educ. Eisenhower School system, Trego County, Kansas, 1981–83 Univ. of MI (no deg.), 1984–85 UCLA (no deg.). All schl. major subj. math, elec-

tronics, and computer engineering. Employed Unisys
1985–87. For full hist. call CGI.955.

Okay, I thought, *so he didn't like school.*

Et cetera, et cetera, et cetera—
Known associates—aha!

Our fax ground us out seventeen faces of known Bandwidth
members at 19804 DPI on 11 × 16 sheets of hard-surface
paper. We spread them flat on the table with more eagerness
than if each had been the last card in five-card stud.

"Kevin Winter," Khalid said, reading the caption on one
photo, a turtlelike man with a receding chin. "Not like any
of our descriptions. Not our fake priest."

"Disguise him to look like the old man?" I asked.

"Neck's too long. Neal and Maggie were sitting behind
him. They would've noticed."

"Yeah. Also, they didn't say anything about tiny little
ears."

"Well, this one certainly isn't either one, the old man or
the priest."

I said, "Show me." She shoved me one of the sheets.

"Supposed to be Raft's right-hand man," she said. "He
calls himself Laser Blue. And I'm sorry to say he popped
up out of nowhere. Or probably Raft found him and between
them they erased whatever background he had."

The photo showed a man with a sharp beak of a nose,
eyes deeply sunken into his head, and a sharp chin.

I said, "For sure none of our witnesses've seen this guy.
You'd never disguise that nose."

Hatch, who was also flipping impatiently through the pictures, barked, "Oh, hell!"

Khalid and I both said, "What?"

Silently, Hatch pushed three photos toward us. He had
lined them up in a row. They were three different men, with
three different names. And if you looked closely, they obviously were not identical. But they were every cop's worst

ID nightmare. Ordinary eyes, average in spacing and size. Middling noses. Ears of a size like most people's, and not especially close set or protruding.

Height? All three were between 5' 9" and 5' 11".

Weight? All three were between 160 and 190 pounds.

Brown hair. Hazel eyes. The Tom, Dick, and Harry of the world. Easily disguised. Essentially impossible to distinguish. With three guys like this, you could have a hundred eyewitnesses and still never prove which one they'd seen.

Khalid said, "We're in big trouble."

"What do you mean? For the first time, we have some real information."

"Information that we're in big trouble. Bandwidth is nothing like ordinary militias and hate groups. It's a lot more like a cult. Ordinarily, we got the citizens' militias, weirdos who can't get jobs or can't keep jobs, so they resent jobs and people who have jobs and think the jobs've been stolen from them by the blacks, Hispanics, and Jews. Then we got neo-Luddites, who blame technology for everything. We got the hate groups. They don't have a plan, just hate. They're just angry and they're armed."

"Hey, Khalid. There are some good people out there with genuine grievances."

"No doubt. But good people don't blow up children."

"Point taken."

"We got the white supremacists, all the angry, poor, unemployed, or underemployed whites who don't fit in. They're enraged. It can't possibly be *their* fault that they're not doing well. Their country has let them down. They deserve better. And they blame the government, the blacks, the Jews, the establishment."

"Who do these Bandwidth people blame?"

"Why, they blame you."

"Me? Me specifically? Cops?"

"No, the people who aren't smart enough to realize that these guys should run the country. The people who don't have enough technosmarts to do what they do."

"But they could get great work in the computer industry. They'd make a hell of a lot more money than I do."

"Under a boss. Who might, God forbid, want them to operate legally."

"Oh."

"They don't want to be employed; they want to *run things*. Bandwidth has been implicated in a lot of disasters. They altered radio transmissions to an airliner during a collision alert—"

"But they can't seriously believe that shooting down an airliner is going to win converts."

"They would never *shoot* down an airliner. They're too cool. They'd sabotage the on-board computers in such a way as to have it drive itself into a mountain and show us how much we need them. The word *Bandwidth* originally was an electrotech term meaning the range of frequencies a device could handle or generate, or the signal-carrying capacity of an optical fiber, or the speed of a gadget. In the cyberrevolution it came to mean the ability of a person to handle information. In other words, intelligence. They believe they're vastly smarter than we are."

"But they can't possibly think that violence will get them any sympathy."

"Hey, did the people who blew up the Murrah Federal Building in Oklahoma City really think they would make a political point or win converts? Did the Pam Am Flight 103 killers?"

"Point taken."

"And Johnnie Raft is their absolute dictator."

"Oh, come on! If they are techsmart people, they may be angry but they wouldn't follow a guy like that slavishly."

Khalid looked at me with scorn. "How naïve can you possibly be?"

"Hey! Don't bust my chops!"

"You are so naïve! Charlie Manson's followers were not idiots. They did what he said because they were smart people with a need. A sick need."

"Well, they were stupid!"

"Foolish, maybe. Listen, cults are not my ticket especially. Kidnappings is what I do. But I put in several years on cults. The people who went down to Jim Jones's compound were not dummies, regardless of what the media led everybody to think. They were smart. They were carpenters, electricians, teachers, people who were alert and questioning. And *more than nine hundred* of them gave their children poison Kool-Aid and drank it themselves."

"They were nuts."

"No, the problem is they weren't nuts. They followed a leader. And there is an even closer example. The Heaven's Gate followers were computer savvy, highly intelligent, highly educated people."

I shifted uneasily. I knew this.

"And they killed themselves," Khalid said, "because their leader told them a star or planet or whatever was coming closer to pick them up."

"All right."

"Johnnie Raft thinks of people as chips and peripherals. And he's the CPU."

"What's the CPU?"

"Central processing unit. The CPU is to your computer as the CEO is to a company."

"Technonerds wouldn't go along with that, would they?"

"Raft has intentionally chosen people who *do* go along with him. It's pretty simple. Set tests and those who don't pass the tests are no longer members. Yes, they'll do whatever he says."

"Jeez."

"If you ask me, the biggest gun these people have is the fact that before they do something crazy, everybody, *including law enforcement,* says, 'Oh, nobody would do that. Oh, no, no. These are intelligent people. They wouldn't do that.' "

"You sound like Senator Gaston."

"No doubt. You ask me, this is personal rage disguised as political action. For all I know, they don't know the difference themselves."

"So you're saying—"

"Militia types and white supremacists are generally los-
ers—not smart, not well-organized, even though they march
around a lot, and not educated."

"And?"

"These guys are *highly* educated. Very organized. Very,
very smart. Some of 'em could have been Bill Gates if
they'd been born ten years earlier, and they know it. Technologically speaking, we are outgunned."

Information on Bandwidth flooded in, a downpour of
databits, an avalanche of datachunks. You could spin down
through the coded and decoded E-mail or just scoop up the
sheets as they were spit out by two faxes, and get info faster
than you could read it.

When technology works, it works big time.

"Pictures of these three guys, Tom, Dick, and Harry,
go to all the witnesses," I said. "Ask everybody who was
in Holy Name—Father Raymond, the women you interviewed, everybody. And, of course, get them over to Maggie
and Neal forthwith."

"Yes, boss," Ainslie said.

"Also Laser Blue, just to be sure whether anybody saw
him."

"They'd have remembered his nose."

"I agree. But let's be on the safe side. Then designate at
least twelve teams of detectives. Grab two teams from each
area and start them reinterviewing car rentals, costume
shops, and all the Catholic institutions where the perps
might have picked up that priest outfit. I realize you won't
find the churches or costume shops open this late at night.
Start with all-night car rentals, but at the crack of dawn you
can hit the ground running. Most churches, church schools,
monasteries, residences for nuns or priests, and seminaries
open up early anyhow."

"Will do."

"And while I'm thinking of it, remember we had some-body check Chicago area theater businesses to find out if there were any plays on right now with priests as characters? The theaters are probably still open. Any of them that told our guy they stored priests' costumes—get the photos over to them."

"I'll have to pull some people off canvassing."

"Then do it!"

I turned to Sam. "Get me an appointment with the su-perintendent for tomorrow. I'm getting sick of having to beg for bodies."

"Um, you want to go over Burkholder's head?"

"You have no idea how *much* I want to."

thirty-nine

It was past 9:00 P.M. and I was half a block from the Knickerbocker Hotel on my way to notify Maggie and Neal about Johnnie Raft and Bandwidth when my beeper buzzed. A message came up in the window to go to the Knickerbocker and meet with them ASAP.

Two minds with but a single thought.

I heard Senator Gaston screaming before the elevator even reached the penthouse floor. What now?

I braced myself and got off.

Senator Gaston was red in the face.

"What the hell kind of sloppy job are you doing here? You stupid cops can't even keep track of one small woman!"

"Who? Maggie?"

"Of course, Maggie, you incompetent idiot! Don't you even know what's going on here?"

"I was coming to tell you about Raft."

"The hell with Raft. Now my *wife* is missing."

I spun away from him to grab a fifteen-second rundown from the nearest cop. Behind him another Chicago cop stood, white-faced with fear and guilt. I shot my finger at him like a gun and said, "What happened?"

The cop, cringing, said, "Mrs. Gaston wanted to go down to the lobby and look at magazines, maybe buy one, she said. Didn't say anything about going outside. Wasn't wearing a coat. I followed her."

"And?"

"She goes to the newsstand and browses awhile. A big guy leans between her and me to get a paper. She slips sideways and out the street door."

I frowned.

He said, "Honest, boss. She just slipped right out. Slick as shi—uh, she was pretty slick about it."

I said, "Get back on the job. I'll talk to you later." I would, but not as harshly as he thought. It would do the cop good to stew for a while though.

We had kept close watch on Neal and Maggie all along. They were suspects in a technical sense, but we mostly rode herd on them because we expected a contact from the kidnappers. My guys were supposed to watch the Gastons, but not be handcuffed to them. The senator had to be allowed to do some confidential Senate business in private.

Khalid, who'd come running in half a minute after me, said, "If the FBI had been watching, this wouldn't have happened."

"The FBI *was* watching!"

"So *now* do you know what's going on?" Gaston sneered.

"Hold it! As I remember, you told us you didn't want to be treated like criminals. We've let you go for walks you said you had to take."

"And sent a cop trailing after me."

"And you have been unpleasant to every officer who went along with you."

"Well, your man should have been more alert!"

"Senator Gaston," I said, getting loud for the first time myself, "*your wife* should have been more cooperative!"

I grabbed my cell phone. "Get me Ainslie and patch him through." I listened. "No, I don't care where he is. I need Operations Command. Get the watch commanders of the Eighteenth District, the First District, Nineteenth, Twenty-first, Twenty-third, Fourteenth, Thirteenth, Ninth, and Twelfth. And get DiMaggio."

"Uh—Deputy Superintendent DiMaggio has gone home for the day." He meant he was probably asleep.

"If he's gone home for the day, call him at home!"

"You know what this means—" Khalid said.

"Not now, Khalid." The FBI was a data-collection organization and a case-development organization and could even mount a task force, but they were *not* an organization of street cops. We had to make a sweep of the streets for Maggie and fast.

I should have anticipated something like this. Maggie had been too controlled, keeping the kind of firm grip on her emotions that eventually just breaks apart. She'd been altogether too *sane*.

The three Chicago police officers and two FBI guys who had been guarding the Gastons' suite were cringing in the corner. Let 'em cringe. Fetterman stood next to me wide-eyed and worried. My cell phone buzzed. Ainslie.

I said, "Maggie's out, Ainslie. I want every human body in your area out on the streets looking for her."

"But they're starting the canvass—"

"Fuck the canvass. This comes first. Everybody."

I punched the power off. Of course Ainslie as an area commander could only get his detectives and other violent crime cops out. Now the district commanders started calling in. They commanded the patrol cops, the uniforms.

"I want everybody out on the streets. You know what Maggie McKittredge looks like but faxes are on their way to every district. She was wearing a brown sweater, black skirt, black shoes. No coat."

Objections from the other end of the phone. Morons! The commander of the Ninth, Carmody, who happened to be in

the station, was incautious enough to say I wasn't his boss.
Which was true. I was taking a real risk.

"Carmody, you will be hearing from your boss. However,
if you have waited *until* you hear from your boss, you will
hear from your boss that your next assignment is out where
God lost his sandals. And if I come by during the night and
find anything more than a skeleton crew in the Ninth, you
are going to smell as good as a dead rat in an air duct."

Unfortunately, I didn't have a leg to stand on. Get it going
first, get permission later.

Fortunately, DiMaggio called back right then and agreed
to make it all okay with the superintendent.

"Had she received any messages?" Khalid demanded.

I said, "Every phone call to that suite, except certain government calls, has been listened to, with their permission,
by the way. Every bit of mail has been read and tested for
hidden codes, too. She's had very few visitors, and they've
all been vetted."

"Do your guys listen in on conversations with live visitors?"

"Usually. But Senator Gaston has had to manage some of
his congressional committee dealings. I mean, he has Senate
business to transact. He has phone calls to make to the State
Department. And the president. And he gets pissed off—uh,
restless—cooped up here. He's gone for walks occasionally,
always under observation. But not Maggie. She never leaves
the TV. She's let us sit in on all her conversations with
visitors, too. Weren't many people that she wanted to have
visit."

"So could the kidnappers have communicated with her or
not?" Khalid said.

"I can't say it's impossible."

Khalid said, "Or—"

"Or what?"

"What I was trying to say before. Maybe this means she
was in with the kidnappers. Maybe she's going to meet
them."

"You're saying *she* kidnapped Danni?"

"Could be."

"Khalid, you utter ass. Maggie's gone out prowling, trying to find Danni. She thinks she can *scent* her. Like a bloodhound."

Instinctively, I knew what Maggie hoped to do. I had almost believed I could do it too when I walked State Street and Pearson. It was as if I could feel Danni's presence, part of the way at least, along that street.

"Check streets and alleys," I told everybody. "Don't bother going into buildings unless we get a specific report. I want every street cruised, both sides, every fifteen minutes. Roll slow. You've got her description. Her code name is going to be Lark. We don't want the media to get wind of this."

I thought for a second and added: "When you see her, don't approach. Drop back but keep her in sight. Call for a second unit to slide in and stop a block or so ahead of her. Get two other units, one on each parallel street."

I thought another second. "And when you get on the air, tell the dispatcher this is urgent. They've been informed to keep all nonemergency traffic off the air on your zone. I don't want you to lose radio contact with each other."

I said, "Switch over to Citywide Seven. Even with the code name we don't want every reporter and drug dealer in Chicago hearing what we're doing."

Last, I said, "After you get your units in place, but before you've taken another breath, *call me.*"

Of course, I was listening to every word of radio traffic on Citywide Seven and heard it before I was called.

"Eighteen, twenty-five, I've got Lark on view. West-bound on the north side of Oak Street, heading for Rush Street."

The dispatcher said, *"Is there anybody with the subject, eighteen twenty-five?"*

"Negative. Not that I can see."

"Who've I got in the area?" the dispatcher asked.

"Eighteen thirty-one. I'm west of Rush. I'll hang here."

The dispatcher said, *"Do I have anybody near Belle-vue Place?"*

"Eighteen thirty-three. Coming off LSD onto Mich-igan. Thirty seconds."

"Thanks, Thirty-three. Who's near Walton?"

"Eighteen twenty-seven. I'm on Wabash at Ontario. I can pick up Walton at Rush. Two minutes."

By then I was pounding down the stairs with Fetterman trailing after me, my radio pressed to my ear.

"Maggie you just can't be out here like this in the dark, wandering around."

"I have to, Polly."

"Why didn't you ask us to go with you?"

"I—thought I'd do better all by myself. Quietly. I could concentrate."

I said, "Look I understand what you're trying to do."

"Do you really?" She didn't believe it.

"You think you can sense where Danni is."

She smiled like an angel.

"But I can't let you do this. Seriously, Maggie. It's dangerous."

"This isn't dangerous." The bright lights of Rush Street were all around us.

"Rush Street can be dangerous. You just came out of a dark side street. And if I don't stop you, you'll wander into another side street. They'll get lonelier and darker as the night goes on. Right now we're two blocks from where Andrew Cunanan attacked and killed Lee Miglin."

"I have to try, Polly. I have to. I can't sit and wait and let everybody else—let everybody else *not* find her."

"But I can't let you. What if the kidnappers are waiting out here to pick you up, too?"

"If they took me to Danni? I'd go in a second."

"But, Maggie, that wouldn't help us find you both."

"How do you know it wouldn't? Anyway, I'd do it."

She meant she'd rather die with Danni than have Danni die alone.

I let her go on looking. It would have been cruel not to. I was aching with exhaustion. For a few moments I thought of getting Senator Gaston out to go with her and some officers. I asked her, "Why didn't you bring the senator along?"

"Because—I'm sorry, Polly, but I thought I could get away better alone."

"You did that all right."

"I didn't mean to make more work for all of you."

"It's okay. Forget it."

She looked closely at my face. "The reason you asked about Neal? You think he's cold, don't you?"

"Not necessarily. People react to stress in different ways."

"You think he isn't like other parents who've had a child kidnapped. He's cautious. He's news-aware. I know you think so. Well, of course he isn't like other parents. You don't realize what it is to be a senator."

"He's very important—"

"I don't mean important. I mean vulnerable. As a politician you spend *all* your time being careful what you say and how you look. If you're a senator and you say *one wrong word* you can be out on your ear."

"I wasn't criticizing."

"But you wondered. I need you to understand him. Look, we aren't very nice to our elected officials in this country. We don't allow them any private life. Or any—any personality. I don't know whether you remember when Edmund Muskie, who was a possible candidate for president, was just reamed out by the press. Somebody had disparaged his wife. And he started to defend her and he started crying. And naturally there was an uproar. Did you want a crybaby holding his finger on the nuclear button? Muskie wasn't

manly, they said. Can you imagine? It was just so wrong!
So unfair!"

"I remember it. Or I've read about it."

"Is it any wonder politicians act so stiff? It's a horrible
life."

"Does Neal want to be president?"

"Sure. In a way. What politician doesn't want to be president? But he's a good guy. And he has a life—with me
and Danni, outside politics."

"Okay, let's get you home."

"No, I'm going on. Polly, I have to do this. And the fact
that I didn't bring Neal along is *not* a reflection on him!
Okay?"

"Okay."

Fetterman, bless his heart, said, "Let me walk along with
Mrs. Gaston."

They didn't go unguarded. Two foot officers dressed like
street people trailed them and two dressed like a partying,
kissing couple preceded them. A squad car trailed half a
block back. Everybody was alerted to maintain watch and
move in if the kidnappers picked Maggie up. To move in,
follow, but not to arrest them. The one potential benefit of
Maggie's nighttime prowl would be a chance, however remote, to follow the kidnappers to Danni.

Maggie probably never noticed that the cops were all
around her. She was like a bloodhound, scenting the air,
stopping at corners, puzzling for a minute, turning right or
left or going straight, according to what some sixth sense
told her. The team ahead of her would rush around three
sides of a block and come up again when they guessed
wrong about which way she would go.

Fetterman held her elbow for support.

day four

helpmepleasehelpmepleasehelpmepleasehelpmeplease

wednesday

ninety-six hours

forty

All across the world people were watching. The major U.S. television channels, CBS, NBC, and ABC, now ran Danni in a permanent corner box no matter what other program was on, as CNN had started to do on Saturday. Many channels bannered their own doctors' updates on her physical condition across the bottom of the screen.

Most people watched, though, on the net. Anybody anywhere who was plugged into the net called up the <**helpmeplease**> web site, and they could see Danni full-screen as long as they chose.

In the Philippines, more people watched Danni than had watched the eruption of Mount Pinautubo. In Canada she had overtaken hockey and curling. Japan television carried a constant written analysis of her condition. Russia, the Ukraine, Uganda, Iceland, Argentina—it was worldwide. In Japan, commentators asked why U.S. police didn't just break into apartments until they found her. In Saudi Arabia, news broadcasts told watchers that such a horrible event could not happen in a state where women stayed home with their small children.

Laser Blue, the man with the hawk nose, smiled at all this. It was as excellent as if he had orchestrated it, which, in a sense, he had. Or to be fair, Raft had. Raft was the master strategist, no doubt about it. There was the deep drum section going doom-doom-doom. It was the end of civilization when such a thing could happen. Pundits told the public that the coming of the cybernetic age had made this possible, and without the publicity, the mechanism to show the child to the world, nothing like this ever would have happened. There would be more such hideous happenings. The world was going to hell.

And the string section—such lovely strident criticism. Why weren't there laws against this sort of action? Well, maybe there were, but why weren't the punishments more severe? What was the Chicago Police Department doing all this time? Four days! Why could they not find a small girl in four days? Nag, nag, nag, nag, like horsehair rubbing on catgut violin strings.

And why, they asked, had her parents not protected her? Didn't they know you should never take your eyes off a child? They were too career-oriented, too rich, too prominent, too selfish. Of course, with all the events they attended as prominent people, they didn't have enough time for their child.

And the brasses! Honk! Honk! Honk! Experts all over the globe told radio and television and the print media what they would have done. We would have flooded Chicago with cops the instant she vanished. We would have searched for the fake priest. We would have traced where that video feed was coming from. We would have asked the public to tell us if they saw a child.

And all of humankind was woodwinds. What now? Oh-oh-oh! Help! Help! Help! What should we do now? What will happen? Can it happen to my child?

Oh, it was wonderful.

There was literally not one news medium on the face of

the earth that was not looking at Danni or talking about her. Danni was everywhere. Danni was everything. It was such wonderful fun. How brilliant this had been, the man thought. How clever of Johnnie Raft.

Laser Blue could see that Johnnie had played the whole thing like the conductor of an orchestra. The build was beautiful. To allow them to feel they were close, as if they had psyched out the leitmotif, then to dash their hopes with a whole new variation. It was an honor to follow such a man. He was as canny as a successful politician.

Most important of all the innovations was the net. The doomsayers were right in one way—it would not have been the same without the net. The immediacy! The pathos! Anybody anywhere who was plugged into the net just called up the <**helpmeplease**> site, and they could watch Danni starve for as long as they chose.

Right in their own home!

The Senate, Gaston's colleagues for twenty years of his political life, met in special session. Senator Polhemus proposed that the Bill of Rights be suspended long enough to invade and search every apartment in Chicago. At the White House news conference, the doyenne of Washington reporters asked why the president couldn't take executive action. "Couldn't you take the army into Chicago under the aegis of your war powers?"

"If we just go around breaking down doors," the president said, "what's to stop them from killing her?"

The governor of Illinois was taking so much heat at news conferences that he went down to the capital, Springfield, which he rarely visited, and stayed in his residence there for thirty hours, incommunicado.

Chicago's Mayor Wallace was taking so much heat that he called news conferences three times a day, at which he said nothing of importance at very great length, and so eventually the press stopped coming.

The Superintendent of Police took the heat at his own daily news conference. Today's first question was: "Who is

Johnnie Raft?" The second question was: "Is there any new lead?" The third was: "Is Polly Kelly able to handle this case?"

Laser Blue watched all the uproar, clicking back and forth between channels to see all the excellent media coverage, and keeping, of course, his own system tuned to the web site that simply ran Danni silently and constantly, with the **FREE JOHNNIE RAFT** words now continuously visible. They had built the suspense to just about the right point.

In the early morning, he had another E-mail message from Raft, the Big Boss. It warmed his heart. It said simply:

<nice job☺>

Maggie had not found Danni. She had given up, had almost collapsed, drooping and sad, at three in the morning. Fetterman had led her back to the Knickerbocker, finally talking her into a cab, trailed by the other cops of course, and he had called for a doctor to meet her there and take a look at her. Fetterman's instincts are all good. In a just world, he will be Chicago's Superintendent of Police in the year 2020.

Fetterman, who had promised me that he would sleep at least eight hours after he left Maggie, whenever he left Maggie, showed up at 9:00 A.M. anyhow.

"Fetterman, since when is 3:00 A.M. from 9:00 A.M., less half an hour to drive home and half an hour to drive here, and from the looks of you, additional time to shave, eight hours of sleep?"

"Well, I just woke up is all."

"Decades of negotiations by the union have specified that we can't work you this much."

"But, boss, that's only if we tell them, isn't it?"

Fetterman had been carrying around his information about Water Tower Place. The events of last night blew it out of my mind and his until now.

"I'll report, huh, boss?" he said.

I wish I were as frisky on four and a half hours' sleep.

"Lemme see," he said, taking out his notebook, a small clutch of brochures, and a pen. His tongue stuck out the side of his mouth as he flipped pages earnestly.

"Water Tower Place," he said, "was built in 1976. The lower twelve floors have the shopping mall—that's primarily floors one through eight—then offices. The offices are mostly dentists, cosmetic surgeons, and cosmetic, uh, paramedical people—like they do facials, and nails, and waxing, which I guess takes off hair, and like that. The tower is sixty-two stories. And that part, the tower, I mean, is condos and the Ritz-Carlton Hotel."

"Big," I said.

"Very big. They say there are over a hundred stores, plus movie theaters and restaurants. It's 610,000 square feet of floor space. The hotel is kinda strange if you're used to hotels where you walk in the front door, like, and there you are, it's all hotel. What I mean is, the Ritz-Carlton has an entrance on the Pearson Street level, but all of the real hotel is way up above there, above the stores. The hotel has its health spa and maintenance systems on the tenth and eleventh floors. The real lobby is on eleven and the restaurants are on twelve."

"Did you look around the Ritz?"

"Oh, yeah. I saw the health spa and all even. It's really, really nice."

"I don't doubt it," I said dryly.

"Plus, I got the fire department diagrams of the fire protection stuff, and of course all the CPD data on security. Store security, building security, hotel security. That's this set of sheets." He plopped down a two-inch-thick pile of papers barely held together by brass-colored pins stuck through three holes in the left margins.

"And this here's the CPD emergency response data."

"This here" was actually a disk for a minicomputer and display screen, like the ICAM one I carried on raids. These tiny disks carry data on specific areas of the city that are displayed on a screen about twice the size of a beeper screen. There are hundreds of buildings in Chicago that are bigger than a small town, and info-disks are made up for the department on all of those. They are intended to provide vital information instantly in major crises like fires, gas leaks, bombs, terrorism, tornadoes—situations that require fast, informed responses. Events where if you put a foot wrong a thousand people could die.

"I can get a regular-size disk of that for the equipment here," he said, pointing to the war room monitor.

"Good. Do that. You did good, Fetterman."

His ears glowed, pinkly happy. "What are we gonna do with this, now, boss?"

"I don't have the least idea."

forty-one

"Ainslie, I want you to get a couple of senior detectives over to Water Tower Place."

He snapped at me. "Which job do I take them off of?"

"Look, I know how you feel—"

"I'm sorry, boss. It's not your fault."

"Well, maybe it's not anybody's fault. Danni is my first priority, but we all know crime in Chicago didn't take a holiday the day she was kidnapped. Look, I don't want Water Tower Place *searched*."

"We couldn't anyhow—except the public areas—without a warrant."

"I just want them to take a few hours, look around, and assess the building. I want to know if it's even possible that Danni could be there someplace. They particularly need to analyze the entrances. How does shipping get into the building? Suppose Danni was in a closed box and was brought inside during those first twenty-seven minutes. Any building takes delivery of big items all the time. Refrigerators. Window frames. Sofas. Display cases. Dental chairs. X-ray ma-

chines. Massive sculptures. So—what is security like for
that stuff? Who watches it? Who has access? How? How
do Water Tower residents get in? If they come in a car,
where do they park? Can they park their own car or is it
valet parking? Obviously, if it's valet you can't bring in a
child by car without being seen. But you could bring in a
big suitcase. Or did somebody bring in a 'sleeping' child on
Saturday? What if you got on an elevator with a child who
was drugged but looked like she was just sleeping? Would
anybody notice? Where are the security cameras located?
What about their security videotapes? Can we get them
ASAP? I know this sounds like a lot of stuff for them to
ask, but it's not as bad as a search. There are only just so
many entrances and I want to know the exact policies they
have for supervising them."

"Policy is one thing. Nobody on earth ever follows a policy one hundred percent."

"Tell me something I don't know."

"Okay. Okay. They'll be in the building in an hour."

The brainstorming session started at ten.

"The Bandwidth members are not from Chicago," Khalid
said. "Most of them are from the Seattle area. A couple are
from Palo Alto and the Route 128 area in Boston. Which
figures since they're disaffected cybertechs. So they had to
find a place to stay here. They're either in a hotel or renting
an apartment—"

"Or squatting in an empty apartment or in one where the
owner's away, or possibly staying with friends who are just
as angry with the world as they are," I said.

"We have to assume they *could* be in a hotel. We'd feel
like idiots if we looked everywhere else and learned later
they were all in a suite at the Hilton."

I said, "Hatch, you've tried credit card charges to hotels?
Bed and breakfasts? Apartments by-the-month?"

Hatch said patiently but firmly, "I've checked every
Bandwidth member's name for any credit card use for any
purchase whatsoever for the entire year up to now and up-

dated it every four hours. They haven't charged so much as a pair of shoes here. But why would they? They are absolute geniuses at sniffing other people's credit card numbers."

"Let's get hotel lobby videotapes."

Khalid said, "If the hotels will give them to us."

"Try. What about those ATM and drive-through videotapes from Saturday?"

"We've had an expert look at them who's studied the Bandwidth people," Hatch said. "He doesn't see them, but we're going to enhanced detail analysis."

"Which means what?"

"They freeze ears, for instance, and compare on a scale of characteristics. It's a lot like fingerprint analysis."

I said, "Bandwidth also must have rental cars. They wouldn't have used their own vehicles."

"Yes, but under a stolen credit card or false name."

"Whatever. Show our pictures to the staffs." I paused for a few seconds and said, "Why Chicago?"

"What do you mean?"

"Why did this happen here? Why pick up Danni here? Why not in Missouri? Or Washington? Do they have support here?"

Khalid said, "They wouldn't want to attack Gaston on his home turf. A stranger would stick out more at home. There's likely to be less security or less predictable security when he's away from home."

"Probably true of Washington, too," Hatch said. "They wouldn't want to do the snatch there. A lot of security there, already in place."

Khalid said, "Plus, the kidnappers would know it's scarier for him and Maggie to have something like this happen away from home."

We dealt the photos of the Bandwidth members around the table, moved them around, looking at them for the fiftieth time. I said, "Which of these guys played the old man?"

"None of 'em look old enough."

"You can do wonders with a little makeup. Stooped posture. Walk slowly and carefully. Sigh when you sit down and groan when you get up."

Khalid said, "Did Maggie or Neal think any of them looked like the old man?"

"These two." I pushed over a picture of one Charles DeGier, fifty-two, a skinny man, to judge by his physical description, with a very thin face. A little shadowing of the wrinkles in his cheeks, a little dark shadow under his eyes, a little white stuff on his lackluster hair, and yes, with the right body language he could look fifteen years older. And a picture of one Heinrich Poole, sixty, who was in fact the oldest of the known Bandwidth members. He seemed to me a little too well-fed to be easily disguised. "Maggie says maybe DeGier. Neal says maybe Poole. Neither one really jumped at a firm ID."

Khalid said, "Did I tell you not one of these Bandwidth assholes is at home? They must *all* be in Chicago."

"Or staying away from home to confuse us. They're smart enough to know we can't tell which ones are here if they've all gone missing."

"True. How many are there altogether?"

Khalid said, "At least seventy. Nobody knows for sure."

I said, "And the only one who we know where he is, is Raft."

"You going to go see him?"

"Today. Right after I talk with Senator Gaston."

"I can tell you one thing. All the members of Bandwidth take their orders from Raft."

"I know that," I said. "You convinced me."

"It's a matter of initial selection."

"Yes, I get it; I get it."

"Somehow he's getting word out."

"Well, maybe we can cut off the flow."

"These people are the worst," Sen. Neal Gaston said. "The very, very worst. Arrogant, cowardly, and vicious."

DiMaggio, Burkholder, Khalid, and I sat on straight chairs in a small interview room in the Knickerbocker. Todd

Haralson held a stack of reference papers for the senator.

Gaston himself paced tensely in front of us as we sat, and he towered over us. Ordinarily you'd think the boss sits down and keeps the employee standing up, but Gaston had this pegged just right. Sitting down, we were like students being taught by a superior.

"I've been involved in tracing hate groups for decades and trying to prevent crimes exactly like this. As you know, my committee has been investigating Bandwidth for four and a half years now. Background material, Todd."

Haralson passed out four stapled reports titled *BAND-WIDTH*, one to each of us.

"This contains everything about them that isn't classified."

"I would think, classified or not, we need to know," Burkholder said.

"I regret that I have to deny that, Chief Burkholder," Gaston said coldly.

"This is *your child* we're trying to save!" Burkholder said. A cruel remark and not necessary.

"Some matters I deal with involve national security," the senator said.

"I'm sure we will give you every respect."

"Some matters are so sensitive that not even the whole Senate knows the details."

"Such as?"

"I will give you an example," Gaston said. "We know that Bandwidth played around with the controller systems for railroad track switching. Just to see if they could do it, they bollixed one in Arizona two years ago and sent an Amtrak train with three hundred and fifty people aboard it off the rails and into an arroyo. Thank God, there were only seventeen fatalities. There could have been hundreds. And no thanks to Bandwidth that there weren't. The cars jack-knifed, and the third car behind the engine caromed off a boulder they hadn't thought it would hit, and only the last four cars went into the ravine. The whole front of the train went off into the desert. Even this information is not to be

made public. How they got hold of the basic access codes
is classified and not for your eyes. The EYES ONLY file
contains railroad codes and security procedures. To put it
another way, it wouldn't help you; you don't need it; you
can't have it."

"Suppose they got hold of some info about Danni the
same way?" Burkholder said.

DiMaggio said, "Oh, give it a rest, Burkholder. He's right.
We don't need that."

"Thank you, Deputy Superintendent DiMaggio."

Gaston was always punctilious about everybody's titles
and careful to use them when he spoke. I suppose that's one
of the things a senator has to be good at.

He went on. "We also know they altered a radio transmission to a plane coming into Miami International last
year."

"The one that went into Biscayne Bay?" I asked, horri-
fied.

"Yes. In effect, they white-noised out a radio warning
from the tower that another aircraft was on a collision
course. The 747's pilot and the on-board collision-alert system saw the other plane, and the pilot took instant evasive
action; but they were already low on approach and one wing
dipped low enough to catch the water. The plane cartwhee-
led. There again, through no credit to Bandwidth, not everybody was killed."

I said, "Over a hundred were killed."

"Suppose the two planes had collided?"

I shivered.

Gaston said, "I've been issuing warnings about these hate
groups for a decade now, and we still care more about their
civil rights than we do about the rights of citizens to be safe.
And now look what's happened to Danni!"

I said, "Senator Gaston, if your committee knows this
about Bandwidth—"

"Not just my Senate committee, the FAA, the FBI, and a
subcommittee in the House."

"If *everybody* knows they're responsible, why aren't they in prison?"

"Well, Chief Kelly, my work is like yours. There's a little matter of proof."

An hour later, Senator Gaston was on network television.

"I have spent the last fifteen years of my life in public service," he said, looking handsome, serious, and calm, "much of it warning about the dangers of hate groups. I have spent ten years on this committee, attempting to warn the American public about the dangers of domestic terrorism."

Cameras flashed. The videocam lights threw his face into half-bright, half shadow.

"The world has changed greatly. The threat in the world today does not come, with some very few exceptions, from rogue nations or criminal governments. Most legally constituted governments today value their place in the family of nations. Even those who might not wish to be part of world culture are virtually forced to fit in because the international flow of goods and money compels them to."

"Senator!" a reporter said.

"Let me finish and then I'll take questions. The real, horrific threat to life comes from hate groups. This is not just scare talk. Real people really blew up the Murrah Federal Building with other real people in it. And the World Trade Center. Groups like this can steal nuclear material, anthrax, botulinum toxin, nerve gas, and more. They can break into and divert the still terribly vulnerable cybernetic transfer of money. They can disrupt or intercept the cybernetic flow of national secrets and personal information."

He paused. "They can kidnap defenseless children."

The room fell utterly still.

"Since they are not nations and may have nothing to gain from what they do but the satisfaction of their hate, we have no way to negotiate with them. Battleships are useless against them. And if they don't want money, we have nothing to trade. Like the group that filled the Tokyo subways with poison gas; by the time we know what they are after, they already have it.

"We need far better information on hate groups. We need to take them much more seriously than we have. Ten years ago, we believed that bombings, poisonings, and political kidnappings could not happen in the United States. And I'm here to tell you that, even after the catastrophe in Oklahoma City, and the six deaths and many injuries at the World Trade Center in New York, we still, as Americans, tend to believe that these are exceptions.

"My purpose today is to say that we need *now*, not next year, right now, to consider the threat at the level that in the past we considered armed nations to be a threat. For these secret, cowardly, venomous hate groups, we need the equivalent of an army, navy, and air force. We need the equivalent of a domestic Department of Defense."

forty-two

A flight out of Midway Airport got me to Springfield by noon, and a state police car whisked me to the Illinois State Penitentiary at Hillsboro. Signs along the road said, PRISON AREA. DO NOT PICK UP HITCHHIKERS.

The prison was set in large grounds with lush groomed early spring grass, but no trees or shrubs. There was not a candy wrapper or cigarette butt to be seen in the broad expanse of lawn. *Plenty of unpaid labor,* I thought.

Ditching my sidearm, wallet, pens, keys, and coins in the metal storage box, I was searched, had my hand stamped, and then I was passed through the double "airlock" doors. Inside, my hand stamp was checked again under ultraviolet light.

Once in the visitor's room, I waited. Waiting is a big thing in prisons, but I resented it. I had a lot to do in Chicago; and more important, every minute was one minute closer to when Danni might die.

Stop. Don't think about that.

Instead, as I waited I thought about the problem of John-

nie Raft. According to Khalid, Bandwidth didn't make a
move without Raft's say-so. Not just say-so; he was more
than the idea man. He told them what to do, even though
they were serious techies who were brilliant at implementing
his vicious notions. He was the CPU and they were the
peripherals. How was he getting instructions out of the
prison to his Bandwidth guys?

There was the famous case of Larry Hoover.

Hoover, from Chicago, is serving two life sentences. Convicted of murder by a federal jury in 1973, he's now nearly
fifty years old and still called "the Chairman" or "King
Larry," the unchallenged, undisputed leader of the Black
Gangster Disciples. They are said to run a hundred-million-
dollar-a-year drug business, and he is believed to be com-
manding it from prison. Hoover is a legend.

Hoover has a complete corporate organization, including
local regents and a board of directors. They franchise operations throughout the Midwest, in Milwaukee, for instance, Indianapolis, Minneapolis, Chicago, Saint Louis, and
so on.

The gang markets casual clothes, including duds with
Hoover's inmate number on them.

There have been federal charges against two hundred pre-
sumed gang leaders between 1995 and 1997 alone.

The Black Gangster Disciple Nation organizes crime very
much like the Mafia. You have to buy your drugs from
them, even though their crack may be selling for 70 percent
more than street crack. Of course the customers object, but
what can they do?

Rumor is that there are thirty-three thousand Disciple
gang members in Chicago.

Knowing that Hoover was running things from prison,
there were many ways tried to keep him from communicating with his lieutenants. In 1996, the gov ordered tiny microphones installed inside the badges required for prison
visitors and taped Hoover's talks with his various directors.
As a result, Hoover was convicted again of conspiracy and
thirty-five of his lieutenants were indicted also. Could we

do something like this with Raft? Tape his visitors? We'd need a court order, but we could get one. Does Raft even have visitors?

Hoover and his gang now run their business with cell phones and computers. They may be good at it, but Raft and Bandwidth were real techies.

How did Raft get word out? How did he run Bandwidth with that much detail?

Phone? Prisoners are allowed to make collect calls only. Is he allowed calls? Can we discover where his calls go?

I had asked DiMaggio about Hoover.

"We always suspected he pays some guards to pass on messages. Also, Hoover may have been using E-mail. Your problem is that your guy is much more sophisticated in cybertech than Hoover. Or the prison. Or me. When I say much more, I mean like ten to the tenth power more. Hoover's genius is organization and intimidation. Johnnie Raft's genius is mathematical and technical, and he's surrounded by brilliant cyberwizards. Seriously, truly brilliant. Laser Blue is known to have been involved in a lot of nasty stuff, but he's never been caught. And the Bandwidth people follow Raft's orders religiously, like Hoover's disciples follow his. If he's light-years ahead of Hoover, he's also light-years ahead of the Department of Corrections. They're at the data-management level of computing and only halfway up the learning curve on that. He's designed systems they aren't sophisticated enough even to *use*."

"But he still would have to get his fingers physically on a keyboard, wouldn't he?"

"Or his voice on a phone."

"Or maybe have something that sends out a beam of light?"

"I suppose. Or go the old black-and-white movie route," DiMaggio said. "Tap Morse code on a water pipe."

Johnnie Raft was brought to me in a glassed-in interview room, ordinarily used by lawyers talking with incarcerated clients.

I was going to be in the room alone with him. He had

passed through a full strip search and "cavity search" as they call it, before being allowed in the interview area, so he was not carrying a weapon. And in any case, I wasn't afraid of violence; he wasn't a violent offender. Johnny Raft murdered people from a distance. Cyberkilling.

He came through the door ahead of a guard. The guard closed and locked the door from the outside. Then he positioned himself outside, where he was visible through the glass window and could see us but couldn't hear.

"Mr. Raft," I said.

"Ah, the cop. The coplady."

He bowed with exaggerated politeness, and sat down opposite me. He was thirty-two years old but looked mid-twenties. He was glossy, slender, and sleek. He had a high forehead, limp, coffee-colored hair, and dark brown, moist, shining eyes.

"Chief of Detectives Polly Kelly," I said.

"Chief of Detectives. Oh, my, my, my. This is a nice change. I don't get out much."

"No. And lately I hear you haven't had visitors."

He grinned, or more accurately, sneered. "I've been on personal lockdown. Individual lockdown is sort of halfway to solitary without the negative publicity for the prison."

"Why?"

"Oh, I ordered some stuff sent to me. Quite a lot of stuff actually. A water bed. A Mercedes. Five cases of 1947 Chateau d'Yquem." He smiled his sneering smile. "They took exception to that."

"I heard they thought you were communicating with unauthorized persons."

"They thought that, too. But they knew for sure I was sending for goodies."

"With a fake credit card number?"

"The warden's number actually. Would you like to know how? It's soooo simple."

"Never mind."

"They've taken me off the grid."

"Which means—?"

"I can't get on the net. You do know what the net is?"

"Heard of it."

"You cops dwell totally in meatspace, don't you? In ten years, you'll all be obsolete."

"Let me get this clear. You can't telephone out? You don't get visitors? You don't have a computer?"

"I can't telephone out and I don't get visitors. I do have my square-headed girlfriend, my computer, as you call it, a lovely laptop that I play with in my lonely cell while the body Nazis work out on the exercise equipment, building pecs and lats. But I don't have a modem. So I can't send messages. So whatever you think I'm doing, I can't be, can I?"

"I don't know. Would Bandwidth undertake a huge world-class crime like this without your guidance? Would Laser Blue?"

His face lost its fake charm and closed down on me. "The short answer is no. The long answer is I guess he just must have, mustn't he?"

"But they are mounting a major public relations assault here."

He didn't answer.

I choked down the anger I felt toward him. For the last several days it seemed to me, I'd been doing just that, containing my anger. But it was more important to suck him in, if possible, than to give vent to my feelings. Worry about ulcers and hypertension later. I asked. "Do you see television? You've heard about Danni Gaston, haven't you?"

"I don't get TV privileges. I can see the communal TV at the end of the corridor from one corner of my lonely cell, if I press my little face right up to the bars. Danni's circling the drain, isn't she?"

I wanted to hit him.

He said, "You're really in a mess. You should never have taken on this case. It's a career-limiting move, you know. When you fail, you'll fail big."

"If you can see the television, can you communicate with the other inmates?"

"Ah, you're so single-minded. No, I can't. They're not allowed to speak to me or even approach my end of the corridor, and they're all far too retarded to know sign language. My only human contact is the guards, and of course they don't count as human contact."

I made a mental note. Ask about his guards specifically. What is known about their personal lives? Could they be paid to take messages out?

"Raft, what exactly are you and your people trying to accomplish?"

"My followers want me out of here."

"No, I mean in general. What's the point of Bandwidth?"

"The point? The point is it's time to let people who can *think* run things."

"You mean *you* should run things."

"I'm talking about a meritocracy. You know the word, don't you?"

"I'll pretend."

"Democracy has really showed its weaknesses. We need a society run by people of merit. People who are intelligent. Of the highest intelligence."

"What do we have now?"

"Well, we certainly don't have that! Does anybody ever run for office on the basis that he or she is smart? Never! If anything, they run on how much they're an average guy. Vote for me because I have a lovely, lovely family. Cute kids and a wife who keeps her hair in place and wears clean, carefully ironed clothes and a string of pearls. Vote for me because I'm like you—I'm the same color you are, or I'm the same religion, or I'm from the same neighborhood. Vote for me because I photograph well or I come across on TV. My voice is deep and my chin is firm. Never because I can figure things out. Never because I can use numbers or reason logically. Nobody runs on their SAT scores. Take my SATs. They are sky-high. You send people to Congress, where they're being asked to deal with the world monetary system, and they can't even do math! They deal with the issues of international terrorism, the potential of biological warfare, degradation of the ecosystem, and a lot of them can't even pronounce 'ecosystem'!"

"What about common sense?"

"People always say, 'What about common sense?' as if only dumb people had common sense. They think common sense only exists in people who are high in irrationality. Or to put it mathematically, they think common sense is inversely related to intelligence. What about requiring that our representatives have an understanding of social statistics and statistical analysis before they vote on stuff having to do with social issues? This isn't asking much."

"You're forgetting moral sense."

"Do you really believe we're electing people for their moral fiber?"

I was silent a few seconds. He said, "Do you really?"

I said, "Don't talk to me about moral fiber! You commit crimes. You kill people."

"We're trying to get their attention."

"Oh, please! That's a goddamned pretext! You're angry that people don't think you're brilliant, and you want revenge against society."

"You're 404, Coplady. You're clueless. You're the carbon community, a cop droid. You been dilberted. You're gonna be uninstalled."

"Hey lose the geek-talk. Every job has its dumb lingo. You just sound stupid."

"I'm running it on you, Coplady. I'm telling you that you're lame. In ten years a person as cybernetically challenged as you will be unemployable. I'm the wave of the future. You're not even delaying things. Your po-lice department is using you, Danni's gonna die, and you're gonna be left everybody's asshole scapegoat."

God! Was he annoying!

"Listen, Raft, I'm not an idiot!"

"Well, of *co-ooourse* you're not," he said, slick as syrup, and I was embarrassed I had risen to his bait.

———

I have to admit I've always wondered why anybody would want to be a prison warden. This guy looked like he should have been a proctologist. But hey, maybe the difference is minimal.

He was also pleasant, even when I asked about his choice of guards.

"We took a good, long look at who came into contact with Raft after the credit card incident," he said. "They are all people who truly dislike hate groups."

"But they might need money. Could they be paid to take messages out?"

"As much as you can be sure of anything in this life, Chief Kelly, I don't think so. He has only three personal guards a day, one on each of the three shifts, who have any contact with him. And even with weekend swings, it's only nine. That's few enough people for me to know them well and for the local cops to know well. And they haven't any of them spent any extra money lately either."

"Visitors?"

"He hasn't been allowed visitors since the credit card thing."

"Or—"

"But actually," he interrupted, "Raft never had visitors. Never. No relatives. No nothing. He always communicated by phone. Or by E-mail. There is a modem in the library, and he was using it outside his authorization area, but he isn't allowed to go there anymore. Not allowed to go to the library at all. We now know that when he had computer-shop privileges, he had worked out a way to get from the info-modem we allow them to some other—uh—some other line. I'm afraid I'm not very computer literate."

"But this route is closed now?"

"We closed it even before we put him in restricted housing. Had an expert in to secure the computer shop."

"What about now? He has a laptop."

"But it doesn't go anywhere. There's no modem and no way to connect a modem. There's no phone line."

"He's tricky."

"You can say that again! But we've had a communications expert from the Illinois State Police scan the room for everything from microwaves to radio waves."

"How about tapping on the pipes?"

"PVC piping. No ring to it." He smiled as if he knew I felt like an idiot asking.

"Blinking his light on and off in Morse code?"

"Lighting is centrally controlled. It goes on at 6:30 A.M. and off at 10:00 P.M. He doesn't have a switch. There are none in the cells. And as far as signaling anybody on the outside by light, like covering the bulb with his shirt, for instance, and uncovering it, it's very high on the ceiling and his window doesn't face outside. It faces inside, toward the administration block. This block."

"It sounds like you've thought of everything, Warden."

"Holy God, I hope so." He waved his hand at the window. "Those guys out there have nothing to do the whole livelong day but figure out how to put something over on us. Doesn't matter if they're in shop or in counseling or in chapel or in French class. They're trying to figure out how to steal or get drugs or escape or kill somebody. This job is one continual effort to stay on top of them."

forty-three

It was two o'clock in the afternoon, but Danni did not know it. All of the time she had been in this room, the light had been bright and unvarying. There was no difference between day and night. Like people kept too long in the twenty-four-hour bright light of an intensive care unit, she was disoriented.

Danni could not quite remember where she was. She had been sleeping, she thought, but then she wondered why it was daylight. Maybe she was taking a nap. Mommy always closed the curtains when it was naptime.

She said, "Mommy, I want to get up."

For some reason, she was on the floor. She looked around the room, but the walls seemed to go away from her as she looked at them. She put her ear to the floor to listen for her friend. Didn't she have a friend under the floor? But there was no sound.

Then she saw the door.

She had to go find Mommy. Danni realized now that she

was sick, with the tummy flu Mommy said she had in the winter. Mommy would know what to do.

Danni got up to got to the door, and she just tipped over and fell right back down. She wondered if there was something wrong with her feet, they felt so far away. She thought that she used to feel hungry. Yes, she was sure she was hungry a little while ago. Maybe she had already eaten breakfast. It was very nice that she didn't feel hungry anymore.

But everything was very far away. The walls, the lights on the ceiling, her feet. Only her hands were in their normal place.

Lying on her back, she put her hands over her eyes so she would not see how strange everything looked.

Three P.M.

Back from Hillsboro only half an hour, and I felt like a side of beef about to be inspected and cut up. The superintendent gave me a push and I walked out to the CPD lobby, in front of more than a hundred microphones and fifty videocameras. My dazzled eyes saw a mike that was labeled Radio Guatemala and another labeled Video Philippines. There were labels I couldn't read, including the Russian Cyrillic.

"You do this, Kelly," the superintendent had said, "or else."

Well, that was clear enough, wasn't it?

"I am Deputy Chief of Detectives, North, Polly Kelly," I said quietly. Not shyly, but quietly. "I am here to answer your questions."

Like, right. Certain questions. The boss had said "Keep it close to the vest." What he really meant was I would refuse to answer a lot of their questions, they'd blame me, and he'd get out from under. Like, "Front for me and we'll serve you up as the dessert when we have to sacrifice somebody."

But it was my job.

CBS asked, "Do you have any new leads to Danni?"

"Absolutely. We're moving ahead fast."

"What are they?"

"Look, I would really like to tell you because I want you to know we're getting somewhere. I know everybody on earth is fearing for Danni. And I want everybody to have hope. But you must understand that if leads are printed or on TV, the kidnappers will know what we know. I ask you to give us some slack here. A little time."

WGN said, "Hey, maybe they're not real leads."

"What can I tell you, Bill? You know me. I do not bullsh—um, blow smoke."

"How do you know there's any time left?"

"We have a physician watching Danni continually and keeping us updated on her condition."

"What about anything the media can help with?" Barbara Conlon from the NBC affiliate in Chicago asked. "Can we help you search for Danni?"

Oh, how I wanted to tell them. Every human being in Chicago should run and search, between the Eisenhower and Armitage, from Pulaski to the lake. But sure as hell Bandwidth was set up and ready to move her. I had to hold my tongue. I said, "Everybody needs to know that they can help. If they see or hear anything suspicious, call us. Even if you noticed something three days ago. Nobody will be mad at you if you waited; on the contrary you'll be a true hero. Senator and Mrs. Gaston have already made that plea, but I wish you would make it again."

"So what about this Johnnie Raft? What're you gonna do about him?"

Another reporter said, "We heard you been down there this afternoon."

"Is that a question? Well, I'm not playing games with you. Yes, I was down there and talked to him."

"Did he help?"

"Did he threaten you?"

"Was there a deal?"

I said, "No deals. None asked; none offered."

"Why *not* deal?"

The *Trib* said, "The letters to my paper want you to let him go."

A chorus:

"Everybody calls the channel says 'free Johnnie Raft'!"

"What's the point of holding him?"

"Is he worth more than a child?"

"Set him free!"

"Is it true Senator Gaston wants him freed?"

A couple of the reporters, guys I knew, lobbed me softballs, letting me get the facts I wanted out, that Bandwidth was suspected of extremely serious crimes. But they knew that already from their own research.

Most of the reporters just wanted to draw blood.

"Danni looks real sick today."

"Yeah, she's weakening, isn't she?"

"Isn't Danni's life more important than some guy?"

"What are you proving by keeping him in prison?"

"Hey!" I said. "Don't yell at me. We have laws in the United States. He's in prison for fraud."

"Fraud! Credit card theft! How important is that?"

"Yeah, isn't a child worth more than a few dollars?"

"Well, it was $117,000," I said. "But it's still not my call. I'm a cop. I don't make policy. Talk to the governor."

"Yo! Kelly! Suppose you did?"

"Did what?"

"Suppose you made policy? Would you let Raft out to get Danni set free?"

"Listen, Drubczek," I said, "you tell me one thing. Are these Bandwidth guys honest people? Whattaya think? If we let Raft out, can you guarantee they'll set Danni free?"

There was a pause of a few seconds. Then he said, "If you don't, you know they won't."

He was right. I said, "I want to find that child more than anything."

"Shit! Tell me this, Kelly. Suppose you don't know anymore than you know now. If you personally had the power and you could take a chance on saving Danni, would you set Raft free?"

Four P.M.

I was bruised and still didn't know the answer to that question. I had said, "Talk to somebody in charge." But that was a cop-out. Excuse the expression.

Every TV channel, every newspaper, every radio program asked their viewers, readers, and listeners whether Raft should be freed. Gordon Holtrup on Chicago's major local radio afternoon drive-home program started his show an hour early, bumping a disc jockey off the air, just to ask that question. He was stacking up calls as deep as his multiple phone lines could hold them. Cell phones everywhere were punching SND. Calls were running five-to-one for setting Raft free. The dissenters wanted Raft kept in prison and members of his gang caught and tortured until they led us to Danni.

Me, I guess—yes—if I were king of the world, I would set Raft free and try to grab him later. Have him swallow a homing device instead of his morning vitamin, something like that. What nobody cared about was that it was not my call. The superintendent sent felicitations via his ADC and stayed as far away from my press conference and me as possible.

I sank tiredly into a chair in the war room, just as Ainslie walked in. He still looked crisp and washed and pressed. How did he do that and how come I couldn't? Every joint in my body ached.

"Boss, I have some bad news," he said.

"Well, it won't be the first."

"My guys really did a good job on the Water Tower ingress and egress."

"We never expected to pin it down definitely that way. What did they find?"

"It's not a matter of what they found."

"Didn't find, then."

"No, boss, it's what I found. I went with them. I didn't

do the entrances; my guys were two senior, experienced detectives who know to paddle their own canoe. I went to the building engineer. Boss, it's just not possible that Danni is being held in Water Tower Place."

"You can *not* have physically looked into every room."

"No. I didn't even try."

"You're very grim. Tell me."

"Polly, I think Water Tower Place was a great idea. An inspiration, connecting several unrelated pieces of data."

"But wrong, huh? Don't butter me up. It won't make me feel better. Just tell me."

"There are no wooden floors in that building."

I felt like I'd dropped twenty stories in an elevator. After a few seconds, I said, "But there *are*. Some of the stores have beautiful parquet. I've been there."

"What I should have said is there are no structural wood floors. You're right, there are wood surfaces. But they are basically 'floor coverings.' Most of them aren't much thicker then linoleum. They're for looks. But the kind of construction where you lay joists, vertical stringers, and then floor across it with thick wood boards—the old way—just wasn't used here. The real subfloor, underneath the various floor coverings, is concrete with metal rebar. There's no doubt whatsoever about this. Water Tower Place was built to be fireproof, and the building management has all the architectural drawings and specs and so on. Water Tower was just built in 1974, and it was thoroughly photographed as it went up. In fact, I think the opening credits of the old *Bob Newhart Show* had Water Tower Place under construction in the background. The engineer has a zillion photographs of it under construction. There's *just no doubt.*"

"Maybe what we see in Danni's room is floor covering."

"No, Polly. Look at the blow-ups you've had made. It's old wood. There are scuff marks. There are uneven spaces between some of the boards. There's been shrinkage over the years. Some warping."

"Maybe these boards were laid to fool us."

"Oh, Polly! A big construction project like that, with the

building management never knowing? Yes, somebody could bring in that video camera and hand carry a whole lot of electronic gear over a few days, a little at a time, without being noticed. I have no problem with that. But loads of old boards, some of them twelve feet long? Oh, Polly, I wish! But it didn't happen. Danni's prison room just isn't there."

I sat still for a few seconds. You can absorb defeat only so long, and then you either have to quit or power up and start over.

"All right. Look on the bright side. This has told us something we hadn't realized before."

"What?"

"That we're looking for a building that's at least several decades old. How old would you think that floor is?"

There was relief and maybe admiration in Ainslie's eyes. I didn't deserve it. Nobody deserved anything until we found her. Alive.

"That's good! That's good," he said, "My guess is that it's gotta be at least thirty or forty years old. But we can have an expert take a look."

"Find one and ask. Right away."

"Maybe we should ask for help from the public now."

"I'd love help from the public. What I don't want to do is tell the kidnappers what we know."

"Maybe it's all we can do."

"No. If they move her now, we'll never find her in time."

Five-thirty P.M.

I thought it over and called back an hour later.

"Ainslie, there's something in this whole affair that's connected with Water Tower Place. I'm not sure what, but it's there. Either that or I have *no* instincts whatsoever."

He didn't answer.

"Do just one more thing for me. Have a couple of our guys ask at each store if there's has been anything strange happening there. Anything out of the ordinary. Ask at the Ritz-Carlton, too, of course. And ask the building manager who takes care of the residences, the condos, in the building."

"Um—sure. Okay."

"Ainslie, I can hear it in your tone. You think I'm crazy."

"Well, you know there's gonna be all kinds of strange stuff. Hotel guests have heart attacks. There are pickpockets. Shoplifters. Credit card thieves. Homeless people hide in the stores to sleep. Once in a while somebody has a baby in the lingerie department of a clothing store."

"Then that's *not unusual*. Just find me anything weird."

"Yes, boss."

He really hated this. He thought it was stupid, and he thought I was making a fool of myself. And wasting valuable cop time.

"Do just this much, Ainslie, and after that I'll let it alone."

forty-four

Six P.M.

I came around the corner from the CPD Building's side door. Just then Hannah Khalid pushed through one of the sets of double doors at the front of the building and marched onto the sidewalk. She saw me and stopped. Hell, shoot-out at the OK Corral?

She put her hands on her hips. I couldn't help smiling.

"Are we gonna argue constantly?" I asked.

"Personally, I'd rather not."

"We shouldn't be wasting energy."

"Where you going?"

"I was going out for a drink," I said. "An alcoholic beverage, and not a moment too soon."

"Drink with me?" she asked.

"Yes. 'Course, I'd drink with the devil right now, if I had to."

She crossed the street diagonally to Zinc's. I hesitated. Was I going to let her dictate the bar we went to? Sure, why not? Get a life, Kelly.

"When I was here before," Khalid said, "this place was supposed to have fifteen kinds of single-malt scotch. I can't swear to it, because I only tried thirteen of them. Buy you one?"

"No, thanks. But you could buy me a beer."

"Consider it done."

"So, Khalid," I said, "should I call you Hannah?"

"I wish you would, Polly."

"So, Hannah, you have children?"

"Two of them. Girls."

"A husband?"

"Yeah, one of them, too."

I smiled. "Was that an unenthusiastic response?"

"No, actually he's a honey. It's not so easy, marriage, traveling as much as I do. He's patient and understanding."

"What does he do?"

"Well, he works, as we say, 'inside the beltway.' "

This meant federal government, of course. I pictured him in the Treasury Department, Naval Intelligence, the CIA, some such thing that you didn't talk a lot about.

"How old are your children?"

"Nineteen and twenty-two. Marie's in college and Emily's in med school."

"What do they think about what you do?"

"You know how kids are. Blasé. Secretly, I think they think it's neat. But they make fun, usually. They call me 'J. Edgar Mother.' "

I drank beer. After a while Khalid said, "You wish you had children, Polly?"

"Yes and no. I realize that's no answer. But I have a lot of freedom. Do what I want at home. At least, I had a lot of freedom."

"What do you mean?"

"My mother has moved in with me."

"Holy shit, woman! Are you nuts?"

"Couldn't afford to keep her house up."

"Good God! Why not?"

"The problem was partly financial and partly she needs

constant watching. She's depressive and potentially suicidal.
The home care with everything else just added up to too
much."

"You've taken Mrs. Gloom into your house?"

"What else could I do? She's my mother."

"Shoot her."

I laughed. "No, I don't think so."

"Lord, you're a better man than I."

After a minute, she added, "No other relatives? No
brother or sister?"

"I do have a sister. She lives in Sacramento now. Used
to live here."

"Could she take your mother?"

"She could, I suppose. She won't."

"Oh? But you will?"

"My sister has three children. A couple of years ago, before she moved, I was baby-sitting Mom and had to leave
on a job. So I asked my sister to fill in. To be fair, she had
already done it a lot. She said, 'Mom is a passive-aggressive,
unpleasant, nasty, negative person.' I said I knew that, but
she couldn't help it. She said how did I know she couldn't
help it? I said, nobody would be that way if they could help
it. She said look at all the assistance Mom gets by being
that way, plus she always gets out of doing whatever she
doesn't want to do, which usually includes anything that
smells like work. I said, 'You still can't know that she can
help herself, plus she's your mother.' "

"Nevertheless—"

"Then I said there was benefit to your heart and soul in
self-sacrifice. She laughed at me. Very loudly. Then she
asked whether I thought Mom really appreciated the help."

"What did you say?"

"I had to say no. Then she asked, leaving aside whether
Mom appreciated it or not, did she really *benefit* from it.
And frankly, I've never seen her benefit from anything, attention included. She wants it, but I can't say she benefits
from it."

"So what was the upshot?"

"My sister said, 'Okay, tell me this. Adrianna has a sore throat and Tim has a soccer game after school he wants me to go to. How many hours out of this particular Tuesday—out of my life and out of *their* lives—do I owe my mother today? One? Three? Five? What do I owe this person who has suffused my life in negativity—exactly how much do I owe her *today?*' And you know, Hannah, I couldn't tell her."

We both drank.

I said, "I often wonder, what is my real mother? The nasty, gloomy one? The only slightly more cheerful one we produce with Prozac? The calm but stupified one we produced with earlier drugs? The one I've never seen—a normal person—who maybe we could produce with perfect drugs? I take other people to be the people they are when I meet them, but I have to constantly pretend that there is somebody else 'in there' inside my mother."

I drank more beer. The subject of my mother was, as my niece liked to put it, harshing my wave. I said, "So, Hannah, can we work as a team and not get in each other's way?"

She studied me seriously. It was okay that she didn't rush into an answer. After half a minute, she said, "Look, I really believe the solution to the kidnapping is going to come out of technology. Some way or other we'll cybertrace where that videocamera is. You think solid police work is the way to go. Okay. That's great, isn't it? Covers all the bases. Mutt and Jeff."

"Meat and potatoes."

"Salt and pepper."

"Bagels and cream cheese."

"Bartender! Another round, please."

Seven-thirty P.M.

Fetterman drove fast, with the Mars Lights on until we left the city boundaries of Chicago. Sam called ahead to tell the Winnetka PD that we were coming.

Ainslie had done it! Bankers don't usually just disappear.

And they certainly don't just disappear when no money has disappeared.

Mr. William Harper Jordan, who had worked at Water Tower Place, had been missing four days. Even though I hoped he would be found, Jordan was not himself the emergency. The urgency, of course, was Danni.

forty-five

"So not even any reported sightings?" I asked the Winnetka cop.

"Zero. Jordan could have fallen off the edge of the world."

"Family problems?"

"Not that we can tell. The whole clan has gathered around Mrs. Jordan, Phoebe, as she always asks us to call her. They all seem to like each other."

"Money problems?"

"Making decent money. Vice president of a bank. Compared to some of our local citizens, he's certainly not rich. But he's not hurting. And before you ask, no gambling that we know of. Not even on the stock market. No sign of another woman. Sober citizen, you might say."

"Mrs. Jordan, I'm afraid I don't have any news." I felt terrible. The woman's face had gone all pink and tight with hope when Fetterman and I had presented ourselves at the door. Now we sat in the living room while Mrs. Jordan composed herself.

She said, "It's just that I'm so sure I'll hear from him. Any minute. We have to hear soon. We just have to."

One of her sons said, "This just doesn't make any sense."

Two young children played out in the backyard, supervised by a pretty woman of about thirty. The house was in good repair, but nothing in it appeared to be new. There was no sign either of a money crunch or overspending, and no sign of some incipient breakdown or breakaway.

"Mrs. Jordan, can you tell me about the last time you saw Mr. Jordan?"

"I guess so," she said in an exhausted voice.

"Please tell me whatever you remember. All the details."

"It was Saturday. You knew that, of course, from the Winnetka police. Bill's half day. He gets home early. Anyway, we had dinner."

"Did he talk about anything in particular at dinner? Anything about work? Anything that happened to him downtown?"

"Well, no. Actually—"

What was coming? I wondered. She seemed a little bit embarrassed. "Yes?"

"Actually, we usually eat in there, not in the dining room." She pointed at a small side room with a television in it. "We like to listen to the news while we eat."

A flicker of hope stirred in my mind. "The news?" I prompted.

"Yes. That was the day that poor child was kidnapped."

"You saw that on TV?"

"Yes, the news report about it."

"What channel?"

"Why—mm—Channel Five."

When I got back, I would get a copy of that newscast and check to see exactly what was shown. My mind was furiously running over what might have been said about Danni's kidnapping.

"What do you remember about the news report, Mrs. Jordan?"

"Phoebe, please. I think that the reporter was speaking

from Holy Name. They thought a priest—or no, maybe I've heard that since. There was a picture of the family, of course, the senator, and Maggie McKittredge, and the little girl, Danni."

Pictures. "Did Mr. Jordan say anything about the kidnapping?"

"No. He just went out a little later. For a walk." She looked like she wanted to cry, but fought it back. "He said he wanted to think."

After several more questions, I ran out of ideas. But something still nagged at me. After a few seconds spent worrying about it, I decided there was no point in sitting here while I tried to figure it out. I stood up.

"Thank you, Phoebe. I know the police are working hard on the case. I really hope everything works out for you." And I was very much afraid it wouldn't.

We walked toward the door.

I stopped stock-still, while my heart fluttered. There was something here. Something—an idea was trying to get through to me. But what was it?

Then I realized I had seen ashtrays on every table, but there was no smell of smoke. Mrs. Jordan hadn't smoked while I was here. The son had not smoked. Were the ashtrays just a Winnetka courtesy?

"Does Mr. Jordan smoke, Phoebe?"

"Oh, yes. He shouldn't. But he does."

Oh, yes. Oh, yes, is right.

Eight forty-five P.M.

"Sam, beep Ainslie to get in here immediately!"

"Should he call on the way in?"

"No, I want his body in this office *forthwith!*"

I contented myself for a few moments with picturing Ainslie in a squad car, tearing through town, Mars Lights whipping out blue and red beams, briefly staining everything in the car's path as they whizzed by.

Thirty seconds of that was enough. I began to pace, staring at the floor to keep calm, with my hands locked together on the back of my neck. Sam stared at me; the detective who was watching Danni on the TV monitor carefully didn't look at me. Hatch was cybersearching and didn't seem to notice. Fetterman, bless his heart, paced along behind me.

After ten minutes I heard pounding feet in the hall. Ainslie raced in, red-faced and breathing hard.

"What? *What? What?*" he yelled.

"William Jordan smoked," I said.

Two seconds of silence. "And so?"

"Ainslie! William Jordan worked at the Copley Water Tower Bank in Water Tower Place. And smoked. And he's missing. I presume dead. Parnella Grant worked at the coffee bar on the mezzanine in Water Tower Place. She had lung cancer. Probably she smoked. She's dead. Your Mr. Edwin Carter who was shot in the drive-by worked at that cigar store in Water Tower Place. He had emphysema. He smoked. He's dead."

"Ahhhhh—" Ainslie was hooked, but the light hadn't quite dawned.

"And, Ainslie, can employees smoke on the job at Water Tower?"

"No. Of course not. It's a nonsmoking building. Nobody smokes inside. Employees, customers, nobody."

"So if you work there and want to smoke—?"

"You go outside."

"*Exactly!* And you stand either on the Chestnut Street side or on the Pearson Street side. In little clumps, with others of your kind. And complain about no-smoking laws *and watch people and cars go by!*"

"Holy shit!"

"Right. And it may not have been a clump of three. Suppose another person, or even two, was there in the smoking group when whatever it was happened and they saw it, too. That person is either dead, and we don't know it yet, or is in deadly danger. And that person, if he or she exists and is still alive, also may remember what they saw."

"What if it wasn't important?"

"If it wasn't important, nobody would have killed them."

"Of course."

"Get every available detective over there right now. Immediately. It's ten of nine. Most of the stores close in ten minutes. Query every single employee of every single store and restaurant, including guards and repair people and janitors. Find out the name of every single human being who Jordan, Grant, and Carter usually took smoke breaks with. Run those names down, latch onto them, and *don't let go.*"

Eleven P.M.

"We've found two."

"Go on."

"There was a woman named Lassiter who usually took smoke breaks with them. But she'd had dental surgery on Friday and wasn't smoking on Saturday."

"Where did they take their smoke break? The Pearson side or the Chestnut Street side?"

"Pearson."

"Damn! I knew it! Tell me the rest."

"The second person is a possible. A man named Darren Black, who works in the Travel Depot, always took a smoke break about that time."

"Did he on Saturday?"

"Yes, he—"

"Where is he? Is he still alive? If he's not at work, we need his home address. Hurry up! He may be in deadly danger. Let's go!"

"Let me finish. He's on vacation."

"Where?"

"He told his coworkers, the owners, Benny and Cindy Gordon, when he went on smoke break Saturday morning, that it was the last one he'd ever take."

"Lord, it certainly was for the other three."

"In his case, he meant he was giving up smoking. His vacation started Saturday at noon. He went back to the Travel Depot just long enough to pick up his backpack, grab his paycheck, and then catch a taxi to O'Hare. He's off on a camping trip. It's a commercial thing, and I think he discovered the company that arranges the trips through his job. A company called Nico-Rid takes you on a strenuous two-week camping and hiking adventure in the wilderness. Rugged terrain. Fifteen miles a day. Climb rocks. Use your lungs. No cigarette within a hundred miles."

"Where?"

"Grand Canyon."

"And he actually left? He isn't dead?"

"Apparently. We phoned his home. His roommate says he called from the Denver airport while he was waiting for his flight to Flagstaff. So he got that far."

"There's something else, isn't there?"

"Yeah. The Travel Depot said we weren't the first people asking where he went."

forty-six

By now anybody who turned on television could see that Danni was failing. She looked cadaverous and she slept all day. The media clamored for the governor to pardon Raft immediately.

Senator Gaston called the governor, asking for Raft's release.

The governor's press aide, in a conversation with CBS, mentioned that the gov might look into supervised release with an ankle monitor. There was an instant fierce backlash from the people who said we would be playing into the hands of the devil. "Should we let criminals get their way if they do something even worse and then hold us up for ransom?" At which point the gov said he had never considered release and had never told his aide that he was. The aide was "just giving his own thoughts." In fact, the gov said, the aide "is planning to leave to continue his good media work in the private sector." But the gov added that he was "looking into alternatives as regards Raft," whatever that meant.

Personally, I thought he had his aide float the idea as a trial balloon, and that the poor aide was about to be a political sacrificial lamb.

A better use for Raft, I thought, was to promise him anything in exchange for Danni's whereabouts. The gov was waffling, but I bet he was leaning that way.

In Las Vegas, where odds-makers had been posting odds on Danni's survival, the numbers had risen to five-to-one against.

Harry W. Bolton had been a guard at the Illinois State Penitentiary in Hillsboro for seventeen years. Harry believed he was one of the best. He kept his uniform clean, with perfect creases on the pants, and his shoes were polished before he went on duty and touched up again right after his lunch. Lunch was what they called it regardless of which shift you were on. If you were on third shift, 11:00 P.M. to 7:00 A.M., lunch was at 3:00 A.M.

Today, fortunately, he was on second shift, 3:00 P.M. to 11:00 P.M. This meant he had eaten lunch at seven, which was almost like suppertime in normal life. He hated working late nights on the graveyard shift. It threw his digestive system off. Gave him heartburn, no matter what he ate, and worse if he didn't eat.

Harry hated other sorts of things as well.

Harry had three daughters—or, once upon a time he had had three daughters. Now there were two. The oldest, Elizabeth, had been a passenger on Pan Am Flight 103.

Tonight Harry had eaten a dinner on his break that should have been a guaranteed heartburn igniter. Barbecued beef, those fat-soaked fries, and cole slaw. He'd also stoked up on three cups of coffee, which ordinarily he would avoid like carbolic acid.

And Harry felt just fine.

Harry walked into cell block C-6 after relieving his relief man—Harry "gave good relief" as the lingo put it, which meant that he arrived on time and the other guy, who couldn't leave until his relief showed up, never had to wait—and Harry had checked blocks C-1 through C-5. It was now 9:30 P.M.

"Hey, guys," he said to the half-dozen inmates watching TV.

"Yo, Harry."

Harry was considered easygoing. By and large the inmates thought Harry was one of the better guards. He didn't read your mail and then taunt you about the contents like some did. He was a stickler for the rules, but he wasn't all eager to write you up for a violation if you did what he told you to do. Basically, Harry was considered a man who did his job, not a guy who had a hard-on for convicts and wanted to make their every living minute miserable.

"Closing it down in twenty minutes," Harry said.

Television went off at nine forty-five and everybody had to be out of the dayroom. Lights out was at ten.

Like all guards, Harry carried no gun. Guns were carried by tower guards, entry guards, and any exterior guards, but nobody on the inside. Nobody who came in contact with the inmates. That way, no inmate could take a gun from a guard.

Harry walked down the long hall to the isolation cells. Only one was in use. Johnnie Raft's.

"Hey, Johnnie," he said.

"What's the good word?" Raft asked in his lazy, half-humorous, sly voice.

"Not much happening," Harry said, "except there's a rumor you're getting word out. Ya know you're supposed to be basically incommunicado. Seems like you're not."

"Yeah, I heard. But we know that's impossible, don't we, Harry?"

"Well, see, I think it is. But I gotta come in there and search."

"Won't find anything."

"Sure thing, Johnnie, but let's make this quick and easy. You move over to the far wall."

"Oh, this is silly." But Raft got up and moved to the far

corner of the cell. "What do you think, I got a short-wave radio in here?"

"A whole TV studio, prolly," Harry said, jovially.

Harry unlocked the door, then when he had entered, carefully locked it behind him, according to regulations.

"All right, my man," he said to Raft, "face the wall."

Raft turned around and faced the wall. "Harry, you aren't monkeying with my laptop, are you?"

"Wouldn't know how. Somebody is gonna go over your files tomorrow, though."

"Shit."

Harry moved closer. "You keep on the wall, Johnnie. Gotta look at your bunk."

"Yeah, yeah."

Harry pulled the thin mattress sideways but not quite onto the floor. Making "Hmmm-mm," sounds, he covered the slight sighing noise of his hand pulling a commissary knife from his pocket. "Stay put," he said, coming closer to Raft as he approached the end of the cot.

He dropped a hand onto Raft's shoulder, brought the knife around in front of him and up into his diaphragm just under the breastbone. Pushing hard, he forced the knife up into Raft's heart.

Johnnie Raft instinctively tried to draw a breath, but couldn't, arched backward spasmodically for a few seconds, and sagged in Harry's arms.

Harry kneed the mattress back into position. He tossed the corpse onto the bed, turned Raft's face to the wall, and threw the thin blanket over him.

He whispered, "Don't get out now. No matter what the governor says. Don't get to kill anybody else."

"Okay," he said, loudly. "They'll be in tomorrow."

Harry walked out and locked the door carefully behind him. Raft wouldn't be found until morning at the earliest. And what with his being on lockdown, it might be that nobody noticed until the morning guard came back to pick up the tray of breakfast they would have pushed through the slot earlier.

Then they might trace it to Harry. Or they might think an inmate had done it before lockup. It was remotely possible they would think Raft had killed himself. They might even trace it to Harry and call him a hero, although he doubted it. The world didn't work that way. Harry didn't really care. He was satisfied.

forty-seven

"Where's Khalid?" I asked Hatch.

"Over at the local," he said, meaning the Chicago FBI office, not the local bar.

"Call her. Get her back here instantly."

"Aye-aye, ma'am."

"When did Ainslie say those people went into the Travel Depot asking about Darren Black?"

"Yesterday afternoon."

Twenty minutes later, when Khalid walked in the door, I said, "All right; this is where you and the feds get to rise and shine." I handed her the hardcopy printout of the detectives' interviews with Benny and Cindy Gordon and Harriet Lassiter.

"We'll want to reinterview these people," she said.

"Oh, please. Forget being FBI-ish, Khalid. There isn't time. We've got a witness. We found him. You catch him."

"I'd like more detail."

"There's no time for that!"

"Then we don't want to waste time running around stupidly. The Grand Canyon has to be a couple of thousand square miles—"

"So contact the Nico-Rid company officers at home. But Khalid, call in the federales first. Bandwidth has killed three people that I know of and maybe a lot more. They're *way* ahead of us. I don't care if you send the FBI or the Arizona State Police or the park rangers. Get them all out if you can. I realize it's too dark now to search, but get them to the staging areas ASAP. And you need somebody to check the Grand Canyon lodges and the campgrounds and the local airports. Send some people to stay in the airports and watch everybody who passes through."

"I'm gonna go with them."

"Really?"

"Yeah. This could be major and I don't want it screwed up."

"Fine."   •

"Plus Bandwidth could be onto this already."

I said, "Bandwidth *is* onto this already."

"You know this for sure?"

"Yup."

"Then I'm leaving now. Hatch can talk to Nico-Rid while I'm in the air."

"Good. We'll get the directions to you before first light. Just get to Darren Black before Bandwidth does."

"Suppose," I said to Ainslie, "you're standing outside Water Tower on the Pearson Street side having your cigarette break."

"I'm supposing."

"Something happens. Say a car comes by and because of some problem inside, it runs into that little iron fence just before the doors to the Ritz. Maybe because Danni tries to get out."

Visualizing it, he just nodded, sadly, which made me like him even more.

"You and the other smokers standing there with you have

seen Danni. Now, Ainslie, we are damn sure there are at least two Bandwidth people in the car. The driver, who was most likely waiting down the block during the mass, and the fake priest."

"Gotcha."

"They know Danni has been spotted. They know that when the news comes on later with Danni's picture, all these people—four or five, I would bet—will remember her. Bandwidth has got to act fast."

"Yes."

"One of them jumps out just a bit down the block, out of sight of the smokers. At the Mies van der Rohe corner, probably. He hangs in a doorway. He watches the smokers finish their break and start back into the building. As you know, Water Tower has both elevators and escalators. But I have become an expert on Water Tower. Only tourists take the elevators. They're slow and get slower when some mother with a stroller gets on. Or worse, twins in a double-wide stroller. All the Water-Tower-expert people take the escalators. The escalators move without stopping, of course."

"No argument from me so far," Ainslie says.

"Our Bandwidth man follows the smokers. We know Parnella Grant gets off at the mezzanine, because she works at the coffee shop there. The Copley Water Tower Bank is on the same floor and the entryway is just past the escalator. This is a piece of cake. Bandwidth-man watches Parnella head toward the coffee bar and he sees William Jordan get off, too. Jordan is wearing a three-piece dark suit, white shirt, and a tie. No problem finding him later, right? Banker's clothes."

"Might have to look, but not much."

"Now, Bandwidth-man is still on the escalator behind Edwin Carter and Darren Black. The cigar store is on the fourth floor and the Travel Depot is on the fifth floor, not that Bandwidth-man knows that's where they're going yet. Carter gets off. Black doesn't. What does Bandwidth-man do now? He's got a major problem. There are seven floors reached by that escalator. So Darren Black could be headed for five, six, or seven. Bandwidth-man makes a fast decision, and a bad decision, thinking he's got Black pinned on the upper floors, and follows Carter to the cigar store on four. Now he knows where Carter works. The only big question mark left is Darren Black, who by now has disappeared. After Bandwidth-man has Carter nailed down, he goes to the fifth, sixth, and seventh floors looking for Black. He doesn't see him. So—okay—he does what he can, checks the coffee bar and pins Parnella Grant specifically. Looks around the mezzanine and pins William Jordan. Makes some calls so that his cronies will follow them and kill them on their way home. Description, location, all that. Now what?"

"Yes, now what?"

"If it was me, I'd do this. I'd go buy a semivaluable item. A small silver money clip, for instance. Or a gold Waterman pen. Lord knows all the priciest brands in the world are available in Water Tower Place. No problem with money; these guys have dozens of fudged credit cards. And I would start going to all the businesses on floors five, six, and seven. By then it would be late Saturday afternoon. The stores probably start to close before he gets very far. It's no wonder this took a couple of days. And, of course, we now know Black had left for vacation almost immediately after the smoke break. He was probably already leaving while the perp followed Edwin Carter. So if Bandwidth-man hung around after the stores closed, watching people leave work, he wouldn't have seen him. Anyhow, over the next couple of days I would go into one store after the other and say I had been walking down Pearson Street on Saturday. I had seen the smokers' group at a distance, and then they went back inside. When I got to where they had been standing, I found this valuable clip on the sidewalk. I would go from store to store asking whether one of their Saturday employees smokes. Oh, yes? And was he here Saturday? Really? Can I talk to him? He's not here? Oh, then where is he now? How can I reach him?"

"Huh!" Ainslie said. "I guess I'm glad you're on our side.

day five

helpmepleasehelpmepleasehelpmepleasehelpmeplease

thursday

a hundred and twenty hours

forty-eight

I had slept on the cot in the room adjacent to the war room. Not aware yet that Raft had been killed at the prison in Hillsboro, I struggled off the stiff mattress at five in the morning and staggered to the war room next door, my left hip and knee aching from the thin, sagging mattress. Mrs. Drobney was staying with my mother. I'd wait a few hours, until 8:00 A.M. at the earliest, then call them and check that everything was reasonably all right. The more I was away, the more depressed my mother became.

A cop on the war room desk answered a ring and immediately handed me the phone.

"Khalid?" I said when I heard her voice. Mental telepathy, calling the instant I walked in.

"I'm at the Grand Canyon National Park airport, off U.S. 180," she said, without greetings.

"Great. Any sightings?"

"In the dark?" Khalid was testy. She probably hadn't slept and had put up with Spartan accommodations on some military plane. The army thinks discomfort makes you a better person. Also, the military makes very bad coffee.

"Not in the dark, no," I said. "Reports. Like maybe other hikers saw Darren Black and the Nico-Rid crew yesterday."

"No such luck."

"Oh."

"But I got everybody here. Two choppers are coming in at first light. The state police and the park rangers are being very cooperative and helpful."

Oh, I understand. They're all right there with you, aren't they?

"Well, that's great," I said with forced cheer. "Five-fifteen here, four-fifteen where you are. When's dawn, sixish?"

"It's at exactly six-oh-seven," she said irritably. "I want to make sure you have my beeper number."

I read it to her off our wall chart.

I said, "We may have some advantage. They have twenty-four hours' head start on us. But we have more and better hardware."

Khalid snorted.

Finally, getting desperate, I said, "What do the locals think? Is there any hope of finding Black today?"

"Nico-Rid is saying they went in—'stepped off' as they put it—near the north rim and were planning to traverse the Kaibab National Forest before going down into the canyon proper."

"Great. That narrows it down."

"The Kaibab is nine hundred square miles."

Before I poured a cup of coffee I stood in the war room and studied Danni on the screen. The cop who was monitoring her, an older guy named Walter, who had told me he had four children, all girls, said, "I don't think she looks so good."

My heart got cold. Somehow this assessment from a father, a man who had walked colicky babies in the night, sat up reading stories to his little girls when they had the flu, and made decisions when they didn't want to go to school as to whether they were really sick or just malingering, meant more to me than the experts. I asked, "What makes you say that?"

"Not moving around much. Healthy kids fidget a lot. She's weakening."

Hatch had been here all night, too. I had seen him lying on the other cot at one point, but I'd bet he'd been up a few hours. He looked slept in or, as a friend of mine used to call it, bed-raggled. His clothes were wrinkled, his hair was every which way, and his eyes were red, which was not terribly unusual for FBI agent Hatch.

Hatch said, "The telco crews are making progress tracing the dark fiber."

I said, "Good." Poor Hatch. He was following their every move by radio and plugging in the trace on a massive cyberchart of the city he had in his system. It resembled a huge "pipes" screen saver and was so detailed that he had to bring up just a block or so at a time or it looked like a dish of worms. He was in constant contact with the phone company. From past experience, naturally I was afraid that as soon as he got close the kidnappers would just make another change and leave him barking up the wrong tree, like a coon dog with no "nose."

He must have read the doubt in my face. "No, no, Kelly. Really," he said, with enthusiasm. "It looks like we've caught a break."

"No kidding!"

"When you want to trace back on unused fiber, you can go really far back and work forward, sending in little diagnostic messages. You can go way back, and have more chance of hitting the right one, but then you have to trace it forward over a larger distance, or not go as far back and hope you've picked lucky. It's guesswork, really."

"And?"

His face glowed with satisfaction. "We got lucky. They're homing in. It could be a matter of two or three hours."

forty-nine

Scramble!

The word from the superintendent was get to his office instantly. At 6:30 A.M.? I'd never heard of such a thing. I ran all the way and slowed only when I was within sight of the superintendent's door.

I already knew it was serious; and when I walked in, I knew not only that I was right, but that the meeting had been going on a long time. You don't need to be a detective to read the empty coffee cups, pulled-down neckties, and, in this case, one full ashtray. I remember the days when you would have had ten full ashtrays. There was the superintendent, of course, and Burkholder and DiMaggio.

But what got my attention was that Mayor Wallace was there, big as life. And on a video-hookup the president of the United States.

The live people looked at me. The virtual president didn't.

"Sit down, Chief Kelly," said the Superintendent of Police.

I did. DiMaggio was there too, and his face was grim.

"Shall I go on, Mr. President?" the mayor asked.

"Sure, Paul," said the president from the screen.

"You will not yet know," the mayor said directly to me, "that Johnnie Raft is dead."

I've had years of experience at keeping a poker face. But it was not easy. "What happened?"

The superintendent said, "He was murdered. Stabbed to death in his cell."

"Do you know who did it?"

"As a matter of fact, we do."

"One of the inmates?"

There was a moment of silence. He glanced at the mayor, whose face was closed.

"We are not giving out that information at this time."

What was this? I was the police, for God's sake. *I'm on your side.* I said, "That means a guard did it."

DiMaggio looked at me with a glance of approval that he quickly squelched. The mayor said, "Speculation is no help. We are not going to release word of this for at least twenty-four hours—"

"But the inmates on his corridor will know."

"They only know that he has been taken to the infirmary."

"The killer will know. The killer's family will know when you arrest him."

"We're not going to arrest him yet."

"But what if—"

"We don't need to. We have him under observation."

"And the senator and Maggie will have to know."

"We will leave it to you to tell them—just that the man is dead."

"Hey!" Burkholder said. "Let's just tell everybody and give him a medal."

Dead silence. With no glance at Burkholder, the superintendent said, "In any case, Chief Kelly, that's not why you're here." His tone not quite hostile, but certainly unfriendly.

The mayor was going on talking, but the president cut in. "Kelly, are you any closer to finding that child?"

Keeping myself calm, I said, "Yes, on several fronts, Mr. President. The FBI technician tells me that they are on the verge of tracing the current video path, some Telco dark fiber, to its source. Second, we have located a witness to the abduction. The witness is out of state, but FBI agent Khalid is in Arizona to interview him. Third, we have greatly narrowed down the part of Chicago Danni's being held in."

The pres nodded. But the mayor said, "How come you haven't already interviewed this witness by phone?"

"He's on a camping trip in the Grand Canyon. The FBI and the park rangers are going to have to locate him."

"About your door-to-door canvass. How close are you to finding the actual building where the child is?"

"Closer. But not there yet."

"How many possible buildings?"

I took a breath, but honesty was the best policy. "A few thousand."

The pres frowned. I waited to hear what he'd say because he had more information than anybody else. But there was no response. The mayor and superintendent gave each other an "anything else?" glance. Then Mayor Wallace said, "You can leave now, Chief Kelly."

As I closed the door behind me, I heard the superintendent say, "Maybe you're right, Mr. Mayor. Maybe it's time to replace her."

I left the door slightly ajar and waited. Surely the president would have more sense than to let me be bumped.

I heard him say, "Don't do that. Give her another day."

By the time I got to my office there was a call from DiMaggio to come and see him. His ADS ushered me into his inner office. Only he was there.

He saw my gaze move around the room.

"No meeting. Just you," he said.

"Oh, okay—"

His ADS left and closed the door.

"I want to talk with you about Burkholder."

"Oh."

"Here, have some coffee."

"Okay." I took a mug, more as a waiting device while he got ready to tell me whatever. I was afraid he would say I was off the case.

"What do you think of Burkholder's behavior lately?"

Oh, gee! "Uh—well, very much as it's always been."

"Come on, Polly."

I knew I could level with him. But there's just so much thin blue line thinking that it's actually hard to criticize a fellow officer. Your throat sort of closes up.

I took a breath, and because I owed DiMaggio honesty, I said, "Burkholder's a liability. He's not informed, he's not on top of things, he's a toady; he doesn't support his people."

"Yes, but he's always been like that."

"What are you asking me?"

"I don't want to put words in your mouth."

What was this about? He had asked me what I thought of Burkholder's behavior *lately*. Well, how had Burkholder behaved last year? The year before?

"I think—" I hesitated. "I believe he is less fawning, but in an odd way. It's as if he's swinging back and forth a bit. He used to be more calculated. He never did much work, but he was more cautious."

"Mm. I think so too."

"So what is it, boss?"

"I don't know. Either somebody has promised him something, or there's something wrong."

"Promised him something! You can't mean they'd make him a deputy superintendent! He's completely unqualified."

Burkholder's sister was the cousin of the mayor's wife. This is not a blood relationship, but close enough to make everybody uneasy. DiMaggio said, "It's happened before."

"He shouldn't be as high up as he is now."

"No kidding. It's either that he's being supported so much that he doesn't care to be careful, or he's losing it."

"Losing it? He never had it. I always thought he's just a natural-born asshole. Plus dumb. He's about as sharp as a Nerf ball."

"I'm not joking, Kelly. He's taking chances with his remarks he's never taken before. Some mental illness? Early onset Alzheimer's? Substance abuse?"

I thought long and hard. "Not impossible."

The hawk-nosed man had received his E-mail and was ready to move. He took pride in always being ready.

Global 9, a geostationary communications satellite hung twenty-three thousand miles above the equator. Global 9 was actually speeding through space at the speed of the Earth, and falling continually around the Earth as the Earth turned. But because it was geosynchronous, making one rotation around the Earth every twenty-four hours, and also geostationary, moving longitudinally neither north or south, relative to the Earth it seemed unmoving, as if there was an unbreakable thread that tethered it to a spot just a few miles north of Quito, Ecuador.

It covered essentially the whole Western Hemisphere.

The satellite itself was passive and had no moving parts. It was "unliving" and largely unreactive. It was not much more than a giant mirror. Earthlings bounced signals off it.

fifty

I had reached the war room and had put out my hand to the phone. I was going to call Maggie and the senator, but 7:00 A.M. was too early. Raft's death wasn't good news; and if there was any chance they were asleep, let them sleep. At almost the same instant, Hatch stopped typing on his keyboard. His hands froze in place.

I heard a sigh go out of him.

For a brief instant, I thought it was a sigh of satisfaction. But a look at his face told me the truth. The screen on the wall had blinked off.

Despairing, I watched. A half minute went by. Then the screen came up again. Danni again. The same room.

And quiet tears were running down Hatch's unshaven cheeks.

The districts in our target area were faxing me lists of possible buildings.

What do we know about Danni's prison?

One, it has a floor made of old, wide, solid wooden

boards. My guy had told me that meant the building was at least forty years old, but more likely considerably older than that. The boards were not only characteristic of older building methods, but looked shrunken and worn. I increased my requested age to forty-plus years.

Two, it was solid. Because of the lack of tremor in the picture, it was well built. Probably this also confirmed that it was older. Look for good original construction.

Three, because of the lack of sway, Danni was not on a high floor. While this might limit our search inside a given building, it didn't tell me whether the whole building was tall or not. It was not useful in finding the building, but it would limit the time spent on searches inside.

What else? There was no sunlight in her room. The light never changed, day or night. Either there were no windows, or the windows were covered with something, maybe plywood or curtains. My guess was that there were windows. Those shapes Danni was fingerpainting in water had certainly turned out not to be the shape of the white patch on the floor.

So—four, let's assume that Danni actually knows what she talking about. Or water-painting about. Let's say the building has tall, rather narrow windows. That's consistent with the age factor. Lund's apartment, the one with the IR receiver but no Danni, was built in the fifties and had wide "picture" windows.

Five, she was not buried, not in some hole or underground room, since she was obviously hearing something by putting her ear to the floor. This was good news.

Could I tell the patrol officers in each district in the target area to look for a building in which some tall, narrow windows on a lower floor were boarded up? Could boarding up be number six? I would bet almost anything that Bandwidth wouldn't let the boards actually show outside. They'd curtain the windows first, and put the boards or drywall inside. The district cops could look, but they'd better look for covering, not boards.

And seven, because Danni often put her good ear to the

floor, I believed she was listening to a child downstairs, maybe a young child who cried often. Khalid disagreed, but she could be wrong.

For a minute my faith left me. *Many* of the buildings in Chicago were over forty years old. Many were landmarks going back more than a hundred years. Chicago was a city of architecture, proud architecture, solidly built. And most of the older buildings had the taller, narrower windows. Many were heavily curtained or had thick shades.

Well, you have to go with what you've got.

Too impatient to wait, I called Khalid. She was in the air, somewhere over the Kaibab National Forest.

"We've only been up twenty minutes," she snapped. "Went up before the sun was even up. We're quartering the area," she said, "and so far we've seen two bears and a moose." Her phone was built into the helmet, as the pilot-to-passenger mike was, so that they could hear over the chopper noise.

"Elk," I heard the pilot say.

"We saw goddamn Bigfoot," Khalid snarled, "but no Nico-Rid people."

"Hey, there's a bunch of ten hikers running around someplace out there," I said. "They're probably wearing that purple-and-chartreuse Spandex stuff and carrying bright yellow backpacks and all that gear. How come you can't see them?"

"This park is a hundred times the size of Chicago. And there are all these stupid deep ditches and—"

"Arroyos," the pilot muttered in the background.

"And the canyon itself is deep enough to—"

"Five thousand, five hundred feet deep," said the pilot.

"Deep enough to hide the Sears Tower!" she snapped.

Nearly four Sears Towers stacked on top of each other, I thought. I said, "But the point is—"

"And *you* can't find Danni in the middle of one-fourth of the city of Chicago."

Low blow, but it was true. "Khalid, the point is, Danni

is hidden. Your targets are outdoors. Out in the open."

"Chicago isn't covered with these goddamn trees. This is like standing two feet away from a sheepdog and looking for a flea on his skin!"

Frederick Hankelin folded his hands. "An uplink is a very simple thing. You see versions of the hardware every day. The television channel vans with the satellite gun on top? That's an uplink. It's basically a laser gun. You find your satellite, get your azimuth—the onboard computer does it for you of course, you don't expect television cameramen to know physics, do you?—you lock on and beam your signal to the Global 9 or any satellite."

"And then?" I said. DiMaggio had come to the meeting with me to lend authority. He folded his hands on his stomach and waited.

"Then? Why, then, it bounces back."

"Why do we need these satellites?"

"Because light moves in a straight line. Radio waves follow the curve of the Earth, which is why you can sometimes receive a superstation like WGN all the way over in Japan. But light beams are straight. So you can't send a video signal from New York to Hong Kong, or even New York to LA. You have to beam it up to a satellite and have it reflected back down over the curve of the Earth."

"So we pick up that signal on Earth and then what? TV channels rebroadcast the signals to televisions sets in people's homes?"

"Well, yes. Ordinarily they take it in and edit it first. But, yes. You've seen live feeds. You know, some person from London on a live feed interviews Madonna as she emerges from Sloane Street shopping. We put our very sophisticated technology to some very base uses."

"Mr. Hankelin, what I'm trying to ask is whether an unauthorized person, completely unknown to you, can bounce a signal off your satellite."

Hankelin didn't say anything. He glanced at the silent Mr.

George. Mr. George said, "Excuse us for a minute, please." Both got up and left the room.

I said, "Hmm."

DiMaggio chuckled, but grimly. Three or four minutes went by. Then our two well-dressed gentlemen came back in and sat down.

"We have decided," Mr. Hankelin said, "to tell you."

"Good."

"In this particular case, the kidnappers didn't just 'bounce a signal,' as you put it. These people went into the system properly. They had our protocol and carrier. Counterfeit, but properly."

I said, "Let's be perfectly clear here. You're telling me somebody got hold of your—what did you call it?—protocol and carrier?"

"I'm afraid so."

"How?"

"How? Well, they may have worked on the system."

I said, "Or known somebody who worked on the system?" He nodded. "Or found somebody who'd worked on the system and bribed him?" He nodded. "Or invaded your office files? Hacked into your office computer? Or broken in? Or may still even work there?"

He nodded miserably. People are so sure they're adequately protected until they find out they aren't. I said to DiMaggio, "This puts us in the business of backgrounding hundreds of people again."

He said to Hankelin, "We'll need an employee list."

You could see Hankelin crumple. Most of his objections up to now, I thought, were caused by embarrassment. "All right. Okay. I can see that's important."

"Damn right."

I said, "Now how do we trace where the counterfeit signal came from?"

He was still more embarrassed, shifting in his chair. "As a company, we don't have any reason to do that. So, uh, it wouldn't be economically feasible to have any such capability built in. It would increase the cost to our customers. And SatCom can't do it."

I placed my hands flat on the table. "You can't trace it?"

"We can't trace it," Hankelin said.

Commander Ainslie came in while I was collating the printout from the districts about the possible buildings. I was dismayed at the sheer number of buildings that fit our criteria. In the central part of the target area alone there were 1,798.

From Ainslie's face, I knew we had another problem. "Tell me," I said.

"The Nico-Rid people just called the Travel Depot people who called nine-one-one and nine-one-one paged me. Why they didn't call you or the FBI directly, I don't know."

"Never mind now."

"It delayed our getting it by an hour and a half, and we don't have that kind of time to waste."

"What's happened?"

"Nico-Rid just discovered that somebody hacked into their computer. Yesterday."

fifty-one

The call from the superintendent's aide reached me in the war room. Somebody who knew somebody in the infirmary at the Hillsboro prison had told somebody who knew a reporter. The long and the short of it was, word was out. Raft's murder was going to be big news any moment.

Fetterman ran me to the Knickerbocker with lights and siren. The gilded elevator seemed much too slow. Trust between the police and the kidnap victim's family is fragile. It gets thinner and thinner the more time goes by and the child isn't found. The very last thing I wanted was for the Gastons to hear about Raft's murder before I could tell them.

Feeling guilty that I had waited and had become so involved in the search, I ran into their suite. But it was clear they hadn't heard. They were sitting together at a table.

Now I cringed at what I had to say, but there was no way out. "Maggie, Senator Gaston, I have some bad news that is *not* about Danni."

"What do you mean?" Gaston snapped. "If it's not about

Danni, why bother us?" They had been eating breakfast, but
a croissant lay broken into pieces on Maggie's plate, and
there seemed to be as many pieces as if she hadn't eaten
any.

"Please sit down, Polly," she said, aware of my mental
discomfort, but only able to deal with possible physical un-
ease.

"Thank you." I sat.

"Well, what?" Gaston said.

There is never any point in being cowardly. Putting things
off usually doesn't help. And for all I knew, they might hate
Raft enough to be glad he was dead, rather than worried
about any information he might have taken to the grave.
"Johnnie Raft has been killed," I said.

Gaston shot to his feet, lost his balance, and clutched the
chair.

"It's a lie!"

"No, Senator. He was killed in prison. In his cell, I believe."

Gaston's face was chalky. His cheeks sunk in, his lips
worked, and then he yelled, "How could you let this happen?"

I was about to say I wasn't a prison guard, which of
course wouldn't have helped, when he swept the table with
his arm, sending glasses and plates and food and hot coffee
shooting out toward the wall. "God *damn* it!" he screamed.
Glass shattered and plates struck like bricks, and the FBI
and CPD agents came rushing in from the anteroom. Two
CPD guys were drawing their guns.

"How could you let this happen? What is the matter with
you people? You incompetent—you incompetent—"

"Neal, please!" Maggie said.

"You incompetent idiots! I *told* you we should have released him!" He screamed, "Shit!" and knocked over the
table.

He picked up a chair and threw it toward the window,
but thank God one of the CPD cops leaped sideways and
caught it by one leg. If it had knocked the glass out, and

the shards had fallen to the street from this height, the twenty-third floor, they might have killed somebody.

"Neal!" Maggie grabbed his arms and physically wrestled him onto the green-and-white sofa. He was sobbing, and by the time she got a good grip on him, he was past resisting very much, melting into hopeless weeping. She held him and squeezed his upper arms.

"Don't you understand?" Neal asked, in a strangled voice.

"What, Neal?" she asked.

"Raft was our link to Danni!"

"Neal, I know—"

"No, he was our *only* link! These cops haven't found her. He was all we had!"

"Neal, they're working hard—"

"We'll never find her now."

"Yes, we will! Neal, we *will!*"

"Oh, God!" he groaned.

The FBI agents and cops and I stood around feeling extremely uncomfortable. After three or four long, long minutes, Maggie looked up at me. Silently, she mouthed, "I'll call you."

I left.

Khalid stared down at the heavily forested plateau. It was so frustrating. Bandwidth had a twenty-four-hour head start on her, the way she figured it. For all anyone knew, they had already murdered the whole Nico-Rid party.

She couldn't see any people, even though this was where the hikers should be. The land beneath her was furred with green. Pines and spruce and God only knew what underneath. You couldn't see anything.

"This is impossible!" she said to the pilot.

"Not necessarily."

She had seen areas that were much less verdant than this as they flew in here. She spoke through the helmet mike and pointed over her left shoulder. "What about the clean rock faces back there?"

The pilot said, "Yeah, you'd see better."

"Well, let's go there."

"Ma'am, with all due respect—"

Khalid hated sentences that started out like that.

"With all due respect, ma'am, that's like looking for your keys under the lamppost because the light's better there."

"Oh, *really!*"

"The Nico-Rid itinerary says they're supposed to be coming this way. So we'd better look this way."

"Shit!"

"Whatever you want, of course. You're the boss."

They swept over the Kaibab forest in parallel lines, quartering it, along with three other copters, which were working adjacent sectors. The copter would sweep along a prescribed path, then slide out to turn and go back on a parallel track. The turn made Khalid feel like a fetus heavy in the womb of a woman turning on her heel. She was spun to the point of disorientation, and was becoming nauseated, but she was too proud to say so to the pilot, who seemed to have no problem at all.

fifty-two

The hawk-nosed man, Laser Blue, walked to the meeting by going around parts of seven blocks—all the way around, two blocks north, one west, three south, four east, one south, one west, and so forth. It took him more than an hour to walk what was effectively four blocks south from his SRO Hotel on Rush. On the way, he dropped a coil of telephone wire in a trash barrel, but with an end sticking out. He figured it would be no more than five minutes before some bag lady grabbed it.

He wore thin leather gloves, the billed cap over his eyes, and a fly fisherman's coat with lots of pockets inside and outside. The pockets were stuffed with equipment.

A block west, he took a cell phone from a pocket and put it down on the doorstep of a stoop-level building. At that corner he turned south, and halfway down he left the biggest item, an amplifier that was a foot long by four-by-six inches and had been uncomfortable in his inside net pocket, plus various small plugs, and some cables with built-in transformers, on the curb in front of a video store.

Moving another two blocks south before turning east, he abandoned a continuity tester and an ohmmeter on a park bench in a yuppie area that was frequented by techies.

He was not going to leave any physical evidence in his hotel room. But the whole crisis, the need to move so fast had pissed him off, let alone the news.

The hawk-nosed man was already furious before DeGier, the false priest, met him at Xanabar for coffee.

"I was *not* coming here," he said, "except I think you deserve some courtesy."

"Or you didn't want to use your cell phone," DeGier said.

"Hey, I could have just split."

"Why? We're on the verge of winning."

"No, we're not."

"What? What's wrong?"

"Everything."

"Like?"

"Something is terribly wrong. May have been wrong for a long time."

"Hey! What are you telling me?"

The hawk-nosed man said slowly and clearly, "Raft's dead."

"I heard. God, what'll we do?"

"I'm getting out."

The other man stared at him. "Just—leaving?"

"Fucking right."

"What about the kid? What about Danni?"

"Not my problem."

"But she doesn't deserve to die."

"Not my problem."

"She didn't make this happen."

"Deserve? She's one of the rich-privileged-no-need-to-do-anything drones."

"She's just a little kid," DeGier said.

"Bullshit."

"There's no point in leaving her there to die. We could tell them where she is."

"No."

"Oh, all of a sudden, you're thinking for yourself!"

"All of a sudden, I have to. Raft is *dead!* He died early last night; don't you understand? Something very strange and scary is going on."

"You could still drop a letter in the mail. We could just—"

"No, we couldn't." The hawk-nosed man was actually thinking, *I couldn't,* because he needed enough time to get far away. When he realized that DeGier was having mushy-minded, stupid misgivings, he said, "All right, all right. Let me see what I can do. You get moving. I'll take care of it."

He had left his satchel with other electronic equipment on the shelf under the coat rack when he arrived. It was a nice, expensive satchel, real, dark brown leather with brass fixings. Now, as he walked out the door, he noticed it had vanished.

Judge Grolsch, who was about sixty years old, was feared and loathed by just about everybody in the criminal courts system. He was rude to witnesses, snapped at court officials, snarled at jurors if they didn't file into their seats fast enough. He thought defense attorneys were idiots and prosecutors were morons. When a jury got itself deadlocked, the snippy or angry notes he sent back were such gems of nasty rhetoric that bailiffs saved them to show their friends.

Judge Grolsch had been rated by the bar association on his qualifications, of course, as all judges were. His rating on the law was "highly qualified." His rating on judicial temperament was "not qualified."

Attorneys all knew this, but he went on judging year after year because, disliked though he might be, judges in Cook County are elected. The body politic doesn't know the names of many judges; and unless there's a truly big stink, voters generally just go down the list punching "yes" in front of every name. Any judge who gets 60 percent or more "yes" votes is reelected. At the last election, all the candidates were retained.

And if you took the time to study his record, he was

reversed on appeal less than any other judge in the system, bar none.

I found him in court, shouting, "If I'd wanted tuna fish, I would have said tuna fish!"

His bailiff or whatever rushed past me carrying a brown bag. I went on into the chambers.

"Polly Kelly!" he said. He was wiry, short, but strong looking, and had eyebrows like Mephistopheles. "Well, you've certainly gotten yourself into a mess this time, little girl. You've got no sense of survival."

"You've got no respect, you old bastard."

"So you want something. What?"

"I want you to take a great professional risk."

"Tell me about it."

"You detectives will each pick up two teams of two patrol officers," I said. "You will receive a list of buildings to inspect."

It was not yet noon. We were in the functional auditorium, plaster walls painted a dull cream, and flat fluorescent lighting, not the smaller, paneled and carpeted auditorium the superintendent used for press conferences. The weather had turned cold in the night. The air smelled of wet wool and hot radiators. A hundred and seventy detectives sat in the plastic chairs. With the 680 patrol cops that they would command, there would be 850 people on the streets in six districts. Little enough to look at every apartment and store in thousands of buildings.

Because detectives are commanded through the detective hierarchy, and patrol cops through the district hierarchy, getting to this point had been a structural and procedural nightmare. Deputy Superintendent DiMaggio had made it work.

"Officer Fetterman is handing out sheets telling you what to look for. For two days officers in the relevant districts have surveyed every building and eliminated those that don't fulfill our requirements. I should tell you now, that if the present survey doesn't yield Danni Gaston, we will go back to those buildings that don't meet every characteristic and look at them in detail. But time is of the essence, and the addresses have been selected because they all have all the elements we want—windows with a tall, narrow, profile; solid buildings more than forty years old; structural wood floors; and so on. Solidly built. We're not even looking into old, rickety wood structures.

"This is the picture. It's all there on your sheets. But you and I and everybody who has ever worked patrol knows that when you get out in the field things are different."

A few said, "You bet," or, "No lie."

"Be flexible. We think the windows will have curtains or shades on the outside, for instance, so that boarding-up on the inside isn't visible. We think that because these guys are smart. But obviously, if you see boarded-up windows from the outside in a site that fits the other characteristics, follow up on it."

"We ask about kids?"

"Of course. Get the supers talking. Now you see these rating sheets. Let's say you and your teams go into a building. Eight floors. The tenants on the first, second, third, et cetera, all let you in to check the units, all except one unit on the seventh floor. Okay? What you do is fill out this sheet with the exact characteristics of the unit. Who it's rented to. When was the last time a maintenance person was inside? Was somebody at home who refused entry, or was it empty and the super refused entry? When were the tenants last seen? Is there a family with children in the apartment below? What's the configuration of the rooms? Are the floors bare? Other info from the owner or super? You modem the whole thing to the war room immediately, and they will score it on a probability scale from one to four, and from that we'll make decisions about how to get in."

"So you figure she's in an apartment where somebody will refuse admission."

"Not necessarily. The kidnappers may have abandoned her. We've never seen any hint of any human being with her. You may have the super unlock a door to a vacant apartment and find her right on the other side."

One detective said, "What if we don't get admitted but really think she's in there?"

"Report," I said. "Fast, by radio."

"What if we want to go in?"

"Yeah. What about warrants?" a cop asked.

"You know better than that. This is a fishing expedition. You don't have probable cause. Probable cause is very specific. Like somebody saw a man taking Danni into a building. Obviously you don't have probable cause because otherwise we wouldn't be doing a broad canvass like this."

"But suppose we get a hot one?"

"Look, get the super or building manager on your side. Use charm. Use the fact that Danni is—uh." I couldn't say it. It was too painful to say "dying." "Tell them we're in a race against time. There can't be three people in the city of Chicago who don't know that already. Convince the supers to let you into any apartments they think are vacant. They shouldn't object to that anyway. Try hard to get them to let you into places where the tenants presumably aren't home."

"What if they are home and won't let us in?"

"Talk with them. Tell them you just want to look. Tell them it doesn't matter if they haven't cleaned the place. Tell them it doesn't matter if they have a roomful of stolen cases of wine. Or a bedful of prostitutes. Beg. Plead."

"Hey, this isn't good enough," said a hefty, middle-aged man in row two. I knew him. Charlie Benaczyk, a long-timer.

"What's that, Charlie?" I said.

"Suppose I get to a place and they won't let me in. And it's got all the characteristics."

"Yeah, Charlie?"

"And suppose I even hear a kid whimpering inside."

"Yeah?"

"I mean, sorry, Kelly, but this is a kid. I got kids. I'm gonna bust down the door."

"No, you're not."

"Yeah, I am. I mean, Kelly, I'm a member of the KMA club."

He meant the kiss-my-ass club, officers who had their twenty-five years in, and had their pensions locked in, and wouldn't lose no matter what happened. Or so they thought.

"You could be sued if you're wrong, Charlie. So could the department."

"I'm gonna bust the door down, Chief."

"No, Charlie, you're not. You're going to get on the radio and tell the dispatcher the emergency code. It's on your sheet."

"Applesauce?" one of the younger detectives said.

"Well, it's not a word anybody is likely to use by accident, is it?" I said. "Okay? Now you contact Hatch with the addresses of apartments you can't get into. Somebody will deal with them."

"Contact Hatch right away or wait to the end of the tour?"

"Right away. I already said that. One last word. Err on the side of calling the emergency code if you have the slightest reason for suspicion."

"I still want to break in," Charlie said. Three other guys said, "Yeah."

"Charlie, you're off the case!"

"No! Dammit, boss!"

"I don't need a loose cannon."

"Please?"

"No. And you other guys," I pointed at the three who'd agreed with Charlie, "you're gonna do as I say or you're out, too. What'll it be?"

"All right, all right."

Right, Kelly, I thought. *If anybody's gonna get jammed up, it'll be me. Set a great example, Kelly. Do as I say, not as I do.*

fifty-three

Hannah Khalid didn't know whether scanning the
ground with binoculars was better or worse than the naked
eye. One way you got detail but no scale, the other way you
got the general picture but felt you might be missing something important. She had used the binoculars for nearly an
hour as they quartered back and forth along an invisible path
the pilot seemed to see traced in the air. But after a while,
staring through the eyepieces while swaying made her
queasy. Once she felt the nausea, the smell of gasoline and
metal made it worse. So she put down the binoculars and
scanned with her eyes, changing over only when she saw a
flash of color on the ground. They had sunk down to check
several possibilities. One was a patch of blue gentian. One
was a discarded backpack. One was a balloon caught in a
tree.

"Damn trees!" she said.

"That's the tenth time you said that." The pilot made a
neat ninety-degree turn.

"How do you know where you're going?"

"GPS."

Oh, the global positioning satellite. Of course. She felt foolish.

"There!" she said. "There's somebody!"

"No, look closer."

"Oh, hell, it's a goddamn pony."

"Nope. Wild burro. Some of the old pack burros escaped, way back, and went wild."

Like I care, Khalid thought, but she didn't say it. This just wasn't her kind of country. Her kind of country was Washington or New York. I'd like to see how this ever-so-spiffy pilot handled himself on Eighth Avenue after midnight.

Wait a minute! Was that a yellow color down there in the bush? It was that hideous Day-Glo yellow-green that the exercise-clothes makers called Saturn. It couldn't be natural.

"See that?"

"Where?"

She pointed. "Right down there."

The color was partly hidden by bushes near a ravine—arroyo—where there were no tall trees. Only a dense thicket of some huge, lush plants that were just leafing out for spring. She hoped the color wasn't some unusual yellow-green vegetation. She grabbed the binoculars.

Through them she got a glimpse of something bright purple.

"Hey!" she yelled.

"Don't scream; I can hear you on the earphones." The copter sank lower. The pilot said, "How are you gonna know if these are our people or some other group?"

"Land this thing and I'll ask."

"Are you kidding? I can't land here. Look at this terrain."

"Then just hang here and I'll count 'em. Nico-Rid is two guides and eight civilians. If it's a group of ten, I'm calling it."

The hikers below them clustered together, pointing at the low-flying helicopter. There were eight; then two more came up from farther along the trail. "It's them!"

"Great."

"I'm getting base on the air. Then I'll let you tell them where we are. The foot teams will have to start hiking in immediately."

The pilot told the base their location. With the GPS it would be within one yard of actual. Khalid punched her hand into the air and yelled, "Yes!" as they lifted higher.

The chopper banked, heading for base. As the body of the helicopter canted sharply over, Khalid found herself staring down into a dense forest some quarter mile from the Nico-Rid party.

"Oh, no!" she said.

"What?"

"Two men in camo gear. There! Right there! Look! And I thought I saw the sun glint off something maybe twenty feet away from them. Probably more men, with guns."

The pilot spun the copter toward them.

"No! Don't!" she said. "Peel off or whatever the hell you call it. We can't let them know we've seen them. Get back to base, fast, and hand me the radio."

fifty-four

"Here we are," Fetterman said, pulling the unmarked car in to the curb.

"And here you are, too," Judge Grolsch said, handing me a piece of paper over my shoulder from where he was sitting in the backseat. "My first felony."

"Don't joke," I said.

"Who's joking?"

"It's not a felony."

"Well, all right. It's just career suicide."

"Look, Judge, I know you could get into trouble. We don't have anything remotely resembling probable cause. I don't think there's another judge in Cook County who'd be willing to take the risk."

"Stop buttering me up, girl. Just pisses me off."

I got out of the car, holding the warrant.

"I'll come with you," Fetterman said.

"Oh, no, you won't. It's bad enough you're here at all."

I had not intended to bring Fetterman. I could be relieved of my job for doing what I was doing. I'd decided to go ahead, but I had no right to involve a kid just starting his career in the department. What I had intended for him to do was stay in the war room and pass along to me the suspect addresses of individual apartments that the patrol officers couldn't get into. He could always claim, or I could claim for him, that he didn't know what I was going to do with them.

But when he heard he was to stay behind, he looked at me aghast and just said, "Please." I could practically see the words go through his mind. *This is why I wanted to be a cop. If I can't save Danni, what good am I? Please. I want to help.* But he didn't say the words, just stared at me with big, brown eyes and waited for me to realize how terribly much he wanted it. And I gave in.

"Remember, Fetterman, I am ordering you to do this. You don't know any better."

He had said, "Thank you, boss!"

Now I said, "You stay here in the car, Fetterman, and get the messages."

"Don't forget to turn on your mike." Then he blushed and said, "Sorry, boss."

"No prob, Fetterman. I can use reminders." With the mike on, he could hear me and whoever I would talk with. If I got into trouble, he could call for backup.

This particular building was one of the 1920s terra-cotta-façade Loop buildings. The windows were tall and narrow, and the floors were wood. Seven stories high, it was mostly offices, except for the top floor, which had been converted to luxurious living space occupied by the owner. He had let the patrol cops in to look around, but he couldn't force his tenants to. Virtually all the offices had let the cops in. People had heard about Danni, and they wanted to help. All over the city, people had been letting the cops come into their businesses, apartments, storerooms, operating rooms, whatever, and search. I felt good about Chicago.

But two offices in this building had refused to admit anybody. And one of the two had opaque curtains. The district cops had noticed that no light could be seen from outside, even at night.

It was a weekday and not yet noon. The offices should be occupied. But in case they weren't, I had the building super in tow, carrying his set of keys. I was carrying my unjustified warrant. I hit the less likely unit first and found nothing but a psychiatrist's office and a shrink who took himself entirely too seriously.

The second unit was on the fourth floor, a lower-rent part of the building, where the lighting was darker and three of the offices were single-practitioner dentists. The patrol cops had seen those. At the end of the hall was a solid door, oak, like all the doors in this old building. I put my ear to it, but heard nothing. There was no company name or any other identifying mark on the door, except Four-D. I had brought the tech guys' explosives sniffer with me and turned it on. I let it suck air under the bottom of the door. No reaction. I knocked. No answer.

"Open it, please," I said to the super.

As the key turned in the lock, somebody pulled the door open fast from the other side. I slapped my hand onto my sidearm.

The man who stood in the doorway was big and dirty.

"Police," I said. He didn't move. I left the gun in the holster and showed him my ID instead.

He said, "Go away."

I showed him the warrant.

He let me in, and I walked into a room filled with VCRs televisions, speakers, turntables, computers, some of it scratched and none of it in boxes. I checked the second room, watching the dimensions for the possibility of false walls. This was the only other room in the unit except for a small, grubby bathroom. More electronic gear.

I knew what this was. A warehouse for stolen property.

When I turned around to ask the big dirty guy who he was, he was gone.

———

At the second address, a deteriorated building in the South Loop, I could hear a child crying as I approached the door. My heart almost stopped. I actually had to stand still a couple of seconds and take a few deep breaths. Then I used the sniffer at the door. Nothing. So, holding the master key, I knocked.

A woman in her mid-fifties, wide in the hips, with dry, straw blonde hair, and a loose blue top with rhinestonelike sparkles around the neck, opened the door.

"Ma'am, I am a police officer. My name is Polly Kelly. This is my ID."

"So?" she said. Her body blocked the whole doorway, intentionally. She was my height, and she stared defiantly straight into my eyes.

"Earlier today you refused entry to two police officers. They wanted to check the apartment to see whether the little girl, Danni Gaston, was here."

"Well, she ain't."

"I'd like to come in." I heard the child, somewhere in a back room, start crying again.

"Well, you can't."

"This time I have a warrant."

She took the paper but didn't look at it. Her face was mulish, but she backed away just enough to let me through the door. I passed so close I smelled her sweat and something like spoiled milk.

There were toys on the living room floor. Before full awareness hit me, I heard, to my utter dismay, a second child start to cry. Then a third in sympathy with the first two.

"You're running a nonlicensed day care, right?"

She just stared at me.

"I'm not going to cite you, and I'm not going to cause you any trouble. I'm just going to look into the rooms and then I'll be out of here."

"Don't do me no favors."

In a medium-sized bedroom, six children from two years old to maybe four were crowded around a television. A seventh child lay on the floor kicking his feet and working his way into a full-fledged tantrum. There were bits of cookies stepped into the thin green rug. Two discarded empty baby bottles lay next to a group of three child-sized plastic chairs. A giant pack of disposable diapers stood near a big plastic barrel. The barrel was full of used diapers, and a smell of urine rose from it.

I looked into the other rooms, of course, and I opened all the closed doors, finding only cluttered closets and another grubby bathroom.

"You know," I said to the woman, "you could have saved us time just letting the officers in here." No answer. "Danni hasn't got much time left." No answer. "Anybody who cares about children ought to cooperate!" I shouted, losing my cool.

Getting no response at all, I left. She slammed the door behind me.

One of the little girls had resembled Danni.

fifty-five

They dropped out of the sky at 10:21 local time—six FBI HRT agents, six state troopers, and six park rangers for guides, six teams of three people, one team from each of six separate helicopters. All the choppers flew low up the arroyo, trying to catch sight of the Nico-Rid party, but also watching for the Bandwidth assassins. There was no chance of keeping a low profile and sneaking up on Bandwidth. Even one helicopter roaring in over this wilderness would be heard for miles.

However, foot parties were setting out from points along the unpaved county Routes 422, 425, and 232 to the north and west, and state road 67 on the east, quietly converging on this area. With the Grand Canyon itself making an irregular barrier on the south, they hoped to trap the Bandwidth crew. But first, they had to save Darren Black and also the nine other innocent people swept up into the crisis.

Khalid was in the lead chopper. It hovered over a half-dry creek near where they had seen the hikers.

When she spotted them again, the pilot took her in fast, directly over them.

She knew he couldn't land. There wasn't a flat piece of land as big as a dinner plate anywhere. But sliding down a rope out of a helicopter was something she knew how to do. She'd been trained for this.

She went first and the two men in her team followed quickly. They wore jackets with POLICE stenciled on both back and front. Despite this precaution, since the FBI and rangers were ringing the area, trying to establish a perimeter, there was danger of shooting each other if shooting started.

"Find Darren Black. Protecting him is the first priority," Khalid had told the teams. They had a photo of him, faxed from Chicago, but it wasn't very good. And it wasn't in color. The accompanying ID said, "light brown hair, brown eyes, light complexion, 5' 9", 175 lb." He looked like a lot of people.

"**FBI!** Everybody listen up fast!" Khalid waved her ID. "Are you guys the Nico-Rid party?"

"Sure are," said a shortish woman with dark hair. She wore a jacket that had white letters on green spelling out NICO-RID. One of the group leaders, no doubt.

The rest were staring stunned at these people dropping out of the air.

"You're in danger!" Khalid shouted. "Get down! Crouch and follow me into this gully." She ducked behind a string of boulders. At the same time her brain was going a mile a minute, counting the group. Three women, one with medium-length blonde hair, two dark-haired, small, with hair cut short, but not sisters. The group leader was sharp-featured and amber-skinned. The other brunette was pale-skinned, blue-eyed, maybe what they called "black Irish."

Seven men. As she herded them in front of her, she cat-alogued them. One was an older man, about fifty, wiry, some white in the hair, saying, "What's going on?"

Two black guys, one tall and slender, one a bit older, with a paunch. One rangy white guy, mid-thirties, with black hair and a Nico-Rid jacket—the other group leader. Three men in their thirties with brown hair. Two of them looked like the Darren Black fax. One didn't, but wasn't very far off, just too tall.

They were funneling between boulders down into the arroyo. The maybe-Darren-Black, the one with lighter brown hair, said, "What's happening?"

"Move faster!" she said. "Are you Darren Black?"

Turning back, he said, "Why—?" And his neck exploded, spattering blood and tissue in her face. He dropped like a sack of flour.

"Aaaawf—!" Sound like a rubber balloon bursting came from his throat.

"Grab him! Move! Move! Move!" Khalid yelled. She took his feet, one of the rangers took his shoulders, and the whole group tumbled down the declivity, backpacks left behind, hats falling off.

I was getting more and more desperate. There were now more than five hundred central Chicago apartments on the prime suspect list, more coming in every minute, and we were bouncing back and forth across the middle of the city like we were a ball in a pinball machine. I'd never get to them all. Never, never, never, never. Never in time. The best I could do is take the descriptions and try to guess which of the already likely sites were most likely.

People have no idea how much stuff there is in a city, how many buildings, how many apartments, how many warehouses. We all know intellectually that an area ten blocks wide, east to west, and ten blocks long, north to south, is a hundred blocks. But even if it's a part of town we're familiar with, we think of maybe a dozen or so landmarks there that we've noticed. We have no real sense of everything else.

And here we were dealing with an area that was an elongated oval shape, maybe a hundred blocks or more wide and forty-five blocks long. At least. Forty-five hundred blocks!

Some of the blocks had one humongous building and some ten to twenty small ones.

We'd been at Chicago Avenue and Ashland, then thirty blocks northeast at North Avenue and LaSalle. Then seven blocks south of that to an old, elegant building on Belleville and State, not far from the Ambassador East. Then two miles and a world away on Flournoy at Halsted. Then two buildings farther west overlooking the Eisenhower Expressway.

And people had the God-damndest stupid reasons for keeping the cops out. People who hadn't dusted today. Or vacuumed today. Or hadn't vacuumed since Eisenhower was president. Like I cared.

One was a lawyer who threw everything in the book at me, and I'm here to say he knew the words "probable cause." But when I threatened to send for a full SWAT Team, he let me in. In his bedroom was a little boy, maybe eleven. This was not good. The question was how to deal with it. My warrant was for Danni. But the child was what we call "in plain view."

I radioed the vice guys and child protective services and ran out to another building and another disappointment.

It was two in the afternoon now, and still more level-one suspicious sites were coming in. I felt like a clock was ticking in my body. There was a hum of fear tick-tick-clicking away that just didn't stop.

Panicky, I called DiMaggio.

"Sir," I said into the phone, "we've got to find a way to get our people into apartments where Danni might be. The uniforms keep coming up with likely places where the tenants won't let us in. This is not a wild goose chase. She's right here."

DiMaggio said, "I'm sorry, Kelly. You can't. We've been over this."

"But I have it all greased! My guys are racking up a list of real, real probables. This isn't just fishing. After they look through a building that fits the characteristics, if they're left with a unit they can't get into, they rank it from one to four on how likely—"

"I understand how you feel."

"It's not how I *feel!* Who cares how I feel? Dammit! This is a child's life we're talking about."

"I know that."

"They're finding more possible places all the time. I'll never get to them all."

"What?"

I remembered that he didn't know I had a rogue judge and was running around acting on unfounded warrants.

"Uh, what I mean, uh, is we can't handle this any other way, sir. Not in time. We have to go in."

There was a silence. My guess was that he suspected what I was doing. I gave him another half-minute, wondering whether he'd tell me to stop. Or tell me to resign. But when there was nothing but silence, I said, "Call somebody important. Call the governor!"

"Kelly, nobody is going to throw out the Constitution of the United States and go breaking into homes. Not the mayor, not the governor, not the president, and certainly not the Superintendent of Police. Nobody."

Danni felt happy. She had been very, very tired, but she stretched out on her pad—or was it her bed? She thought it was her bed at home, her real bed, and it just felt so nice. And then her mommy came to see her. Mommy sang to her.

Mommy was so beautiful. She was all sparkly like stars and light and warmth, and Danni felt wonderful. They sang songs together—"Momma's Little Baby" and "Hush, Little Baby" and some songs that Danni couldn't quite remember because maybe she sort of fell asleep or dozed off or whatever.

Then her mother was singing again and Danni felt like singing along, but she thought she really was all dreamy and happy and warm and not making any sound.

But she knew Mommy would understand.

It had been so wonderful. So wonderful. So wonderful that what she wanted to do most now was sleep. Even with her eyes closed, she could still see Mommy all sparkly, like the stars, and she could watch her as she fell asleep.

fifty-six

Ainslie said over the radio, "Uh, Polly, we have sort of bad news."

"What?"

"Khalid is in Arizona—"

"I know that!"

"Uh, well, they found the Nico-Rid party."

There was something in his voice—anger, maybe—that warned me. "Go on. They're all dead, right?"

"No, no, not that bad. But Khalid and the FBI HRT guys and some other rangers and the Nico-Rid party are pinned down, under fire from Bandwidth."

The building fit every element of the profile. It was an old, five-story brick structure, built around 1900. The windows were tall and narrow. The floors were old wood, solid but worn, exactly like the ones in Danni's prison room. It had been a warehouse until the recent near North boom when all these old manufacturing and storage buildings on Franklin Street next to the el had been converted into art galleries on the lower two or three floors and condo apartments or artists' studios above. The high ceilings and brick walls appealed to the upwardly mobile.

Because it had been built to be used for heavy storage, the building was extremely sturdy.

And one apartment on the top floor, the fifth, had some opaque material covering all its windows. It was the one apartment in the building that the cops hadn't been able to get into. It was owned by an "R. Gostling," who was said by the uniforms to be a woman in her thirties.

She was slender and sharp—sharp little black eyes, sharp pale nose, sharp red fingernails. Pretty, but brittle looking.

"I told you people you couldn't come in," she said when I identified myself.

I showed her the warrant.

"I don't see how you could get this." She had a sharp mind, too.

"I assure you it's legitimate. If you'd like to call the judge, I can give you his number—" *He's down in the car with a cell phone.*

"Oh, never mind." She stepped back and waved her arm ungraciously.

The main room was huge. Old wood floors had been varnished with a zillion coats of polyurethane directly over the old stains, scars, and dents. Probably this showed that the place had character. The windows were covered with white-painted plasterboard. Two huge skylights in the ceiling provided ample light. There were two heavy wooden easels, one aluminum portable easel, canvasses stacked against the wall, and a long table with paints, jars of chemicals, knives, brushes, stretchers, and so on. No child was hidden in here.

I walked through the big room to a door that stood open. A bedroom. No Danni. A door in the bedroom opened into a bathroom. No Danni. At one side of the main room was an arch. Beyond it was the kitchen. No Danni. No false walls. And no other rooms.

"Why do you have the windows covered?"

"I don't like people looking in. The building next door is ten feet away. I value my privacy."

She had cost me fifteen minutes, fifteen precious minutes, for no reason at all that I could see.

"Why didn't you just let the patrol officers in?"

"I told you, I like to be private."

"Didn't they explain that they were looking for little Danni Gaston?"

"They told me. She isn't here."

"But you'd have saved us time to just let us see that."

"Not my problem." She folded her arms.

"She's a little girl. She may die. Don't you care?"

"I didn't steal her."

"Goddammit! You could put aside your stupid *privacy* for ten minutes! You're a poor excuse for a human being!" I felt blood rushing to my head and my hands clenched.

Don't hit her, Kelly. Don't pound her tiny little head until her sharp nose sticks in the cracks in the floor. Don't even take the time to tell her what you think of her. Just move. Hurry.

fifty-seven

A cold creek ran through the bottom of the arroyo, making sucking sounds as it curled over rocks. Khalid had landed with one knee down in the water. Other than the water sounds, there was a dreadful silence. Nine Nico-Rid people—stunned, exhausted, and nicotine-deprived—stared at the dead man, as Khalid slowly lowered him to the pebble-strewn bank of the creek.

A couple of bedrolls, which had come loose from packs, lay in the wet sand. A water bottle, dropped by one of the hikers, rolled down the hill behind them with bumping noises and came to rest in the mud at the edge of the creek. For a second, as she saw it, Khalid had a flash of Danni and the water bottles in her room.

One of the women bled from a cut over the left eye. The younger black man held one hand in the palm of the other, trying not to scream, his teeth bared in agony. Judging from the bent-back angle of his right index finger, he had broken it in the frantic scramble down the hill.

A canyon wren sang a mournful sound, then stopped.

The Nico-Rid party was in silent panic, some cowering behind tilted slabs of granite at the base of the incline. They were trying to stay quiet, but after a half minute with no more gunshots, they became bolder.

"What's going on?"

"Who's shooting us?"

"This is awful! This is awful!"

One of the men was crying. Two of the women hugged each other, each shaking too hard to stand alone.

"I think we're safe here," Khalid said, "but stay low."

"Why were you asking for Darren Black?" the group leader asked.

"He was in danger. I guess that's obvious now that he's dead."

"That isn't Darren Black."

A second man said, "I am."

Suddenly there were crashing noises above them. Shots struck the rocks. One of the other men cried out.

"Down! Down!" Khalid yelled. She pushed the men behind two boulders, while the ranger shooed two women and a man, and the HRT guy pushed a man down and threw his body over the other woman.

Bullets spanged off the rocks. They didn't whine like flying lead in movies but made chunk! noises, like bricks falling onto concrete.

"You two guys stay low!" Khalid shouted at Darren Black and another man. Black was on his knees in the cold stream and the other man some ten feet away from him, lying in the water. "They're after you."

"Why me?" Black said.

"I'll explain later. You! There! Stay low or they'll shoot you!"

"I don't understand. I haven't done anything!" the man yelled back.

"You look like Black. All they have is a description."

One of the women was crying now. The HRT man returned fire, but shots came back at him and then they heard the stutter of machine rounds. The water kicked up in the creek.

Darren Black yelled, "Shit! I'm hit!"

Khalid looked around, trying to see if she could get to him. Their position here wasn't good. The creek was the only place they could have run to when the shooting started, and there was some cover from all the boulders. But still, they were low here, and Bandwidth held the high ground.

She crouched, then sprang and bolted at a flat-out run over to Black. A couple of rounds followed her, but she was not hit.

He was swearing at top speed. This was a good sign. It was when they got all sleepy and mellow that they were going into shock.

"Where're you hit?"

"Arm."

His sleeve was red with blood. She enlarged the rip made by the bullet.

"It's a graze. You're lucky."

"But why is this happening?"

"It's a long story," Khalid said. Just then she heard a scream from the ridge above. There was an exchange of gunfire, but none of the rounds were coming down to the creek.

"I think the cavalry has arrived."

I was exhausted and angry. Angry at all the people who felt they had to make some kind of statement about their personal space at the expense of a little girl's life. Fetterman remained positive and efficient, but he was worried. His weather-barometer ears were pale.

Judge Grolsch was as crabby as ever, and somehow that was reassuring.

There were four possibles in the Ukrainian Village area around Western and Huron. Two in Greektown. More on the Gold Coast and then more near some disheartening public housing. And nowhere, nowhere, did I find Danni.

Late afternoon. The high-rises along Lake Shore Drive

cast lengthening shadows into the lake. I realized that I was whispering "Oh, my God, oh, my God," under my breath over and over and over.

Then the phone rang. Fetterman answered.

"It's Agent Khalid," he said.

"You're okay?"

"Yeah. And I've got Darren Black."

"Thank heaven!"

"He doesn't remember the license plate."

"Oh, shit!"

"But he remembers that it was a rental car."

"How?"

"The rental agency logo."

I held my breath.

Khalid went on. "Regal Rentals. He remembered it because his mother's maiden name was Regall, he says."

Thank you, God. "Tell me what he saw."

"He was smoking outside with the other people like you said. The car was a white Toyota, going east on Pearson. It swerved and hit the railing next to the street there, also like you said. The back door had started to open, just before the car swerved, and he says a little girl tried to get out. He hasn't heard about Danni yet, of course."

"Uh-huh."

"And the man in the backseat reached over and pulled her back in. He said something to the smokers. Something like, 'Forgot the car seat.' "

"Oh, man!"

"And he slammed the door and took off and turned out of sight at the corner."

"Where he got out and doubled back."

"Probably. He must have sedated Danni first."

"So did Darren Black see this guy clearly? Or the driver?"

"Sorry to say, it was one of our look-alikes."

"Tom, Dick, or Harry?"

"Yeah. But there's good news."

"Tell me."

"The driver was a man with a sharp chin, beaky nose, deep-set eyes, wearing a baseball cap."

"Laser Blue!"

"Yep. This is the first time we've been able to place him at the actual scene of an actual crime. Black can ID him, no doubt about it. We've got him cold!"

"Excellent!"

"I'm calling you from the air. We should land at O'Hare in about an hour."

"We?"

"Black's with me. Black's willing to be available to ID Laser Blue in person and make a try at Tom, Dick, and Harry."

"Great! So he's willing to cut his trip short to help us?"

"Kelly, he's given the trip up entirely. The first thing he did after the doc sewed up his arm wound was bum a cigarette from the ambulance driver and light up."

Had Bandwidth tracked down the smokers and killed them because they saw Danni? Or because they saw the car? Or because they saw Laser Blue?

fifty-eight

It was now fully evening, the air violet and the streetlights beginning to brighten.

Regal Rentals was on North Avenue, adjacent to the Gold Coast, about fifteen blocks north of Holy Name Cathedral. It specialized in fine cars for rental to the wealthy and near-wealthy who lived in the area. Why Bandwidth had chosen it particularly, I wasn't sure, except that, not being a national company, its record-keeping might be different in some way. We'd worry about that later. Right now I didn't care.

As far as its location, though, it was very clever of Bandwidth to put Danni near Holy Name, giving themselves a short distance to travel and less chance of being seen. And being close and yet waiting seventy-five minutes to begin televising would confuse us. We would not know how close they were. In fact, we'd tend to believe they'd traveled a good distance.

The place was swarming with cops going over the records for the last two weeks. The manager had come in. The owner was on his way from Morton Grove where he lived.

Cops with pictures of our suspects were on their way to the homes of every clerk, secretary, mechanic, and car washer who worked for Regal.

But I didn't care about that either. I had Fetterman drive by just to have a place to start.

Ainslie and Hatch were categorizing our apartment possibles, ranking them in distance from Regal Rentals. The closest would be our first visit.

I was no longer reacting with anger. I'm not sure I was reacting like a normal human being. All I cared about was how fast I could move. Each place where I went it was hurry, hurry—should I take the elevator or would the stairs be faster?

Time was running out. The war room said Danni had not moved in two hours.

The people who delayed us by not letting us in I now just blew off. I ran through their apartments without even seeing them as people.

I said, "Fetterman, try to narrow these down to places where there's a child in the apartment underneath. I think Danni's been hearing a child cry."

I was taking a gamble. Danni's life was on the line. But what else had we been doing all along other than gambling? And it was a necessary one. Time was running out.

I wasn't angry. I was obsessed. Racing down the stairs in a building off Franklin Street, I encountered, coming up the stairs, what a lot of Chicagoans would call Mr. Nightmare. Six feet six, huge, three hundred pounds and none of it fat, shaved head, earrings, and nose studs, he was wearing black leather and a necklace of horse teeth. I said, "Out of my way! Move!" and pushed him back as I plunged down the stairs.

He faded against the wall with a look of stunned astonishment.

The first place I chose from the revised possibles, the short-list of places near Regal Rentals, was on Lake Shore

Drive, called the Gold Coast. It was a beautiful apartment in a beautiful old building with plaster egg-and-dart moldings and a tessellated entry hall.

The woman who owned the apartment was outraged, and I could see why. It was a mess. The living room and bedroom were filled with boxes, tipped-over lamps, fast-food cartons, Styrofoam Thai and Chinese and Italian restaurant containers, used tissues, spilled popcorn, and bits of food ground into the antique Oriental rugs.

The kitchen was worse. It smelled of food left rotting in the sink, in the disposal and in the garbage cans. And all over the counters and floor were empty scotch bottles. The very best. Laphroig, Macallen, single malts.

The woman kept saying "Bitch. Bitch. Bitch. I'm a friend of the mayor, you know. Bitch."

I checked all the closets, including one that is peculiar to these old places built for the rich. In these apartments, near the front door, there is usually a narrow but deeper-than-usual closet or a sideways closet. They were intended for fur coats, which were too bulky to fit in closets of normal depth.

I was out of there in no time.

I hadn't expected Danni to be that close to the car rental anyway. My theory was Bandwidth would pick a place close enough to walk from if they had to, but not too close.

Ten o'clock. It was fully dark. We drove and I climbed stairs and I found that I was again muttering, "Oh, God, oh, God, oh, God."

Word from the war room was that Danni still had not moved.

Eleven o'clock.

At 11:15 I had a call patched through from my office line. It was Mrs. Drobney.

"I'm sorry but I had to call."

"What's wrong?"

"Your mother—um—she grabbed up a knife. I got it away from her."

"She's all right? You're all right?"

"Yes, but she says she wants to die. She says you're never here."

"She's been saying she wants to die since 1972."

There was a silence on the other end. Mrs. Drobney disapproved of this response.

Finally, she said, "What shall I do?"

"Look, I'm not a monster, Mrs. Drobney. But Danni Gaston wants to live and my mother—my mother is an adult who has a choice. Danni has been deprived of all her choices."

"I know, dear. I'm sorry."

"Call her doctor. The number's on the pad near the phone."

"I know."

"If he wants her hospitalized, call the ambulance."

"Yes. All right, dear."

Oh, hell.

I found I could do an apartment every seven or eight minutes if the super was right there when I rang. If not, it took about ten; and no matter how much faster I ran, it averaged out to six an hour. Not fast enough.

And then one building on North Rush Street was perfect. Ten blocks from the Regal Rental, fifty-five years old, solid construction, and windows covered with curtains in an apartment on the fourth floor, no light visible through them, and on the third floor a family with a new baby.

Oh, Lord, let it be.

fifty-nine

There it was! There was the sleeping pad, glued to the floor, the water bottles, mostly empty now, and that little scrap of humanity, a tiny girl in a dirty dress that had once been blue-and-white checks. Her hair was matted, her skin sallow and stained.

She looked dead.

"Oh, Danni!" I said.

I tiptoed to her, wanting to scream or sob, but very careful not to frighten her. Was she still alive?

"Danni, sweetheart?"

I knelt down beside her and touched her forehead. It was cold. Her chest didn't seem to move. Was she breathing? Gently, I touched her neck where the carotid pulse should be.

She opened her eyes.

She said, "Mommy?"

All over the earth, people saw a woman wearing navy blue pants, white shirt, and a navy blazer tiptoe over to

Danni, and although there was no sound, they could see her say, "Danni, sweetheart?" and kneel down beside her.

They saw the woman touch the child's forehead, then brush some stray stiff hair from the little girl's eyes.

They saw Danni's mouth move as she said, "Mommy?" and they knew she was alive.

Then the woman took a phone from her belt and spoke.

I said, "Fetterman, I've got her! Call Dr. Brunschner to get here immediately. Call the paramedics. And call Maggie and the senator."

"Right away, boss," Fetterman said.

His voice came from the hall door, not the radio. He and Judge Grolsch stepped into the room. Fetterman was crying so hard he could barely speak, but he sobbed and sniffled into the radio contact with the war room.

Judge Grolsch was gasping for breath and looked like a man on the verge of a heart attack. "We heard you," he said. "I've never run up four flights of stairs so fast in my life."

"Judge! People will see you here. The video is still on."

"Frankly, my dear, I don't give a damn."

Astonishingly, he was crying too, big rivers of tears from both eyes. His ugly, satanic face was wet all over and he swiped at the tears, driving them into the creases of his wrinkles.

"Hi, Danni," he said. "We're gonna take you home to your mommy and daddy."

Danni seemed to think he looked beautiful. She smiled, weakly but happily, at him.

sixty

"I'd be happier to have her in a hospital."

The senator looked Dr. Brunschner in the eye and just said, "No."

We were in the Gastons' suite at the Knickerbocker, Danni lying on the sofa with an IV in her arm. Knowing hospitals from many unhappy experiences, I sympathized with Senator Gaston. But Dr. Brunschner was indignant.

"There are problems with refeeding after starvation," Brunschner said. "There is edema in the early stages of refeeding and rehabilitation. You can have all sorts of problems with electrolyte balance."

The senator said, "Yes, yes, but how *is* she?"

Maggie said, "It's all right, Dr. Brunschner, Mr. Haralson has called an agency for a registered nurse to stay with her. They said she'd be here in an hour."

"I'll stay here myself for the first twenty-four hours."

"Thank you."

"I don't want to take any chances. I have her on antibiotics for the bronchitis. We should get the results on the blood draw back soon."

"All right."

"Mrs. Gaston, I want to emphasize again that you *must not* feed her! You'll want to—"

"Yes! I want to! But I understand."

"I'll allow a teaspoon or two of yogurt every three hours."

"Oh, yes."

"It's very important. Feeding starvation victims too much can kill them. This happened to people when the concentration camps were liberated after World War II. The GIs gave out food and people died from it."

"I do understand." Maggie smiled at him. Nothing could diminish her joy.

"Refeeding has to be slow until GI function is restored. I'm starting her on a formula made of forty-two-percent dry skim milk, thirty-two-percent edible oil, twenty-five-percent sucrose, plus mineral, vitamin, and electrolyte supplements."

"Oh, yes," Maggie said. "Certainly. Of course."

I could tell she didn't even hear him. She just held Danni's hand and glowed. I think if we had turned off the room lights we would have seen a big pink neon aura of happiness around her.

Fetterman had been watching Maggie and Danni, his ears red with happiness and a grin stretching between them. He walked a few feet to the side of the room, probably thinking to give them privacy. Suddenly, he said, "Boss! Look!" and pointed at the television in the sitting room.

Everybody else looked too, except Danni and Maggie.

It was a place I knew better than my own house—the steps in front of Eleventh and State, the headquarters of the Chicago Police Department. There was a dense, pushing, shoving, shouting mob of reporters, but we were seeing it through the camera of some video photographer close in. Hannah Khalid was talking.

"—very pleased with how it turned out," she said. "My job here is done and I'll be leaving tonight."

There were several shouted questions, but like politicians do, she just answered the ones she liked.

"The agency was able to determine where the child was being held because of our extensive technological expertise, particularly computer searches through FBI databanks that are growing more and more useful every day." Somebody yelled a question about Raft, but she went on.

"As a result, we were able to supply the Chicago Police Department with the address where the child could be found."

"Did you catch the kidnappers?" somebody yelled.

"We've arrested five Bandwidth members involved in the kidnapping—"

"Did the Chicago Police help?"

"The Chicago Police were extremely supportive, and I am glad to say that the agency and the police here worked very well together. We thought it was appropriate to permit them to make the rescue."

Fetterman turned to me with his mouth open.

sixty-one

At noon the next day, I visited the Knickerbocker for the last time.

Danni was lying back in the overstuffed chair, weak, but they had removed the IV. I said, "Hi, sweetie. You look great."

"My mommy got me this. His name is Derby."

"He's beautiful."

He was a little stuffed horse.

"And at dinner I get to have a really, really little peanut butter and jelly sandwich."

"Oh, that's wonderful."

"We do want to thank you, Chief Kelly," Senator Gaston said in his formal way.

"Senator, can I talk to you for a minute? Privately?"

"I don't see why not."

He walked into the sitting room, the room with the television. I clicked it off and when I turned around I noticed that Maggie had followed, saying to the nurse, "I'll be right back."

This wasn't what I had wished for. But there was little point, in the long run, in telling her to leave. I closed the door behind her.

"Senator Gaston, there are a hundred senators, all told."

"Yes. Why?"

"And over four hundred congressmen in the House of Representatives. Five hundred people who would like to be president."

"Many. Probably not all."

"Whatever. Plus governors of fifty states plus a few odds and ends of army heroes, Gulf War veterans, and so on, plus more odds and ends of captains of industry, a few famous actors and other oddballs who would like to be president. Maybe seven hundred presidential hopefuls with reasonable aspirations."

"Are you going anywhere with all this?" Gaston had not sat down, and now he paced toward the window and turned to face me.

"Yes. Unfortunately. How does one person among seven hundred stand out? Suppose you, Sen. Neal Gaston, want to be president?"

"I could take it or leave it."

"Really?"

"What are you trying to say?"

"Let me switch topics a little. I wondered when I first met you why you were so interested in the media response. But I thought either it was fear for Danni or maybe a politician's habit. But you went on to court the media. Why did you keep talking about your experience with the domestic terrorism committee? When the 'Free Johnnie Raft' words came on the video feed, you said free him, but you weren't very excited about it. If it had been my child, I would have kicked and screamed. Free him now! Get Danni back. Do whatever we have to do. But you said, 'See, that's how these people are. I've been warning you.'

"The only thing that sent you into a rage was the *death* of Johnnie Raft."

"He was our connection to the kidnappers."

"No, he wasn't. He had never given us one tiny clue that he was in contact with his group, and he wasn't going to. Johnnie Raft could *not* call out. He could not communicate with anybody. I went there. I checked. Experts checked his cell. He was not giving orders to Bandwidth."

"There's no way to know that. He was very, very slick."

"And when I asked him whether Bandwidth would act without him, he was troubled. Raft prided himself on being the brains of the organization. He caught himself, and he tried not to show he was upset, but he was. They wouldn't have acted without *believing* it was on Raft's orders."

"It couldn't have been anyone else's."

"Well, yes, it could. That was one thing that really got my attention in fact. When I had the helicopters quartering the city, once they were in the air, Khalid insisted that we come and tell you about it. Let you know we were doing something. I can understand that. And ten minutes after we left you, the sound feed was cut."

"So?"

"So you told them to cut it."

"That's absolutely absurd!" Gaston stood stock-still, his feet planted wide apart. He looked like he wanted to hit me.

"I'm afraid you did, Senator."

"Watch it. You're getting above yourself, Detective."

I carefully did not look at Maggie, but I was aware of her out of the corner of my eye. Her way of dealing with disaster was familiar to me now. She was very strong. Maggie was not a person who screamed or threw things or dumped her misery on other people. She held it in. She thought and prayed. And right now she was as silent as the grave.

"You had your private connection to the Senate and the Pentagon. National security. We couldn't take it away from you."

"That's irrelevant. I couldn't reach Johnnie Raft."

"No one could. No one did. I just told you that. You *could* reach Bandwidth."

"How?"

"You learned a lot about them in your years as chair of the Senate Committee on Terrorism. You knew how to get into their E-mail."

He said nothing.

"So you knew Raft's code. You represented *yourself* as Raft to them and gave them instructions. They thought they were taking orders directly from Raft."

Still no response. I heard a sigh from Maggie.

"When Raft was killed, you didn't find out about it right away. I had decided to let you sleep, and I was busy with a lot of others things. So you didn't find out until I came here several hours after he was dead. You had already told Laser Blue to go ahead with the satellite uplink *after Raft was dead.* When Blue realized that, he knew there was a rat in the pipeline. And he split." I paused. Still nothing.

"Your reelection in Missouri is certain, but being a senator has become old hat. It's not enough for you anymore. You want to be president. So does every politician in the country, so that's no surprise. How could *you* get attention out of hundreds of hopefuls? How could *you* get sympathy? Why, to be hit with a crisis, which you could bravely fight, and to be proven right at the same time. Have your *own child* captured by terrorists."

In the faintest of voices, Maggie whispered, "But Neal loves Danni."

"I think he does, too. That's why he was so furious and terrified when Raft was killed. He intended to 'negotiate' and get Danni back. To do some magnificent deal with the kidnappers and save her. Pretending to be Raft, he could order Bandwidth to release her. Unfortunately, Neal didn't know where Danni was; Bandwidth was not able to E-mail into the prison. They never expected to, and Neal wouldn't have wanted them to anyway. They might have asked the ostensible Raft something Neal didn't know how to answer. So now there was no way to find out where Danni was. He couldn't reach the kidnappers as himself, of course. Now that Raft was dead, he couldn't communicate with them at all."

She gaped at me. If she believed what I was saying, her world was falling apart, except that she had Danni back, and maybe that meant everything right now. She said, "Neal? You didn't, did you?"

Gaston didn't even look at her. He said to me, "You can't prove it."

Maggie breathed, "Oh." My heart broke for her. But I had to go on. I said, "Actually, I can. I tapped your congressional line."

"You can't tap it. It's under a national security umbrella."

"True. I called the attorney general a couple of days ago when I got suspicious. The attorney general called the president. There was a tap installed, and it's legal, and it's admissible in court."

"But Neal loves Danni," Maggie said again, in a whisper.

"I think he does, but he's not her biological father, is he? Danni looks like you, but not like Neal. The treatment you had for infertility was artificial insemination. By a sperm donor." Neal had had mumps as a child, according to the medical records. It had left him sterile.

"As I said, I believe he does love Danni," I told Maggie. "He never meant it all to go this far."

epilogue

Three Bandwidth members were caught in Arizona over the next two weeks, as the rangers and state police slowly drew the net tighter and rounded them up. Several evaded the patrols however. The rangers' best guess was that three to six got away. One who got away actually staggered into the Tuweep Airport later in a state of near starvation and was pathetically grateful to be arrested and fed.

Fetterman received four "attaboys" to go into his personnel jacket. One from me, one from Ainslie, one from DiMaggio, and one big, major, letter of gold-plated importance from, believe it or not, *the superintendent.* Hoo-boy! It may have helped that I asked DiMaggio to put in a word with the big boss. Fetterman deserved it.

Hannah Khalid, of course, received a promotion.

Judge Grolsch was called to the office of the chief judge who is in charge of judicial conduct and reamed out for issuing unfounded warrants. Then the chief judge took him out to dinner and bought him unlimited glasses of Chivas Regal and all the steak and lobster he could eat.

Sen. Neal Gaston is in federal prison.

Maggie and Danni are doing well. Maggie just sent me
her new album, and Danni sent me a picture of me. In it I
have purple hair and an angel's halo.

And speaking of Maggie. It's strange how the human
mind works. It was several days after the whole thing was
over, and I was retracing the kidnappers' route, that I realized how eerily close Maggie was to Danni's prison room
when she went out walking. From the Knickerbocker Hotel
at Fifty North Michigan she could have walked north or
south, up or down Michigan, or east to the lake or west. But
she walked north, then northwest up Rush toward North
Avenue, which was within three blocks of where we finally
found Danni. I sent her a note about this when I realized it,
saying I believed there was a true psychic bond between
mother and daughter.

Chief of Detectives Burkholder was asked to quietly re-
tire. Surprisingly, he did so without fuss. I was promoted to
take his place.

My mother still lives with me.

The hawk-nose man, Laser Blue, was never found.

William Harper Jordan was found. Unfortunately, his
body was recovered in Lake Michigan in July, when it
washed up against a pier in Gary, Indiana. I wish I could
have made things all right for him and his family, but of
course, before anybody knew about it, it was already much
too late.

You do what you can.